A Window to the World

Susan Meissner

HARVEST HOUSE PUBLISHERS

EUGENE, OREGON

Cover by Left Coast Design, Portland, Oregon

Cover photo © Christiana Ceppas/Workbookstock

A WINDOW TO THE WORLD

Copyright © 2005 by Susan Meissner
Published by Harvest House Publishers
Eugene, Oregon 97402
www.harvesthousepublishers.com

Library of Congress Cataloging-in-Publication Data

Meissner, Susan, 1961-
   A window to the world / Susan Meissner.
      p. cm.
   ISBN 0-7369-1414-5 (pbk.)
   1. Female friendship—Fiction. 2. Kidnapping—Fiction. 3. Witnesses—Fiction. 4. Girls—Fiction.
I. Title.
PS3613.E435W56 2005
813'.6—dc22   2004015871

Printed in the United States of America

05 06 07 08 09 10 11 /BP-KB/ 10 9 8 7 6 5 4 3 2 1

For Kathy Sanders Zufelt
— I can't imagine my wonderful San Diego
childhood without you in it, dear friend —
and
For all those who wait for someone they love
to come home.

Acknowledgments

Special thanks to

- Bob Meissner, my husband; and my children, Stephanie, Joshua, Justin, and Eric, for never complaining about all those hurried meals or all the times you wanted to use the computer and couldn't because I was busy using it to write this book. I love looking at the world with the five of you beside me.

- Nick Harrison, Kimberly Shumate, Carolyn McCready, and everyone at Harvest House for your constant flow of encouraging words.

- Jon Rose, a defense investigator with the law offices of the public defender for San Diego County, for helping me with the police procedure details.

- The National Center for Missing and Exploited Children for answering my questions in such a kind and timely manner.

- Judy Horning, my mother, for expertly proofreading every line.

- God, who never tires of seeking the lost.

"Come to the edge."
"We can't. We're afraid."
"Come to the edge."
"We can't. We will fall!"
"Come to the edge."
And they came.
And he pushed them.
And they flew.

GUILLAUME APOLLINAIRE

PART ONE
Winter 1988

*T*wenty-one silent first-graders perched on elfish, aquamarine chairs waited without wiggling as their teacher, Mrs. Fredericks, welcomed the new girl into the classroom. Mrs. Fredericks had her arm across the girl's shoulders and was engaged in a hushed conversation with the girl's mother. It was the first day back from Christmas vacation, and there were still wreaths made of green handprints stuck on the wall behind the trio of teacher, pupil, and parent. Outside slightly open windows, an expected January sun was bathing the San Diego neighborhood in rapidly increasing warmth. By noon it would be sixty-five degrees without a cloud in the sky.

"We're so glad to welcome you to our class," Mrs. Fredericks was saying as twenty-one sets of eyes took it all in, their teacher's familiar one-armed embrace, the dulcet tone of her voice, the long, golden braids that fell from the girl's head, and her calm, blue eyes that surveyed the room with no trace of apprehension.

It was the girl's relaxed demeanor that kept the children awed and silent. She seemed completely at ease.

Only moments before, wide-eyed Mrs. Fredericks had admonished the class to "show our new student how quiet you can be," like being quiet would utterly amaze the newest member of their class. But the girl did not seem to be amazed at all by the silent stares.

For Megan Diamond, last chair, table three, keeping quiet wasn't difficult. "She's our quiet one," her mother would say when someone spoke to her and she rewarded them with just a nod. It was not like Megan to speak out of turn in class. It was not like Megan to speak at all unless spoken to first. It was one of the things she liked least about herself. And she hated being called shy. It was a short, marshmallow-soft word, and she felt the word for shyness should instead have a hard edge to it, like "wasp" or "scab" or "spinach."

Megan stared at the new girl like all the others in her class did but without so much as a bridled whisper on the tip of her tongue. She instinctively figured she could stare at the new girl as long as she pleased, completely unnoticed, because that's how she lived her life—quietly, anonymously, invisibly. At seven, she was not consciously aware of how she was acting. She didn't really notice that her parents—and now her teacher—were somewhat concerned with Megan's quiet manner and apparent inability to initiate a friendship. She didn't know that she had been described as "compliant, but withdrawn" by her kindergarten teacher, or that Mrs. Fredericks daily looked for little ways to engage Megan in social interaction with her classmates.

Megan only knew that most things she did in class went unnoticed. And so she stared.

Megan noted the deep, golden hue of the girl's braids, the tiny pearl earrings in her pierced ears, her jeans edged with red trim, the daisies on her white knit top and the smooth, unfreckled cheeks on her perfect face. Subconsciously, Megan reached up to her own cheeks and flicked a few hated freckles away, aware and yet unaware that they stayed just the same.

But then something amazing happened. The new girl locked her eyes on Megan's, and for the first time in a very long time,

Megan did not feel invisible. She felt exposed. It was a scary feeling and yet nice at the same time. The girl had noticed her. She had been discovered. Then the girl lifted up the corners of her mouth and offered a grin that was nearly imperceptible. But Megan saw it. The new girl was smiling at her.

Megan let the corners of her mouth rise in response.

It was a shared moment that was too quickly swept away into the next. The girl's mother squeezed her daughter's shoulder, backed out, and left. Mrs. Fredericks closed the classroom door and gently ushered the girl farther into the classroom.

"Class, this is Jennifer Lovett," said Mrs. Fredericks. "She likes to be called Jen. Can you tell her hello?"

A chorus of commanded greetings filled the room. As Megan said the name Jen for the first time, she felt strangely drawn to this new word, its lyrical quality, and its beautiful owner. She watched Jen take a seat across from her at another table. As Jen slipped into an available chair at table two, she cast a glance back at Megan, as if to reassure Megan that, yes, she had indeed noticed her. Mrs. Fredericks then instructed the class to stand one at a time and tell Jen their first and last names, starting with table one. When it was Megan's turn and she stood and whispered her own name, the boys at her table snickered, and one of the girls said, "Say it again. She can't hear you!"

"I heard her," Jen said, surprising everyone. "Her name is Megan Diamond."

~ ~ ~

Megan had a hard time concentrating on making acceptable Ws that morning, and later she kept dropping the colored beads she was using to make a patterned sequence on a string. She kept looking at the new girl, wondering why in the world she had smiled at her. Was she teasing her in some way? Was she strange? Was she just being nice? Finally it was story time, and Mrs. Fredericks instructed the students to each take a seat on one of the carpet squares in the reading circle.

Megan moved to the circle and sat on one of the gray squares because no one liked those and she wouldn't have to worry about defending it. Two squirrelly boys plopped down on either side of her, oblivious to her. Megan drew up her legs closer to her body, not daring to look at either boy but wishing with all her heart they would move. Jen was suddenly standing by the boy on Megan's right.

"I'm sitting next to Megan," she said to the boy, plainly and confidently.

The boy, who hardly realized he had sat down next to a girl, cast a glance at Megan and quickly scooted away. Jen dropped to her knees on the open purple square next to her.

"Look!" Jen said, pointing to her ankles as she folded her legs. "We have the same socks!"

Megan, nearly transfixed by the preceding moment, silently looked down at her own feet. It was true. She and Jen had the same white socks dotted with rosebuds and edged in lace. Megan could hardly believe Jen had noticed when even she hadn't.

"I got mine at Penneys," Jen said quietly, as if divulging a wonderful secret.

"So did I," Megan replied, barely above a whisper.

"Do you have a cat?" Jen continued, like it was obviously the next question to be asked. Megan could tell Jen wanted it to be so, that Megan did indeed have a cat. She couldn't contain the smile that spread across her face.

"We have a tabby cat. His name is Pippin. He's orange." The three sentences fell from Megan's lips like an invitation to wonder.

"You are so lucky," Jen said in reply. "We can't have a cat 'cause my brother Charlie has *nallergies*."

Megan had wanted very badly to ask Jen what *nallergies* were, but their conversation ended then because Mrs. Fredericks took her place at the top of the circle and held a finger to her lips.

But Megan couldn't concentrate on the story Mrs. Fredericks read. Or anything else they did that day in class. Jen's words kept replaying themselves in her mind, over and over.

You are so lucky. You are so lucky.

~ ~ ~

Trina Diamond was not used to her older daughter rattling on about school, friends, or anything else, so she found it rather odd when Megan came home from school full of news about the first day back from Christmas vacation. Trina listened attentively but with a fair amount of astonishment. This was not like her daughter.

Megan had always been quiet, reserved, and somewhat untrusting. It was an attribute Trina had decided was not a bad thing, especially when it came to her daughter's safety. Megan hardly spoke to adults she knew and never spoke to strangers, whereas her other daughter, three-year-old Michelle, was a non-stop chatterbox. Megan's shyness caused Trina some concern, but it wasn't something she agonized over. Megan was only seven. Trina was sure a time would surely come when Megan would come out of her shell. And if she didn't, well, that was okay. There was nothing wrong or shameful about being shy.

Trina had held out hope—and still did—that school would draw out her quiet daughter, but when it finally seemed to have happened, she felt uneasiness, not relief.

From the moment Megan slipped into Trina's car when school let out to when she sat down in the kitchen a few minutes later for a snack, Megan talked. First grade had been fun that day. There was a new girl named Jen. She and Jen were now friends. They had made an ant farm. Jen had sat next to her at reading. They had played together at recess. Jen pushed her on the swings. She pushed Jen. They drew cats at art time. *Look, here's Pippin. This one is Jen's. They can't have a cat. Can Jen come over?*

Megan, sitting on a kitchen stool and carefully placing raisins on a peanut-buttered length of celery, waited for an answer.

"And who is this girl?" Trina asked, surprised at her apprehension.

"She's the new girl," Megan repeated.

"Well, yes, I mean, where does she live? Where did she move from?"

"She came from *Lost* Angeles," Megan said, obviously proud to know so much. "She lives across the canyon. That way." Megan waved in a westerly direction, toward the ravine of sagebrush, tumbleweeds, and pepper trees that separated their housing development from the one that sat on the rim of the canyon's other side. Less than half a mile of open air separated the two housing tracts though the length of the canyon from rim to rim spanned nearly twice that. It was untamed, undeveloped, and rumored to be home to rattlesnakes, scorpions, and black widow spiders. Megan and her sister were forbidden to play in it.

"So *can* she?" Megan said, crunching down on the celery stalk.

Trina inwardly berated herself for feeling so overly cautious. This was exactly what she and Gordy had been hoping for. In their moments alone when she and Gordy prayed for their kids, they never failed to ask for good playmates for their quiet first-born. As she was reminding herself of this, Trina suddenly understood why she had reservations: She didn't know anything about Jen or her family. Megan had so few friends. None, really. It mattered a great deal what kind of friend this Jen would be.

Trina hated thinking that only girls raised in Christian homes like theirs would be suitable friends for Megan. It didn't seem like a very magnanimous attitude to have toward the little girls in Megan's class, especially this one, whom Trina had not even met. But she couldn't help thinking that Megan's shyness made her vulnerable in a way that confident kids were not. Megan would surely be the loyal, obedient follower in any friendship. The wrong kind of playmate would be worse than no playmate at all. In that moment Trina decided she would proceed with caution. She carefully worded her next question, giving no indication of what she was really thinking.

"Well, we can call her mom up some day and invite them both over so her mom can meet us too, okay?"

"I have her number," Megan said, licking peanut butter off her index finger. "She gave it to me. And I gave her mine."

Trina didn't like the speed with which this was going. She needed time to think. She wanted to talk it over with Gordy. Michelle started to whine from her bedroom down the hall where she had been sent to take a nap.

"Maybe we should let them settle in before we call," Trina said, getting to her feet and almost thankful for Michelle's interruption.

"What's 'settle in'?" Megan asked.

"Well, honey, they just moved here from Los Angeles, and they probably have a lot of unpacking to do. We can call in a few days, okay?"

Trina started to walk away before Megan could answer. The phone rang.

"I'll get it!" Megan said, scrambling off her stool and reaching for the phone. Trina couldn't remember the last time Megan volunteered to answer the phone. Michelle whined louder. Trina set off to attend to her. As she walked down the hall she heard Megan say hello and then, "Hi, Jen!"

Trina kept walking toward the sound of Michelle's complaints, but her thoughts were far from her younger child's refusal to take a nap.

"Michelle, what is all this about?" Trina said as she reached the room and pushed the door open.

"I'm not tired!" the three-year-old whined. Michelle was lying backwards on her bed with her bare feet massaging the wall above her headboard. Picture books lay scattered about the floor and around her head and torso.

Trina sighed. She could hear Megan saying, "I'll go ask her!" and she knew there would be no nap for Michelle. There would be no waiting to talk this over with Gordy, either. Megan came flying down the hallway.

"Jen and her mom can come over now and meet us!" Megan said. "Can they come? Can they come, Mommy?"

"I am *not* tired!" Michelle said again.

"Can they come, Mommy?" Megan said.

"All right," Trina said, and both girls yelled, "Yay!" each assuming she had received the desired response to her request.

Michelle slid off her bed as Megan ran back down the hall.

"Michelle, if you're going to skip your nap today then you'll need to show me you're a big girl who doesn't need one," Trina said, picking up her younger daughter's socks, which Michelle had rolled up into little cloth biscuits and thrown at her dresser. "Put your socks back on. We're going to have company."

"I *am* a big girl," Michelle said taking the socks and plopping down on the floor with them.

Trina made her way back to the front of the house, taking stock of the condition of her home as she walked. Toys in the hallway. Toothpaste droppings in the bathroom sink. Mail in an unorganized pile on the kitchen table. Folded laundry on the back of the couch. Cat hair all over the ottoman.

There was no time to make much of an improvement, so Trina decided to go back to the kitchen and make a pot of coffee and at least clean up the mess from Megan's snack.

Megan had run outside to await their guests' arrival, and it seemed barely a few moments had passed when she pulled open the door and announced they were there.

Trina ran a few fingers through her shoulder-length permed hair, using the face of the microwave as a mirror. Moderately satisfied, she followed Megan's excited voice and stepped into the entry to welcome the guests.

"Mom, this is Jen!" Megan said, grabbing her hand and hastening her way into the entry.

Jen was a little shorter than Megan, with long golden braids that fell halfway down her back. She was tanned and perky. Her jewel blue eyes were shining, and she was quite the picture of confidence.

"Hi," Jen said, waving a hand with tiny painted fingernails. Behind her stood her mother, with the same golden hair, the same bronzed skin, and the same self-assurance. She wore the same shade of nail polish as her daughter. On her left ankle was a tiny tattoo of a pansy. She wore a short denim skirt and an electric red, short-sleeved pullover.

Trina imagined herself looking quite ordinary by comparison with her monochrome brown hair, light brown pants, and lighter brown cotton shirt. Brown everywhere. Like cardboard.

"Come see my room!" Megan said, grabbing Jen's hand and pulling her down the hall. They brushed past Michelle who stood aside to let the older girls pass.

Trina watched the girls go and then turned toward Jen's mother.

"I'm Trina Diamond," she said, extending her hand and offering what she hoped came off as a genuine smile.

"Elise Lovett," Jen's mother said, taking Trina's hand and grasping it warmly. Elise had perfect shimmering teeth.

The two women exchanged a few more familiarities, and then Trina asked Elise Lovett if she would care for a cup of coffee.

"You are so kind to offer," Elise said. "But I don't drink coffee. Actually I don't drink anything with caffeine. And if it's all right with you, I was hoping I could leave Jen here to play awhile. I need to get back to the house, I'm afraid."

"Of course," Trina said, slightly taken aback. "You must have a lot of unpacking to do."

"Unpacking?" Elise said at first, like the word was foreign. "Oh, we've been in the house for three weeks already. I'm just expecting a kiln to be delivered today so I need to get back, if that's all right."

"Certainly." Trina said, and then added, "A kiln? You must be into pottery."

Elise laughed. It was easy and effortless. "You could say that."

"For fun or for business?" Trina asked as they started walking toward the front door.

"Oh, I don't do anything unless it's fun!" she said with that same easy laugh. "But lucky for me I can sell what I make."

"I'd like to see what you make sometime," Trina said, genuinely interested.

"Certainly…anytime," Elise said as she opened the front door and they stepped outside. "I'll come back for Jen in a couple of hours. Is that all right?"

Trina suddenly had an idea.

"Why don't you and your husband come for supper later?" she said. "You've had a busy day, and I'd love to properly welcome you to the neighborhood."

"Oh, I don't know," Elise said, looking off toward the canyon. "It seems like such an imposition."

"Not at all," Trina said. "It would be a great way for our families to get to know each other better. I have a feeling our daughters are going to want to spend a lot of time together."

"I think you're right about that," Elise said, grinning.

"Please say you'll come," Trina said.

"Well, I'll have to run it by Nate—my husband. And we have a son, too. Charlie."

"He's welcome too, of course."

"Well, let's say we're coming unless I call, okay?" Elise said, as she turned to walk away. "Any particular time?"

"How about six-thirty?" Trina asked.

"That works for me!" Elise said with a wave of her hand.

Trina watched Elise get into a vintage turquoise VW Beetle convertible with a white vinyl top. Every inch of chrome on the little car shined like glass.

"Nice car," Trina called out to her.

"My oldest and dearest friend!" Elise said as she got inside and started the motor.

Elise backed out of the driveway and took off down the street at a speed Trina usually complained about when performed by other drivers.

She stood there for a few moments as the Beetle sprinted out of sight, wondering if something wonderful had just begun or something that she would never be able to trust. When the street was quiet again, she turned and stepped back inside her house.

2

At five minutes to seven, with no sign of the Lovetts, Trina began wondering if she had heard Elise wrong and that she was not to expect them *unless* Elise called, rather than the other way around. Everything was ready and had been ready for nearly half an hour. She sighed and cast a quick glance through the kitchen doorway to the dining room and the eight settings of Fiesta Ware waiting to be used. Two pans of lasagna, baked to perfection, sat on top of the stove, blanketed in heavy-duty aluminum foil. Twin baking sheets of untoasted garlic bread were nearby, ready to be slid under the broiler at the last minute. The united aromas of garlic, sweet basil, and Parmesan wafted through the house. She would give the Lovetts ten more minutes, and then they would simply have to start without them.

Michelle, who had been in and out of the kitchen every ten minutes since six o'clock, wandered in again to say she was hungry. Trina placated her with yet another half a graham cracker. Megan and Jen were still in Megan's room where they had been all afternoon. They had only emerged once to ask for help getting a Barbie hair salon down off Megan's closet shelf.

As soon as Michelle was shooed away, Trina's husband, Gordy, stepped in from the living room, the television, and a

UCLA basketball game. He stopped by the tossed salad Trina had sitting on the breakfast bar, carefully picked out a slice of cucumber, and popped it into his mouth.

"So, you're sure they're coming?" he said, with a hint in his voice that he knew it wasn't the best question to ask. He reached into the salad bowl again and snagged a cherry tomato.

Trina knew Gordy wasn't overly thrilled with surprise dinner guests at the end of a stressful Monday. His job as a senior buyer with Sony kept him busy with long hours, most of them challenged by the constant struggle to perform miracles for an ungrateful manufacturing floor. She also knew the prospect of making small talk with Nate Lovett, a man he hadn't even met yet, made Gordy squirm with uneasiness. Megan's shyness was likely an intensified extension of her father's reserved nature.

"Elise said to expect them at six-thirty unless she called," Trina said firmly, as much to reassure herself as Gordy. She turned to the sink and for no apparent reason ran water into it and wiped down the sides with a dishrag.

"Maybe she forgot," Gordy ventured, stealing a circlet of carrot.

"She might've forgotten dinner, but she certainly couldn't have forgotten her *daughter*," Trina snapped back, growing more annoyed by the minute. Not with Gordy, though. With the uncertainty of what lay ahead with this new friendship of Megan's. She was quick to apologize.

"I'm sorry, Gordy," she said. "I didn't mean to take it out on you."

Gordy shrugged.

"No permanent damage," he said, relaxing against the breakfast bar. He crossed his arms across his chest and studied his wife's countenance.

"So what's really the matter?" Gordy said.

Trina turned to look at him, grateful that he knew her so well, yet peeved she couldn't get *anything* by her husband. In the ten years they had been married, she had never been able to truly surprise Gordy. He knew her deepest insecurities, what she feared most, what she drew strength from, and how she concealed concern. It was this kind of intuitiveness that first attracted her to him when they were students at San Diego State University. They had met when she was a sophomore library-sciences student and he, a senior in business administration. They attended the same on-campus Bible study. The questions Gordy asked and the depth of his understanding of the Bible had intrigued Trina. He could spend hours in debate on a single issue, arguing it from all sides even when he was convinced of none of them.

When they married a year later, Gordy had long hair, drove a Datsun pickup, and nurtured big dreams. A decade later he had far less hair, drove a four-door sedan, and his dreams of success had been tempered by reality. Trina knew Gordy didn't particularly like his job at Sony, but they were both thankful he had it. He wasn't making the big money he had dreamed of in college, but he did keep a modest roof over their heads. And in Southern California, that was in itself an accomplishment.

She could see him studying her through the rimless lenses of his glasses, waiting for her to answer.

"I'm afraid for Megan," Trina said, folding the dishrag and draping it across the sink faucet. "I'm afraid she's been so starved for friendship that she'll just disappear into the first friend she makes. I'm afraid it will change her."

Gordy blinked and said nothing. Trina knew he was deciding how to say what he was thinking without getting into trouble.

"They've known each other for a day, Trina," he said gently. "What has this little girl done in one day that has you so worried?"

"It's not so much what Jen has done," Trina answered in a hushed tone, glancing down the hall to make sure they were truly alone. "It's what Megan has done. She seems different, Gordy. She *ran* to answer the phone today."

"What's wrong with that?" Gordy said.

"There's nothing wrong with it," Trina said with a sigh, wishing the conversation would just end. Gordy was a realist, an analytical thinker, and though she loved him, she sometimes wished he could imagine things different than how they appeared. "It's just that it's not like her."

An arc of headlights swept across their faces through the window above the sink as a car pulled into their driveway.

"I think they're here," Gordy said and then added, "Oh man!"

"What is it?" Trina asked coming to stand by him so that she could look out.

"He's got a BMW," Gordy replied, in a tone heavy with a mixture of awe and disappointment.

Trina watched the Lovetts step out of their car. Nate, tall and athletically built, sported the same healthy glow as his wife and daughter. His sandy brown hair was flecked with a trace of gray at the temples. He wore twill slacks, a navy blue polo shirt, and a brown leather jacket. In his hands he carried two dark green bottles of wine. Trina hadn't even thought of getting out wine glasses. She and Gordy rarely drank. She grimaced at the thought of how dusty the glasses would be.

Trina sighed and watched as Elise stepped around the car to join Nate. She had changed into a gauzy, flowing dress printed with a batik pattern. It fell nearly to her ankles. She had a pair of gold sandals on her feet though the temperature had dropped to the low fifties. Trina silently wondered what Gordy would think of Elise's little tattoo.

A boy of about nine or ten followed Elise and Nate up the steps to the front door. Charlie looked every inch a miniature of his handsome father, sans the graying temples. Elise saw Trina at the kitchen window and waved.

"Well, let's do it," Gordy said, motioning with his hand for Trina to go first.

~ ~ ~

It wasn't the evening Trina had hastily planned that afternoon. The meal never made it to the dining room, and the Fiesta Ware sat untouched and unappreciated. No soothing dinner music. No cozy but unnecessary fire adding a little ambience.

Instead, Nate and Charlie were thrilled that Gordy had the basketball game on and they never made it past the family room couch and the television. Gordy was only too happy to oblige. The lasagna was served buffet style on Trina's everyday stoneware. The girls ate at the kitchen table, the men and Charlie balanced their plates on their knees, and Trina and Elise settled at the breakfast bar. It was the casual kind of evening Trina usually loved. But tonight it made her restless. And she knew why. She couldn't conduct the veiled interview of Jen's parents that she felt she needed to set her mind at ease.

She did manage to learn about the Lovetts' move from Los Angeles to San Diego, Nate's career in software design, Elise's knack for shaping clay, and her new job in set design at the Old Globe Theater in Balboa Park. But it was hard for Trina to get at what really mattered. She wanted to ask Elise what she believed about life. About God. About parenting. About values and morals.

The closest she got was asking Elise if they were looking for a church.

"No," she said and then took a bite of garlic bread.

"So I guess church isn't important to you?" Trina asked, as gently as she could.

"God, no!" Elise said, and then she laughed heartily. "Did you hear what I said? I said, 'God, no!'"

Trina managed a grin. She had heard it.

"Sorry!" Elise said when she had composed herself. "I can see that it *is* important to you, Trina. I don't mean to make light of what you believe. Honestly. It's just that formal religion doesn't do it for me. I'd much rather go parasailing or rock climbing on a Sunday afternoon and completely surround myself with what God has made, not what man has made. That's where God is for me—in the beauty of the natural world around us. Not in a building… Wow! This bread is amazing. You use fresh garlic, don't you? I can tell. I'm going to have some more. You want some?"

Trina knew in that moment there would be few future conversations with Elise about spiritual things without Gordy present. He knew how to talk with someone who loved God's creation but not His church. Trina felt painfully inadequate to complete her secret evaluation.

"Sure. I'd love some more bread," she said.

Later in the quiet of their bedroom, when the guests were gone, the basketball game over, and the girls tucked in bed, Trina sat quietly on the edge of her bed, waiting for Gordy to ask her what was on her mind. She knew he would.

He turned off the light in the master bathroom and crossed over to his side of the bed. Fluffing up two bed pillows, he slipped under the covers and then reached for *Confessions of Saint Augustine* on his nightstand, his current bedtime read.

But he didn't open it.

"C'mon. Let's have it," he said softly, motioning for Trina to come alongside him.

Trina crawled under the covers and cuddled up against Gordy's chest. His flannel pajamas smelled like Polo. He wrapped his left arm around her and waited.

"They're nice people," she began and stopped.

"Yes, they are," Gordy said.

"But they're so different from us. I don't think I've ever met anyone like Elise," Trina said thoughtfully.

Gordy closed his eyes and leaned back against the pillows and headboard.

"I meet guys like Nate all the time," he said.

"You do?" Trina asked.

"*All* the time," Gordy answered. "Nate will be a millionaire someday. I can guarantee it. He knows what he wants, and he isn't afraid to go after it, even if it means risking everything he owns. I see guys like that at work every day. They're the corporate ladder-climbers. They'll climb that ladder without even knowing what waits at the top, if they think they can make it."

"I'm glad you're not like that," Trina said quickly, snuggling closer. "Those kinds of men make lousy husbands and fathers."

"Sometimes," Gordy said.

After pondering that exchange, Trina said, "Do you think you and Nate will ever do anything together? Like go golfing maybe?"

"Doubtful," he said, grinning. "Nate doesn't golf. He skydives, he surfs, he skis. I think he likes to live life—every part of his life—on the edge of danger and disaster."

"Do you know where they went on their honeymoon?" Trina asked, and before Gordy could answer, she continued, "Kenya. They went on a safari in *Kenya*. Can you believe it?"

"Yeah, I can," Gordy said. "I think the only thing Nate and I have in common is a fondness for basketball... and pretty wives."

Trina cuddled against him, enjoying the compliment. Gordy started to chuckle.

"What is it?" she asked.

"I asked him if he enjoys anything by C.S. Lewis, and he asked me if Lewis is a jazz piano player."

Trina laughed softly at the idea, but yet another reminder of the differences in the two couples regarding faith. Gordy sensed this and held her tighter.

"We can't shield Megan from everything, Trina. And we shouldn't want to," he said. "We will continue to do what we've always done for our girls: Guide them, teach them, pray for them, and commit them to God for safekeeping. Maybe God has placed the Lovetts in our life so that through our daughters' friendship, they'll come to a deeper faith."

"Maybe," Trina replied softly.

Each was lost in personal thought when a soft knock at their door interrupted them.

"Mommy?" It was Megan.

Trina sat up. "Come in," she said.

The door opened, and Megan stood there, framed in a soft yellow glow from the hall night-light.

"Sweetie, what's up?" Trina said.

"I can't fall asleep," Megan said, grimacing. "Can I have a back rub?"

Trina had been giving back rubs as sleeping agents since the girls were infants.

"Sure, honey," Trina said, rising out of bed.

"C'mere, Muffin," Gordy said to Megan as Trina slipped on a robe.

Megan ran to her dad and put her arms around his neck.

"Sweet dreams," he said, kissing her on the forehead.

Megan and Trina then made their way to Megan's room. Pearly moonlight peeked through the curtains that covered the bedroom window, splashing Megan's blankets with luminescent streaks.

As Trina helped Megan get into bed, she asked her daughter if the moon was keeping her awake.

"No, I like the moon. It's like God's night-light. That's what I learned in Sunday school," she said.

Trina smiled and began to gently massage her daughter's back. A few moments of silence followed.

"I'm so glad I met Jen," Megan said softly.

Trina said nothing at first; she just stroked her daughter's back.

"I'm glad you're glad," she finally said.

"Mommy, can you sing the horse song?" Megan said softly.

"Sure, sweetie," Trina whispered.

Bathed in filtered moonlight, Trina softly sang "All the Pretty Little Horses" until her daughter's breathing became slow and even.

She rose gently from the bed and made her way down the hall. Just outside her own bedroom door she could hear Gordy's barely perceptible snore. She turned and walked back down the hall, through the family room, and into the kitchen. For a few moments she stood there, silently reviewing the day. She poured herself a glass of water and drank it, leaning against the doorway into the dining room where the Fiesta Ware glowed in borrowed moonlight.

In the next few weeks, as January slid into February, Trina reluctantly eased into a wait-and-see mode that gave her periods of peace in between scattered moments of seemingly unwarranted anxiety. Megan's friendship with Jen Lovett continued to blossom in ways that alternately awed and alarmed her. Gordy was surprised as well by the speed with which Megan seemed to be emerging from her shell.

Taking an active role in a social relationship was normal, Trina told herself. It was what she had always wanted for Megan. But she couldn't help but be stunned by the pairing. To her, Megan and Jen seemed as opposite as night and day.

The morning of Valentine's Day, Megan walked into the kitchen with her hairbrush, two ponytail holders, two red satin ribbons, and a spray bottle of water.

"What's all this?" Trina asked as she set out a bowl and a box of Froot Loops.

"Jen and I want to have matching braids today," Megan said, setting everything down on the breakfast bar except for the brush, which she handed to her mother. "Can you make them really tight?"

"Okay," she said. "But what's the water bottle for?"

"You have to wet my hair first and then braid it," Megan said as she chose a bar stool and presented the back of her head to Trina.

"It doesn't have to be wet for me to braid it, Meg," Trina said, brushing Megan's hair in long, even strokes.

"Yes, it does!" Megan said, whipping around to make sure Trina picked up the spray bottle and used it. "Jen says if you braid your hair when it's wet, it will be extra curly when you take the braids out. We want to have extra-curly hair!"

"Okay, okay," Trina said, grabbing the bottle and misting Megan's brown hair.

"Make 'em tight," Megan said again.

"I'll make them tight," Trina answered as she set to work on the first braid.

Gordy came into the kitchen then and headed for the coffee pot.

"How are my Valentines this morning?" he asked.

"I can't be your Valentine, Daddy. Mommy is," Megan replied, handing her mother the first ponytail holder.

"Okay, Pocahontas," Gordy replied, winking at Trina and taking a sip of coffee.

"These are French braids, Daddy," Megan said. "Pocahontas wasn't French."

"Neither are you, *mademoiselle*," he said, kissing her on the forehead and then giving Trina a look that said, *When did our daughter become such an expert on everything?*

Trina returned a look that said, *You know exactly when our daughter became an expert on everything.*

Gordy walked over to the toaster, placed two halves of a bagel into it, and pushed the lever down.

"I'm going over to Jen's after school, remember?" Megan said to her mother.

"Yes, I remember. Hand me a ribbon," Trina said. "Is Elise picking you girls up?"

"We can walk," Megan said, holding one ribbon up.

"I'd rather she picked you up, Meg," Trina replied.

"Mommy, Jen only lives a couple of streets away from school. She and Charlie walk all the time."

"I'm sure they'll be fine," Gordy said as he retrieved his bagel from the toaster and cast a look at both daughter and wife.

"Will Elise be there?" Trina said.

"She gets home at four. But Charlie will be there. He's almost ten."

Trina looked up at Gordy as she secured Megan's second braid with a ponytail holder.

It's okay, he mouthed. Trina looked back down at their daughter's head.

"All done," she said.

"Did you make them tight?" Megan asked as she hopped down off the stool.

"Yes, they're tight," Trina said, noticing for the first time that Michelle had wandered into the kitchen. She held a blanket, a doll, and a stuffed elephant in her arms. "Well, good morning, sunshine," Trina said to her younger daughter.

"I want blades," Michelle said, frowning.

"Your hair's too short for braids," Megan said to her sister, picking up the Froot Loop box and filling a bowl.

"I want blades!" Michelle said again, louder.

"Megan, I will take care of this. You just concentrate on breakfast," Trina said. "Why don't you come eat some breakfast, Michelle. Then we will work on your hair, okay?"

"I want blades," Michelle said for third time, softly though, as she made her way to her booster seat at the kitchen table.

"Can I take you girls out for dinner tonight?" Gordy asked as he poured another cup of coffee.

"I want IHOP!" Michelle said.

"I don't want pancakes. I'm tired of pancakes," Megan countered.

"Well, since Mommy is the Valentine, we'll let *her* choose," Gordy said. He walked over to Trina and kissed her goodbye. "Okay, Mommy?" he said, giving her a knowing look.

"Okay. Bye, Daddy," she said, with a grin.

"Bye bye, Daddy," Michelle echoed.

"Bye, Muffin," Gordy said, tugging on one of Megan's braids.

"Bye, Daddy," she replied.

Gordy headed for the door that opened into the garage, opened it, and then pressed the garage-door opener. Giving Trina one more *don't worry* look, he closed the door behind him.

"Okay, girls," Trina said. "Let's finish up. Megan, make sure you put your Valentines in your book bag. You don't want to forget them."

"I already did," Megan said, taking her bowl to the sink. "I put them in my book bag last night. You saw me."

"So I did," Trina said, shaking her head and then turning to Michelle. "C'mon, Michelle. Let's get some clothes on you."

"I want blades," the three-year-old said.

"I made a special Valentine just for you," Jen whispered in Megan's ear at the reading circle later that morning. "It's different than everybody else's."

"I put *Little Mermaid* stickers on your envelope!" Megan whispered back.

"Jen, Megan, this is listening time, not talking time," said Mrs. Fredericks, giving both girls a disapproving look.

"I put a *peso* in it!" Jen said under her breath.

Megan's eyes widened. She loved looking at Jen's Mexican money. Jen had a jar full of it on her dresser a result of the Lovetts' frequent trips into Mexico to visit with friends, shop, and stay overnight on the beach in Baja California. Megan had never even been across the border.

"Jen, this is the last time I'm going to warn you," said Mrs. Fredericks.

"Yes, ma'am," Jen said obediently and then turned to Megan and grinned. All thoughts of the reprimand faded, and only special Valentines glowed in her shining eyes.

~ ~ ~

Megan opened Jen's special Valentine at the party that afternoon in their classroom. Jen had made it out of a paper doily, a piece of vellum, glitter, red lace, and a tiny, gold heart earring whose mate Jen had lost last summer. Inside was the chocolate brown *peso*, dull and old, but bigger than a quarter and totally unlike any coin Megan had ever owned before.

"Your parents don't mind if you give this to me?" Megan dared to ask.

"I have lots," Jen said confidently. "Daddy says they aren't worth much."

This made no sense to Megan. It was money. How could it not be worth much?

"Thank you," Megan said to Jen, closing her hand around the big coin.

"You're welcome," Jen said. "You're my best friend, Megan."

Megan nodded her head.

"And you're mine," she said.

~ ~ ~

Having to spend part of the afternoon with Charlie was the only part of the day Megan didn't like. Charlie spent most of the walk home trying to give Megan and Jen flat tires by walking up behind them and placing his foot on the back of their sneakers so their heels would pop out.

"Cut it out!" Jen yelled at him. "Or I'm telling Mommy."

"Cut it out or I'm telling Mommy!" he mimicked in a high voice.

"Shut up. You're a moron," she yelled back at him.

Megan winced. She wasn't allowed to say shut up to anyone. And she had no idea what a moron was.

"Look who's talking!" Charlie replied, taking a giant step and successfully giving Jen a flat tire.

"I'm telling!" Jen said.

"I'm telling!" Charlie echoed and took off down the street ahead of them.

Jen sat down on the curb to slip her foot back into her shoe. Megan sat down beside her.

"What's a moron?" Megan asked.

Jen tied the bow on her shoe with vehemence.

"I'm not really sure," she answered truthfully. "But whatever it is, it's not good. Charlie calls people morons all the time when he doesn't like them. You definitely *don't* want to be called a moron."

Megan nodded and filed away the information in her head.

"C'mon, let's go," Jen said, rising from the pavement.

When they arrived at Jen's house, Charlie was waiting just inside the front door. He jumped out at them when they stepped inside and both girls screamed. Charlie began to laugh.

"You're going to get it when I tell Mommy!" Jen said.

"Oh, I am so scared!" Charlie said, pretending to shiver.

"One of these days I'm going to put a *cat* in your bed!" Jen said, narrowing her eyes.

"Yeah? Well, one of these days I'm going to put a snake in yours," he retorted back. "In fact, I think I will go into the canyon right now and find one. A big one."

"Liar," Jen said.

"Here I go!" he said and ran for the French doors in the family room that opened onto an expansive redwood deck.

The Lovetts' backyard bordered the canyon that stretched between Megan's neighborhood and the Lovetts'. A perimeter fence that included a hinged gate the previous owners had installed so they could walk their dog in the canyon lined the edge of the yard. Megan was not allowed in the canyon and had never minded the restriction. The simple notion that rattlesnakes lurked in it was incentive enough to stay out. Jen and Charlie weren't allowed in the canyon alone, either, although Megan knew Jen's parents went for walks in the canyon, and sometimes Jen and Charlie accompanied them.

"C'mon!" Jen said, grabbing Megan's hand and following Charlie out the door.

Charlie sprinted across the sloping lawn beyond the deck, jumped over the diving board that stretched across the Lovetts' black-bottom pool, and headed to the corner of the yard where the fence was.

"Here I go!" he said, reaching for the latch on the gate.

"I'll tell!" Jen yelled.

"So what?" he said, his hand on the latch.

"You'll get in trouble."

"I'm opening the gate!" he said, raising the lever.

"Don't do it, Charlie," Megan said, surprising herself and Charlie.

"He won't," Jen said.

"Bye!" Charlie said, looking now at Megan.

Megan's heart was pounding.

For a moment the three children were absolutely still.

"You know, I think I'll wait until dark to get a snake, and then I'll put it in your bed while you're sleeping!" Charlie finally said, letting the latch fall back in place.

"You're such a liar," Jen said.

"You're so ugly," he shot back.

"C'mon, Megan. Let's get a snack," Jen said and turned to walk back into the house with Megan following. Megan turned back to Charlie to make sure he hadn't suddenly changed his mind, and for a moment her eyes and Charlie's met. Something odd passed between them that Megan would remember many months from then, when her world would be caving in around her. Then the moment passed, and Charlie stuck his tongue out at her.

Megan followed Jen into the family room, through the living room and dining room, and into the Lovetts' kitchen.

The Lovetts' house was newer than Megan's, and Elise had decorated it in neutral tones of taupe, ivory, and mocha. Above their gas-powered fireplace was a huge oil painting of a blazing sunset with giraffes and elephants in the foreground.

"That's the *Serengeti*," Jen had told her once when she caught Megan gazing at the painting. Megan didn't know what a Serengeti was. It looked like the most thrilling and wild place on earth. After the canyon, of course.

There were no bookshelves in the Lovetts' living room, no calico blue pillows or dusty rose curtains, no country oak furniture that was all the rage in the late eighties. The expansive living room was furnished with two enormous leather couches in a hushed ivory shade and a matching chair. Throw pillows the colors of coffee with varying amounts of cream were carefully placed on the couches. The coffee table was a slab of gray marble sitting atop a gangly stump of petrified wood. It sported a charcoal black statuette of a kneeling woman with her hands raised to heaven. A five-foot, carved wooden giraffe sat in one corner of the room and a potted palm tree in another. A mahogany cabinet held a stereo system and a collection of recordings of jazz musicians Megan had never heard of. There were no curtains on the long panes of glass that offered a view of the backyard patio. It was a room that Megan both loved and feared. It was the kind of room kids aren't usually allowed in.

As she followed Jen into the kitchen, Megan couldn't help but stare back at the black statuette of the woman on the coffee table. Was the woman praising God or begging God? It was anyone's guess—the face was smooth and featureless.

The girls munched on Doritos, drank Kool-Aid, and watched some cartoons on the little television in the kitchen. Then Jen decided it was time to take their braids out.

They started giggling as they freed their hair from the tight braids, and then they ran into a nearby bathroom to look in a mirror. Untamed, kinky curls fell from their heads like tangled telephone cords.

They giggled some more.

"Let's brush it!" Jen said, opening a drawer and handing Megan a hairbrush and reaching in again for one for herself. "Then we can be wild girls!"

The hairbrushes turned the kinky-curled heads into wild mops.

"We're wild girls!" Jen yelled and she ran into the amazing living room. She began to dance under the Serengeti. Megan followed her.

"We're wild girls! We're wild girls!" Jen chanted and danced. Megan chimed in and began to dance as well.

"You guys are nuts!" said Charlie, who had come back into the house and was watching them from the dining room.

Elise walked in at that moment, holding a bag with tulips sticking out of it. Megan wondered only for a moment where Elise had found such beautiful flowers. Then she froze, thinking Elise would surely tell them they were not supposed to be dancing in the living room. But Elise was laughing.

"What are you girls doing?" she said.

"We're wild girls!" Jen yelled.

"You wild girls need some music!" she said, setting the bag down on the dining table and walking to the mahogany cabinet where the stereo was. In a matter of seconds the room was filled with strange, lively music, and Elise started dancing with them.

"C'mon, Charlie!" Elise said.

"No way!" he said, but he stood there at the edge of the dining room watching.

Elise danced over to him and grabbed his arms, dragging him down the two long, carpeted steps into the living room. She began to dance around him until he finally gave in and began to wave his arms in the air and kick his legs.

"We're wild girls! We're wild girls!" Jen and Megan yelled over and over until they were breathless and sweaty and the song died away. They collapsed on the floor by the fireplace with the majestic Serengeti rising over their weakened, contented bodies.

Trina sat at the breakfast bar with a late afternoon cup of coffee and raised her eyes from the birthday invitation Megan had brought home from school. She didn't bother to minimize the sigh that escaped her body.

Outside, a late February drizzle made occasional taps at the window over the sink. She could hear Megan and Jen laughing in Megan's room and Michelle knocking on the door, begging to join them. Trina was surprised when she heard the door open and Michelle was welcomed in.

She looked back down at the invitation and couldn't help but shake her head. Megan had been invited to go skiing with the Lovetts for Jen's seventh birthday the first weekend in March. Skiing. As in snow and mountains and skis. The Lovetts were renting a condominium in Big Bear—an hour and a half away—for the weekend. Megan wouldn't have to bring anything but pj's and clean underwear.

"Jen has lots of extra ski stuff, Mommy!" Megan had said breathlessly when she and Jen emerged from the car after school that afternoon. "She has extra skis, too!"

"But Megan, you don't know how to ski," Trina had said gently as she got out of the car and opened the passenger-side door for Michelle.

"I can show her!" Jen said quickly. "It's not hard!"

Jen then turned to Megan. "We can stay on the bunny hill all day if you want!" she said. "We can have hot chocolate at midnight and sit in a hot tub!"

"Let's check it out with Daddy when he gets home, okay?" Trina had said, but the girls had raced into the house, offering no evidence that they had heard her.

Trina took a sip of coffee and wondered for a moment what it would be like to spend seven or eight hundred dollars on a little girl's birthday and think nothing of it. For Megan's seventh birthday just two months before, Trina had invited a few of Megan's Sunday school friends to the house for a tea party. Megan hadn't wanted any of her classmates from school to come and actually didn't really want a party at all.

The tea party had been Trina's idea. She had taken her grandmother's china tea set with the yellow rosebuds down from its forgotten perch in the hall closet and shown it to a reluctant Megan the Saturday before her birthday.

Trina absently stirred her cup as she remembered trying to convince Megan that a party would be fun.

"See how pretty it is?" Trina had said, holding up a tiny white cup with a curlicue handle. Megan had reached for the cup and held it in her hands.

"And we can have little sandwiches cut in circles and tiny cakes and strawberries dipped in chocolate," Trina had continued.

"And tea?" Megan said, studying the inside of the cup.

"Sure! And tea, too," Trina said.

Megan gave her a rather puzzled look.

"I don't think those girls at Sunday school like tea," she said softly.

"Well..." Trina said, thinking fast. "We can use apple juice."

"Then is it still a tea party?" Megan said, looking now at the fat little teapot.

"Of course," Trina answered confidently. "We'll just pretend the apple juice is tea."

In the end, Megan agreed to inviting three little girls from Sunday school who came to the house the following Saturday, dropped off by grateful mothers eager to do a little Christmas shopping. Megan even allowed Michelle to dress up for the party and to receive a little favor bag when the party was over.

Trina got up, walked over to the coffee pot, and refilled her cup.

It had been a nice party, actually. The little guests seemed to enjoy the games Trina planned and decorating their own little teacakes. But Trina couldn't help but notice that day how much Megan let the party just play itself out around her; how it seemed the party really was for those little girls Megan saw once a week for just an hour.

When she tucked Megan in bed that night, she asked her if she had enjoyed her party.

"I liked the chocolate strawberries," Megan said, after a moment's pause.

Trina said nothing at first. She looked down at her quiet, composed daughter and decided that was okay.

"I liked them too," she said and then she kissed her good night.

That day seemed light years away from the present, Trina thought as she added a little milk to the coffee. Jen's friendship had changed everything. And most of the time it seemed like a good thing. Megan and Jen spent almost every afternoon together, and every Friday night Jen's parents took the girls out to eat or to the movies or other fun places.

Trina suddenly realized she and Gordy had really done nothing special with the girls since the two had met in January.

She set the cup down as an idea came into her head. She set off down the hall and stopped in front of Megan's door.

"Megan, it's Mommy. May I come in?" Trina said.

Laughter erupted from inside.

"Okay!" Megan answered.

Trina opened the door to find Pippin, the cat, dressed in baby-doll clothes and Jen snapping the tenth or eleventh barrette into Michelle's hair.

"We're the mommies," Jen was saying, as she grabbed another barrette and the last tiny handful of Michelle's hair.

"This is my daughter Janet," Megan said, holding up Pippin and fixing a bonnet that had fallen over one green eye. Pippin looked ready to bolt.

"And this is Catherine," Jen said, pointing to Michelle.

"I'm not *Caffrine*," Michelle said, like she had said it many times already.

"*You* wanted to play," Megan said to her sister as she plopped the cat into a doll bassinet and patted him to make him stay.

Trina knelt down by Jen and smiled at her.

"Jen, would you like to stay overnight Saturday and come to church with us on Sunday?" Trina said. "We can go out to eat afterward."

Megan and Jen looked at each other and grinned.

"A sleepover!" they both said.

"I want IHOP," Michelle said, yanking out a barrette that was poking her in her left ear.

"Can we sleep on the sofa bed?" Megan asked Trina excitedly.

"Sure," Trina answered. "We'll just run it by Jen's mother when she comes to pick her up."

Trina stood up and started to make her way to the door.

"Why don't you girls put the doll clothes away while I make you a snack, okay?"

"Okay," Megan and Jen chimed.

Michelle followed Trina out the door. Pippin also made his getaway, tripping over his smocked baby-doll dress.

~~~~

"So, what do you do at your church?" Jen asked as she scooped up a handful of doll clothes and tossed them into a large Rubbermaid container.

"We sing songs about Jesus and learn stuff," Megan said casually. "Haven't you ever been to church?"

"I went to a wedding once," Jen said. "It was boring. But the cake was good. And they had a swan made of ice."

"Oh," Megan said thoughtfully, trying to picture a frozen swan sitting on a church pew.

"So, do you have to learn new stuff about Jesus every time you go?" Jen asked.

"Well, lots of the stuff I already know, like the Bible stories and Jesus' dying on the cross," Megan said proudly.

"I like Bible stories," Jen said. "I have a book of Bible stories. My mom reads them to me sometimes at bedtime."

Then Jen furrowed her brow and clamped the lid down on the Rubbermaid tub.

"How come Jesus died on a cross?" Jen said, turning to Megan.

Megan was suddenly glad she paid attention in Sunday school. She actually knew the answer.

"To take away our sins," she said solemnly.

"What sins?" Jen asked.

"Well, all the bad stuff we do." Megan said. "It makes God sad, and we can't get to heaven. Jesus died on the cross to take away the sins so we can go to heaven when we die."

"How come He couldn't take the sins away with His magic powers?" Jen asked, clearly interested.

Megan was stumped.

"I don't think it works like that," she finally said.

"How come?" Jen asked, pushing the container into Megan's closet.

"I don't know," Megan said. "The Bible says it had to be the cross."

"That doesn't seem very fair to Jesus," Jen said, picking up her shoes. "If I had been there in Bible times, I would have hidden Jesus in my house and not let those people put nails in Him."

Megan had never considered what she would have done. She had never pictured it any other way. It was Jesus on the cross. It was always Jesus on the cross.

"But then the sins would still be there," Megan said.

"God made everything, didn't He?" Jen said, after thinking a moment.

"Yes," Megan said.

"Then He can make the sins go away without a cross. He can use His magic wand," Jen said, slipping on her shoes.

"I don't know if God has a magic wand..." Megan said pensively.

"Of course, He does, silly!" Jen said. "He has everything!"

Jen took off down the hall, enticed by the smell of fresh popcorn.

Megan followed but didn't notice the aroma. She knew something wasn't quite right with what had just happened. But she wasn't sure what it was.

∽ ∽ ∽

It seemed to Megan that it took a lot of talking before her parents said it was okay for her to go skiing with Jen on her birthday. First the mothers had to talk about it at the door when it was time for Jen to go home that afternoon. It seemed to Megan like her mother had a million questions. Megan couldn't see what the big deal was. People skied all the time.

Then there was more talk about it when Daddy got home. Finally they told her she could go. She ran to phone Jen with the news, and they talked about how much fun they were going to have until Megan was summoned to dinner.

At bedtime, after her mother kissed her and tucked her in, her dad came in to read a chapter from *The Voyage of the Dawn Treader*. The chapter that night was a little scary: the boy Eustace turned into a dragon, and the chapter ended with his desperately longing to be a little boy again.

"Will he always be a dragon?" Megan asked when the last page of chapter six had been read and her father had closed the book.

"Do you really want me to tell you what happens?" Gordy said, smiling.

Megan nodded, her eyes wide.

"He won't always be a dragon, sweetie. Aslan will save him," Gordy said, smoothing the hair around Megan's forehead.

Thinking of Aslan's rescuing a boy who had been turned into a dragon made Megan think of her conversation with Jen earlier that day about Jesus' rescuing people by dying on a cross.

"Daddy," she said. "Why didn't God use a magic wand to take all the sins away? Why did Jesus have to die on the cross?"

Her father placed the book on the nightstand and turned back to her.

"What brings this up?" he said gently.

For some reason, Megan didn't want him to know Jen had asked. She shrugged her shoulders. "Just wondering," she said.

"Well," he began. "How bad do you think sin is? Is it really bad or just a little bad?"

"Really bad," Megan said.

"And how do you feel after you've done something wrong, something you know God doesn't like? Really bad or just a little bad?"

"Really bad," Megan whispered.

"Okay, now how about this? How would you feel if God just used a magic wand to take away your sin? No cross. Just *zap!* and it's gone. Would you feel really bad about your sin, just a little bad, or maybe not bad at all?" her father said.

Megan blinked. "Maybe not bad at all," she said.

"Maybe that's part of the reason why Jesus had to die on the cross, don't you think?" her father said, stroking her cheek.

"So that I would feel really bad about bad things?" Megan said thoughtfully.

"Something like that," her father said, bending down to kiss her. "There's more to it than that, Meg, but I think for tonight that's enough for you to think about."

Her father ruffled her hair as he rose from her bedside.

"Goodnight, Muffin," he said as he walked to the door and turned out the light.

Megan lay there for quite some time before she fell asleep. So many thoughts were swirling through her head: Jen's upcoming birthday at Big Bear, Eustace turning into a dragon, God using a cross instead of a magic wand to rescue her. Why couldn't God just use a magic wand to *make* people feel bad about bad things? Or why couldn't He just use a magic wand so that there *are* no bad things? It didn't seem to make sense.

It wasn't until the whole house was quiet that Megan finally succumbed to sleep. She feared she would dream of dragons that night, but she didn't. She dreamed instead of snow, birthday cake, and white socks with rosebuds—edged in lace.

PART TWO

Summer 1989

The afternoon sun shimmered over the surf at La Jolla Shores, as Trina held a hand above her eyes, watching to make sure Megan and Jen hadn't wandered too far into the waves.

"Seaweed!" she heard Jen yell, followed by Megan's familiar squeal.

She watched as the girls hopped across a length of greenish brown kelp. Jen reached down, grabbed two rubberlike leaves, and snapped them loose from the floating vine. She held them by their bulbous stems and brought them up to her ears.

"Look!" she said to Megan. "Earrings!"

Megan laughed, grabbed two leaves, and did the same thing. The tide whooshed the slimy vines around their calves and they shrieked, running to the shore with their oversized earrings.

Trina smiled and called out to them.

"I think it's time for more sunscreen, girls!" she said. "Bring Michelle up with you." The girls skipped over to where four-year-old Michelle was building a sand castle.

Trina watched them bend down and ask Michelle a question. When the little girl nodded, Jen and Megan laughed and stuck their seaweed leaves in the top of Michelle's volcano-like castle, like pennants on a fortress. Then the girls all stood up and ran through the sand to Trina.

"Whoa, girls," Trina cautioned them. "Don't kick sand on your towels! Here, dry off a little, and I'll put more sunscreen on your backs."

"We're hungry!" Megan said, teeth chattering. The chilly waters of the Pacific never warmed up enough for Trina's liking. Not even on a balmy, late-June day like this one. She put her own towel around Megan's shoulders.

"Well, I have lots of snacks," she said. "You want a tangerine or some Cheetos?"

"Tangerines!" Megan and Jen said in unison. Michelle reached into the snack bag and pulled out the bag of Cheetos.

"Here," Trina said, handing the girls a tangerine each. "You peel and I'll rub."

She rubbed in more sunscreen on both girls while they peeled and ate the fruit.

"Let's go back in," Jen said a moment later, bending down and grabbing her rubber raft.

The girls began to run off.

"Not too far!" Trina called. "Stay where you can see the life-guard tower!"

"We will," they called back to her.

"Wait for me!" Michelle yelled as she struggled to get up off her towel.

"Wait, Michelle," Trina said. "I'll take you."

"I want to go with them!" Michelle whined.

"Honey, they know how to swim. They go out farther than you," Trina said.

"I'm big enough!" Michelle said, crossing her arms and frowning.

"C'mon," Trina said cheerfully. "Let's sit in the waves and look for moonstones, okay?"

"Okay," Michelle said grudgingly.

Trina and Michelle walked to the surf's edge. Trina grimaced as she sat down in the ankle-deep surf. It felt like ice water. Michelle waddled around on her haunches, digging into sand to uncover the smooth white pebbles she and Megan called moonstones.

"I found a little crab!" she yelled. "Look!"

Trina took a quick peek at the pearly gray crab no bigger than a dime.

"Okay, sweetie, let him go."

"He's going in my castle," Michelle said and she ran to her lopsided creation.

After a few minutes, Trina's legs grew used to the chill of the water, and she began to relax. She watched Megan and Jen out in the water, side by side on Jen's red raft. They rode a wave in, jumped off the raft, waved to Trina, and then ran back into the surf to catch another.

It was hard to believe the girls were eight already, that school was out, and they would be in third grade in the fall. They had grown up so much this past year. Especially Megan.

Trina couldn't deny that much of her daughter's newfound confidence was due to Jen's friendship. The past year and a half with Jen a part of her everyday life had sparked a dramatic change in Megan. She was polite to adults she did not know well, less afraid to try new things, and more assertive in her relationships with other kids her age.

Most of the time Trina was exceptionally glad Megan had Jen as a friend. There were moments, however, when she could sense Jen was restless, that Megan's adoration of her wasn't quite enough. Sometimes Megan would call Jen's house to talk to her or ask her over, and the call would be cut short because Jen had another friend over. Megan seemed to take this as well as could be expected, although she didn't seek out other friendships like Jen did. On occasion, a third, and sometimes a fourth, playmate would join them on their play dates. But Trina could tell it was always Jen's idea to invite other girls to play with them.

Megan was loyal to a fault, Trina often thought. On those days when Jen was unavailable because she was with her family or another friend, Trina encouraged Megan to call one of the other girls from her class or Sunday school. Most of the time Megan declined and just resigned herself to playing with Michelle. A few times Megan would agree to invite a little girl named Tracie to fill the void Jen left when she was otherwise engaged. But those times were few and far between. There simply was no one else for Megan but Jen.

As she watched Megan and Jen ride wave after wave, she couldn't help but think, in spite of her earlier reservations, that Jen had been an answer to prayer. Trina wondered, though, how far she should let that thought travel. Jen wasn't a typical believer, nor were her parents. Trina really didn't know what Nate Lovett thought about God or spiritual things. They never discussed it on those few occasions when the two families were together. Usually when Trina picked Megan up from Jen's, it was Elise who came out to say hello, if she was home. Trina got the impression Nate was gone from home a lot.

And Elise? Elise was a mystery. She occasionally read Bible stories to her kids. She sang when she did housework. She made beautiful things out of clay. She didn't swear. She loved her kids. But Trina couldn't convince Elise to come to a ladies' Bible study with her or to attend a Sunday-morning service. She seemed content with the little of God she knew. Trina was glad Elise had no qualms about letting Jen come to church with Megan as often as she wanted, but that's as far as their influence as a family went with the Lovetts. It seemed to Trina that the Lovetts liked their God big in global terms, but small when it came to having a personal relationship with Him.

When Trina figured it was after three o'clock, she rose from the water. If they didn't leave soon, rush-hour traffic would guarantee a slow, boring ride home. She turned to Michelle who had abandoned the castle and was now writing the alphabet in the sand.

"Time to go, Michelle," she said.

"I have four more letters," Michelle said, drawing a huge V with a stick.

"Okay, but make them quick."

She called out to Megan and Jen.

"One more ride in, girls, then we need to go!"

"Two more times!" Megan called back.

Trina gave her the thumbs up sign and trudged back through the sand to their towels and beach chairs.

⌇⌇⌇

Traffic on Interstate 5 was nightmarish, despite leaving as early as they did. By the time Trina got back to her North County neighborhood, it was nearly four-thirty.

"Why don't you girls run through the sprinkler to get the sand off," she advised, as the girls piled out of the car.

"I want to turn the water on!" Michelle called out as Megan and Jen raced across the lawn to the spigot.

Trina shook the towels and blanket on the driveway, walked back into the garage, and dumped them by the washer. It would be a good night for grilling hot dogs, she suddenly thought, and she pushed the gas grill out the side door and onto their backyard patio.

"I'm going inside to take a shower," she called out to Megan who was dashing through the spray of the lawn sprinkler. "Watch your sister, Megan. Don't let her go into the street."

"Okay!" Megan said, laughing as Jen slipped and fell giggling onto the wet grass.

Trina lingered in the shower, letting the hot beads of water massage her neck and back. It felt good to get the sand and sticky salt water off her hair and skin. Afterward, she dressed, towel-dried her hair, and ran a pick through the tight curls of her perm.

When she came back through the house, Michelle was sitting in front of the television watching cartoons, wrapped in a clean towel and eating Cocoa Puffs out of the box. The rest of the house was quiet.

"Go get some dry clothes on, Michelle," Trina said, looking about the room. "Where are Megan and Jen?"

"They went on their bikes."

"Where did they go?" Trina asked.

"I don't know," Michelle said, not looking away from the television.

"Dry clothes," she said to Michelle as she started to walk away.

She stepped into the garage from the kitchen door, and then walked out into the late afternoon sun. No sign of the girls.

Trina sighed. She didn't like the measure of independence bicycles had given the girls. Ever since they had learned to ride two-wheeled bikes last summer they had begged to be allowed to ride to each other's houses. Elise hadn't minded from the beginning, but Trina hadn't been ready for Megan to take off alone on her bike. It wasn't until May, just one month ago, that Trina had finally given Megan the okay to ride alone to Jen's house. *It's all neighborhood streets,* Gordy had said. *She'll be okay. She knows how to watch for traffic.*

Yes, it was all neighborhood streets. But it was still several blocks to Jen's adjoining neighborhood. And those neighborhood streets were never quiet. There were always cars zooming up and down them. No one ever seemed to drive the speed limit. Not even on her own street, which she simply could not understand. The street on which she and Gordy lived dead-ended at the edge of the canyon. And yet people still sailed down it like it stretched clear to Nevada.

She gazed up the street toward Jen's neighborhood. It wasn't like Megan to take off on her bike and not tell Trina where she was going. Trina looked at her watch. Five-fifteen. Elise would be calling any minute to have her send Jen home, and she had no idea where the girls were.

Trina could just picture Elise saying, *Well, just send Jen on home when you see her.* Like it was no big deal that Trina didn't know where she was.

Trina was suddenly reminded of the time last fall when Elise commented that for a woman of such strong faith she sure worried a lot.

She sighed and went back into the house to thaw hot dog buns.

⌣ ⌢ ⌣

Megan and Jen stood with their bikes between their legs, scanning the horizon that lay before them. The yawning canyon lay at their feet, its mouth shielded by dented, gray guard rails that had kept more than one drunk driver from plummeting to the sandy depths below.

"I think it's that one," Jen was saying, pointing to a fence line on the canyon's other side, directly ahead of them. To their right, the canyon extended as far as three more neighborhood streets. To their left, it stretched to an unknown length.

"Which one?" Megan said.

"See?" Jen said, putting her head close to Megan's. "You can see the little black latch."

"I don't see it," Megan said, squinting.

"Right there," Jen said. "Right by that big bush with the yellow flowers. That's my fence."

"I see it," Megan said. "Are you sure that's your house?"

"Yep, that's my house."

Jen suddenly had an idea.

"Come back here when it gets dark, like nine o'clock, and shine a flash light, okay?" she said. "Blink it three times, and then I'll blink mine three times. I can stand on a deck chair and reach over the fence to do it."

"Okay!" Megan said, and then she added, "If my mom will let me."

"If she will let you what?"

"Come out here at nine o'clock."

"It's your own street!" Jen said in amazement.

"Yeah, okay," Megan said.

"I bet if there were a trail in the canyon, we could get to each other's houses in no time," Jen said, as she wheeled her bike away from the canyon's edge.

"But there are rattlesnakes in the canyon!" Megan said, turning her bike around also.

"I've never seen one," Jen said, almost like a challenge.

"I'd rather ride my bike," Megan said carefully, not wishing to spoil Jen's optimism about what lay behind them.

"Hey! You want to ride my bike back to your house?" Jen asked.

Megan smiled, glad that Jen knew how much she admired the new bike Jen got for her eighth birthday. It had three speeds, hand brakes, and a glittering violet seat and chain guard. Megan's was a hand-me-down from her cousin Leah who lived in San Jose. It was a hazy orange color, and the kickstand was broken. Her dad had told her that when she was older, he would buy her a nice ten-speed, but for right now, Leah's old bike was just fine. Fine, yes. Beautiful, no.

"Okay!' Megan said.

The girls switched bikes and pedaled away from the rim of the canyon, their still-damp hair flying easily in the breeze.

The first part of July passed agonizingly slow for Megan. Jen and her family spent five days in Santa Barbara visiting Jen's grandparents and then had taken off for an eight-day cruise in the Caribbean. Megan had seen Jen only once in the first fifteen days of the month.

Megan's parents kept telling her that lots of families go away for a little while in the summer. They reminded her that they would be going on a trip of their own in August to visit family in San Jose.

"It's taking too long," Megan said, more than once.

Megan declined Trina's offers to arrange play dates with other girls while Jen was gone. Most of the time she played by herself or with Michelle.

On the day the Lovetts were due to return, Megan began calling their house, hoping to catch Jen when she first walked in the door. It was late in the evening, past Megan's bedtime, when the Lovett phone was finally picked up by Elise.

Jen was already in bed, Megan was told. But she could call back the next day.

Megan hung up the phone and, without saying anything to her parents, crawled into bed herself.

Jen was back home, and she hadn't called.

Her mother came looking for her a few minutes later and seemed surprised that she was in bed with the light out.

"Did you talk to her?" Trina asked.

"She was in bed," Megan answered softly.

"It *is* kind of late, honey," she finally said.

Megan nodded.

"Can I invite her over tomorrow?"

Megan heard her mother draw in a breath like she was about to deliver bad news.

"I promised to help paint the nursery at church, remember, honey? You and Michelle are going over to the Wilsons'."

"I don't like going to the Wilsons'."

"It's just for one day, Megan."

"I hate those boys," Megan said, staring out the window across from her bed.

"Megan…"

"I do! They're mean."

"If they're mean, Megan, you should tell Mrs. Wilson," Trina said firmly.

"Why? She never does anything," Megan replied angrily.

"We'll talk about this tomorrow, Meg," she finally said. "It's late."

"I can go to Jen's. Elise said I could call tomorrow," Megan said.

"We'll see," Trina said as she rose to leave. "Let's wait and see what Elise says, okay?"

"I want to go to Jen's," Megan repeated, clearly wanting the last word, but her mother wouldn't let her have it.

"I said we'll see," Trina said evenly.

In the end, Megan spent the day with Jen.

Megan called the Lovett house in the morning as soon as Trina would let her. Elise told Megan she could ride her bike over anytime and stay as long as she liked. Trina had asked to speak with Elise herself.

Megan heard her mother suggest that perhaps the first day back from vacation wasn't a good time for a friend to visit.

"Mom!" she said crossly.

Trina looked at her and frowned.

"Well, if you're sure it's okay..." Trina said, her voice trailing off.

Apparently, it was okay. Her mother hung up, and then paused for a moment before telling Megan she could go.

Trina offered to take Megan over to the Lovetts on her way to drop Michelle off at the Wilsons', but Megan insisted she needed to take her bike.

"What if Jen and I want to go for a ride?" Megan said.

"Please be careful," her mother said as Megan rushed off to get dressed.

Her mother said those three words so often that Megan didn't even hear them anymore.

The next few days passed like Jen had never been gone. The two girls spent every day together—usually at Jen's, where they tried to avoid Charlie as much as possible. Most of the time that wasn't a problem. But Elise was gone a lot, and Charlie was always left in charge, a role Megan thought Charlie took on more like a cruel despot than a responsible older brother. He barricaded them in Jen's bedroom, locked them out of the house, chased them with his Super Soaker water gun, and threatened to throw them into the pool and then tell Elise they had jumped in when he told them not to. And that was just the short list.

Megan wanted to complain to her mother how wicked Charlie could be, but she knew if she did that, it would reveal how often she and Jen were left alone with only eleven-year-old Charlie for supervision. She decided it wasn't worth it. Besides, what could her mother do? No one got after Charlie for anything. Jen never even tattled on him, though she always threatened to.

One afternoon that first week was spent at Megan's, where life seemed more predictable. Megan liked it that way.

But even Megan could tell Jen was used to a more independent life, a life filled with surprises, even if some of them, like Charlie's tricks, weren't that pleasant. Jen was used to managing her own day. Waking up when she wanted, getting dressed when she wanted, getting her own meals on her own timetable. When Trina called the girls into the kitchen for an afternoon snack on the fourth day Jen was home, Jen turned to Megan and said, "Why does she do that?"

"Do what?" Megan replied. She and Jen were in Megan's backyard, coloring pictures atop Megan's wooden play structure.

"Make a snack when we didn't even ask for it?" Jen said, putting the pink crayon she had been using back in the crayon box and rising to her knees.

Megan wasn't quite sure what to make of Jen's question. She rose to her knees, too. They slid down, one after the other, on the structure's plastic yellow slide.

"'Cause she probably thinks we're hungry," Megan replied as she landed.

"But if we wanted a snack, we could just go in and get one," Jen said as she skipped over to the sliding door that led to the kitchen.

It didn't appear that Jen was doing anything more than making an observation, which was good because Megan had no philosophical answer for why a mother would make a snack that no one had asked for. Megan followed her into the kitchen where a plate of apple wedges, slices of cheese, and Triscuits awaited.

That night as Trina tucked Megan into bed, Megan toyed with the idea of telling her mother that sometimes Jen said and did things that surprised her. Sometimes Jen would ask a question or say something or do something that Megan would never dream of saying or doing. Like suggesting there was no need for Jesus to die on a cross. Like wondering if there really were rattlesnakes in the canyon. Like questioning a mother's motive for making an unrequested snack. But then Megan played the conversation in her head as she figured it would go, if she were to say such a thing.

"What kinds of things?" her mother would ask.

What kinds of things?

Megan watched her mother rise from her bed and walk to her bedroom door. She switched off the light.

"Good night, Meg," she said.

The imagined question hung heavy in the air.

Megan knew she could not put it into words her mother would understand. She didn't know how to express how uncertain Jen made her feel sometimes. How she sometimes felt unsafe with her. It made no sense.

She let it go.

" 'Night, Mommy," she said and turned over on her side, toward the window, toward the canyon, where the sun would rise in the morning.

The following day dawned bright and balmy. It began as the kind of late-July day that the San Diego tourism industry loves; hot and dry with no bugs and no humidity. A trademark beautiful day.

As the morning wore off, however, and the mercury still climbed, it became the kind of day that makes kids complain there's nothing to do and that makes mothers wish school would hurry up and start.

It was a day like the one before it, only hotter.

Megan rode her bike over to Jen's after lunch. It was the earliest her mother would let her go since Elise wasn't home and wouldn't be home until after four o'clock.

"Besides," Trina had said, "You can help me pick out the wallpaper border for the church nursery, Megan. You can help me find something fun. Say, maybe you and Jen can come to the church with me this afternoon and help me put it up. Want to do that?"

Megan had declined.

"That does *not* sound like fun, Mom," she said, shaking her head.

Megan went to the home-improvement center with her mother as requested and helped pick out something "fun," but as soon as lunch was over, Megan pedaled as fast as the heat would let her to Jen's. She was glad Jen answered the doorbell instead of Charlie. Jen enthusiastically let her in.

Neither girl noticed the full-size van parked in the shade of a Chinese elm across the street from Jen's house and two doors down. It was dark blue. Splotchy paint. It had been there since late morning.

It had been there the day before for a while, too, but no one had noticed then, either.

By two that afternoon, Megan and Jen had seemingly exhausted all there was to do inside the house. It would be two more hours before Elise got home from her art exhibit and they could go swimming.

The girls went outside, and Jen dared Megan to run across the street barefoot and run back.

"I don't want to do that!" Megan protested, but Jen said she would do it, too.

They did it twice—Jen to prove she could, and Megan to prove her loyalty. As they soaked their scorched feet in Jen's swimming pool, they tried to think of something else to do.

"I want a Slurpee! A big one," Jen said.

"I don't have any money," Megan said, which was only partially true. She had ten dollars she was saving to spend at Disneyland, which she and her family would visit on their way to San Jose in August.

"I have some in the bank," Jen said at first. "Hey! Let's get on our bikes and look for money in the gutters. I bet we find all kinds of dimes and nickels. Then we can go to the 7-Eleven and get Slurpees!"

It sounded like a hopeless cause but Megan said nothing. At least it would give them something to do until Elise got home and they could go swimming.

They slipped their sandals on, got on their bikes, and pedaled away, one on each side of the street. After canvassing the curbs of ten houses each, Megan announced she had found a penny.

"Let's go to the street the school is on," Jen said. "It's busier there. More people to drop their money."

Jen was off, so Megan sighed and began to follow her.

They didn't notice that the blue van had started its engine and was pulling away from the curb.

By the time they reached the street by the schoolyard, Megan had found a very dirty dime and Jen had pocketed a nickel and three pennies.

"I'm going to check by the bus stop!" Megan yelled to Jen as she pedaled off some yards from Jen to check under the bench at a city bus stop.

She eased her bike to the ground and crouched down to peer at the bench's steel legs. She thought she heard Jen say something behind her.

She turned.

Jen was talking to a lady on the passenger side of a blue van that was idling by the curb.

Megan stood up.

Jen was pointing to something across the street, but the lady didn't turn her head. She didn't look in the direction Jen was pointing. She looked only at Jen.

Megan wondered what the lady was trying to find. She also wondered if Jen had found any more money. She was getting really hot. The lady had very strange hair. All black, very straight. Where was the driver?

These random thoughts cascaded in one or two seconds, as the side door of the van slid open in a rush. Two thick arms reached out, grabbed Jen by her middle, and pulled her inside. Jen's head hit the top of the doorframe as her bike clattered to the sidewalk so that the sound the bike made coincided with her head's crashing into the metal frame.

Jen's mouth opened, but no sound came out.

Megan opened hers, too, but couldn't make a sound.

The lady with the funny hair had slid over to the driver's side and was starting to pull away as Jen was pulled in.

The sliding door was slamming shut and zooming past her when Megan finally found her voice.

She screamed Jen's name.

The man inside looked at her as the name exploded off Megan's lips, and then he disappeared behind metal and steel.

And so did Jen.

Adele Springer was annoyed with herself that she hadn't come out earlier in the day to water her geraniums. San Diego's dry heat was notoriously hard on hanging plants, and she didn't usually let stuff like this go. She fingered the flimsy head of one of the biggest blooms, its pungent odor practically begging for attention.

"Well, it couldn't be helped," she murmured to the striped Martha Washington variety that hung above her head.

She had spent most of the day in her garage-turned-upholstery shop, working tirelessly on an antique fainting couch that had arrived the day before in deplorable shape. The heat of the day finally drove her into the house. Chet had never wanted to get air conditioning for the house, but it was the first thing she changed after he died last winter. Actually it was the only thing she changed.

As she watered, she pondered how many days the couch would take her. Sometimes her customers expected nothing short of a miracle. Her problem was, and she knew it, she usually gave them what they wanted. And so they kept coming back. Chet had once opined that he thought her "little upholstery business" was just a great little way to keep her occupied, to keep her mind off the children they didn't have and, therefore, the grandchildren they also didn't have. But Adele was really good at what she did. She was at the point where she could pick and choose her projects. She smiled at the thought that the year Chet retired from the post office, she had made enough for the two of them to take an Alaskan cruise to celebrate. First class all the way. It had been a wonderful trip. It was the last they would take together. A year and a half later, Chet was dead of a massive heart attack. She was glad he never suffered beyond the initial pain of the attack. And that he died fully ready to meet God.

Adele was still getting used to the idea of being a widow, although she hated the way the word looked—with those two Ws on either side, like metal brackets stapled to her heart and soul. She hated the way it sounded off the tongue, too. That "oh" sound at the end was hideous. Like it would forever and always be, "Oh! Chet is gone!"

Oh!

She almost said it audibly.

But then she thought she heard a scream.

And another. And another.

Adele set down the watering can and looked up the street toward the school near her house, toward the sound of the screams. A little girl was standing there. Two bikes were by her, lying on the ground. The girl was screaming.

"Good Lord!" Adele whispered, and then she began to run. She was heavier than she used to be and her ankles ached when she was in a hurry—but she ran nonetheless. A brown UPS truck was pulling up behind her as she reached the shrieking child.

"What is it?" Adele said between breaths when she reached the girl.

"Is she hurt?" the UPS man asked as he jumped out of his vehicle.

"I don't know," Adele yelled above the little girl's screams.

"Honey, what is it?" Adele repeated, dropping to her knees and taking the girl gently by her shoulders.

The girl looked at Adele's eyes and abruptly stopped yelling. Adele almost fell over backward at the immediate silence.

"Did you boys see what happened?" the UPS man said to two boys who had been shooting hoops in the schoolyard and had run to the fence.

"Nope. We just all the sudden heard screaming," one of them said.

Adele searched the child's face for a clue as to what was going on inside her mind.

"What's your name, precious?" Adele said softly.

The child blinked.

"Why do you suppose she has two bikes? That doesn't make any sense," the UPS man said.

Adele looked at the bikes. One was a few feet from the girl; the other, a few yards. There was no one else around.

She tried again.

"What's your name?"

The child opened her mouth. For a moment there was no sound.

"Megan," she finally whispered.

~ ~ ~

The lady in front of Megan, with her hands on her shoulders, smiled at her. It was a nice smile. The lady smelled like her Grandmother Lewis.

"Hello, Megan," she said. "My name is Adele Springer. Can you tell me why you were screaming?"

Megan's eyes filled with tears. She began to shake. This lady was not Grandma Lewis. This was not happening. *This was not happening!*

"Megan, are you hurt?" Adele said softly, but firmly, her arms still on Megan's shoulders.

Megan looked deep into Adele's eyes, the eyes of a stranger. And yet somehow she knew Adele was not like the strangers her mother had warned her about. She was not like the strangers in that blue van.

Jen.

"Megan, honey, you need to tell me what's wrong so I can help you. Okay?"

Megan's heart was still racing, her breathing still accelerated. This was a dream. This was a nightmare. *I want to wake up.*

"Am I sleeping?" Megan said, barely whispering the words.

Adele's eyes widened. The man in the brown shirt took a step backward.

"No, Megan, you're not," Adele said.

Megan sank to the pavement with Adele's arms still around her.

"Megan?" Adele said her name loudly.

Megan closed her eyes and then opened them.

"They took her!" Megan croaked.

"What?" Adele said.

"They took her," Megan repeated, and she began to sob.

"Who took who?" Adele said as she frantically tried to get Megan to look at her.

"Jen. They took *Jen*." Megan moaned.

"Jen?" Adele said, her voice rising. "Is Jen your sister?"

Megan thrashed her head from side to side. Adele must have quickly decided it didn't matter who Jen was.

"Who took Jen?" Adele said firmly.

"The people in the blue van. They grabbed her. They took her!"

Adele looked at the bikes. The UPS man did the same.

"You have a radio in that truck of yours?" Adele said to the man.

"I'm on it," he said, and he ran to his vehicle.

Megan wanted her mother.

Adele had her cuddled against her wide, soft chest as they sat on the sidewalk. Waiting. But Megan wanted her mother.

The man in the brown shirt was talking to the boys on the other side of the fence. It seemed very quiet.

"I want my mommy," Megan said faintly.

"Of course you do. The police will help you get to her, okay, Megan?" Adele said.

A few minutes later, two San Diego Police Department squad cars arrived, without sirens but with lights twinkling like a Christmas display.

Two policemen got out of the nearer car. When they opened their doors, their radio squawked a message in code. It was loud. Megan flinched.

The man in the brown shirt walked over to them and started talking. He pointed to Megan. He pointed to the bikes. He looked at his watch.

"Maybe ten minutes ago," he said as he looked back toward Megan.

One of the policemen walked over to Megan and Adele.

"Let's stand up, sweetie. This policeman is here to help you," Adele said, helping Megan rise to her feet.

"Hello, I'm Officer Powell," he extended his hand to Adele. She took it.

"Adele Springer."

"And who is this?" Officer Powell said, lowering himself to Megan's height.

Megan said nothing.

Officer Powell looked up at Adele.

"This is Megan. I'm afraid I don't know her last name. We just met," Adele said rubbing Megan's shoulder.

"Can you tell me your last name, Megan?" the policeman said. He had the blackest sunglasses Megan had ever seen. She couldn't see his eyes.

"It's okay, honey," Adele said, reassuringly.

"Diamond," Megan said.

"Megan Diamond? And how old are you, Megan Diamond?"

"Eight."

"Do you know your address and phone number, Megan?"

Megan nodded and rattled the numbers off.

The policeman motioned for his partner. He gave him the phone number and told him to give the house a call.

"Can you find her?" Megan suddenly said.

The officer whipped his head back around.

"Tell me what happened, Megan."

It seemed like a long time had passed, and yet the policeman was still asking her questions. People in cars were slowing down to look at her standing there with the policeman and his twinkling car. Megan didn't like it.

"Are you sure you've never seen these people before, Megan? Maybe the man is Jen's uncle? Or a good friend of the family?"

It was very hot. Megan was starting to feel sick to her stomach.

She shook her head.

"And you didn't see his face?"

"I saw a little bit. He had a moustache. He had big arms."

"Did he have skin like mine or skin like Officer Trumbull over there?"

Megan looked over at the policeman talking to the man in the brown shirt. Officer Trumbull was black.

"Like yours," she said.

"And the lady had black hair?" Officer Powell asked as one of the cops from the other squad car came up to stand by him.

"It was funny hair," Megan whispered.

The policeman looked up from his notes.

"How was it funny, Megan?"

"It was like Cleopatra. It was all black and straight. Like spaghetti."

"A wig," the other cop said tersely.

"We better move on this, Kel, or we're going to lose her," the new policeman said.

Lose her.

Officer Powell stood up. "Did you get the APB out on the van?" he asked the other policeman, and his colleague nodded.

Then he turned back to Megan.

"Megan, we need your help to find your friend, so we're all going to go to our police station now, okay?" He took her hand and started to walk with her toward the squad car.

"Maybe I should come?" Adele said.

"I want my mom!" Megan wailed, fresh tears filling her eyes.

"I think maybe I should come," Adele said again.

Officer Powell stopped and bent down again to look at Megan.

"Megan, I know you're scared, but I'm going to take good care of you. And together we're going to try and find Jennifer. We're going to bring your mom to you, okay? We called your house, but she's not there, so we're going to find her for you. Do you know where your dad works?"

Megan couldn't get past the thought that the policeman kept calling Jen "Jennifer." He had asked her if that was Jen's real name and Megan had said it was. But it really wasn't. She was *Jen.* No one called her Jennifer.

"Megan, can you tell me where your dad works?" the officer said again.

Megan had to think for a moment.

"S-Sony," she said.

"Good girl," the policeman said. "We'll find your dad, too, okay?"

"I want to come with her," Adele said for the third time.

"Is it okay with you if Ms. Springer comes with us?" Officer Powell said.

Megan nodded.

"Okay, let's go," Officer Powell said, and they started walking toward the police car. Officer Trumbull was talking into the radio as he stood outside the car.

"That's affirmative on the possible abduction," he was saying. "We're bringing in an eight-year-old witness. Still trying to locate parents of both girls. Missing child's name is Jennifer Lovett. Looks like she may have been kidnapped. See you in ten."

Jennifer Lovett.

Jen.

Kidnapped.

Megan turned away from Officer Powell and Adele and vomited into the street.

8

To Megan, the police station looked more like a restaurant than a focal point for law and justice. The creamy-colored stucco exterior and red tile roof let it blend in with all the houses, businesses, and shopping centers that surrounded it. It was also very cool inside. Almost too cool. Megan drew close to Adele as they walked through a heavy glass door that buzzed loudly when they walked through it.

"Can she have a cup of water?" Adele was saying to Officer Powell as he ushered them through.

Megan could still taste bile in her throat. She was glad Adele knew she needed a drink of water.

"I'll get her one," said a lady police officer who had joined them.

They were shown to some chairs by a desk where still another policeman sat. Another man in a suit was standing by him. He was on the telephone, but he hung up when Megan and Adele sat down. Officer Powell knelt down to Megan's eye level and handed her the cup of water that the lady police officer brought. Megan drank it in one gulp.

"Megan, this is Detective Fuentes," Officer Powell said, pointing to the man in the suit. "He's from our downtown office. He's a policeman like me. He's going to help us find Jennifer, okay?"

Her name is Jen.

Detective Fuentes was nice, but he asked all the same questions Officer Powell did. It was like reliving the horrible afternoon for the third time. Megan's head ached.

"I want my mom," she said during a lull in the questioning.

"We're trying to find her, Megan," Detective Fuentes said. "She's not at your house. Do you know if she had to go somewhere today?"

Megan could not think. Her head was throbbing.

"How about her father?" Officer Powell said to the lady police officer.

"We've contacted the plant. He's out on a vendor call. His supervisor is trying to reach him," she replied.

Megan looked up. Four officers besides Detective Fuentes were standing by her.

Adele rubbed her shoulder in sympathy.

"Megan, do you know if your mom had to go somewhere today?" Officer Powell tried again, kneeling back down to Megan's eye level.

Megan suddenly remembered the wallpaper border. The church nursery. The church.

"She's at church," Megan whispered.

"Which church?" Officer Powell said.

"My church," Megan said.

"What's your church's name?"

Megan couldn't think of her church's name. It was just her church.

"Who's in charge of your church?" Detective Fuentes asked.

Megan looked around. Was this some kind of test?

"God," she said.

The officers smiled. One of them laughed. Even Adele grinned.

"Megan, is there someone at your church you call 'Father' or 'Reverend'?" Detective Fuentes asked, still smiling.

Megan looked at Adele.

"Do you have a pastor there, Megan?" Adele said.

"Pastor Lacey," Megan said.

"I'll check the directory," the lady police officer said as she walked off.

Detective Fuentes said Megan's name. She looked up at him.

"Are you sure you can't remember where Jennifer's parents work, Megan?"

Megan shook her head.

Megan had no idea where Nate Lovett worked. She barely ever saw him. She knew Elise worked in Balboa Park somewhere, but she also knew Elise was at an art exhibit that day. Charlie knew where the art exhibit was, but one of the policemen said they had been to the Lovett house and Charlie wasn't there. Jen knew where the art exhibit was, too.

Jen.

The lady police officer came back.

"I found Megan's mother. She's on her way," she said.

Adele squeezed Megan's shoulder and leaned in close to her.

"She's coming for you, Megan. Your mom's coming for you."

⌐◡◡◠⌐

Trina's heart was pounding as she angled her car into a marked space at the police station. Terrorized thoughts ran through her head. She had lived in this suburban corner of San

Diego for almost a decade and had never been here before. She could hardly believe she was here now. Megan was in there. The police had Megan. The police had to come looking for her. She hadn't been home.

She scrambled out of the driver's side, noticing how abysmal her parking job had been, but slamming the door shut anyway. She sprinted to the entrance and went inside.

"Where's my daughter?" she said nervously to a uniformed woman who sat behind a wall of glass.

"Your name, please?" the woman said. Her voice sounded far away and near at the same time.

"Trina Diamond. I'm Trina Diamond," Trina said, shouting her name through the vented circle that carried her voice through the bulletproof glass. "Megan Diamond is my daughter! Where is she?"

"Just a moment, please," the woman said calmly.

Trina paced while the woman pressed a button on a console and said something into a mouthpiece.

"Someone is coming for you, Mrs. Diamond," the lady said in the same calm voice.

Trina nodded. There were two doors, one on either side of the glass. She didn't know which one would open for her. She paced between the two, tears threatening to burst from her eyes.

The door on her left made a loud, clicking sound as it opened slowly. A female police officer stood in the middle of its frame.

"Mrs. Diamond?" she said. "Can you come with me, please?"

Trina looked at the woman who knew more than she did. This woman looked old enough to have children. She probably did have children. But this female police officer wasn't coming to her as one mother to another. She was a cop. She had been with Megan inside the police station. She was probably the police officer who had to search for her because she hadn't been home when Megan was brought here.

Megan had been in incredible danger, and she had not even known it.

Trina followed the police officer inside.

~ ~ ~

Megan's eyes were tired. She wanted to go home. Why did she have to look at picture after picture of frowning men and women? They looked mean. They looked sad. She leaned against her mother.

"Just a couple more pages, Megan," Detective Fuentes said, sensing Megan's exhaustion. "Anything familiar about any of these people?"

He had asked her that five times already. She didn't know these people.

She just wanted to go home.

Her dad had arrived a few minutes after her mom. They couldn't stop hugging her. Her mother couldn't stop crying. Megan figured it out. They were thinking the bad people in the blue van could have grabbed her, too. Or instead.

What if they had grabbed her instead of Jen?

What if they had?

It was hard to concentrate on the pictures of the sad people.

What if they had grabbed her instead of Jen?

She turned the last page.

Detective Fuentes took a sip of coffee.

"No one in that book looks like the man or woman you saw in the van?" he said, setting the cup down.

Megan shook her head.

"Can we take her home now?" Trina asked.

Detective Fuentes was reaching for another notebook.

"I know this is hard for all of you, but we have to act very fast whenever we suspect there's been a stranger abduction, Mrs. Diamond," he said. "The information your daughter gives us may be the key to finding this little girl."

The key.

He opened a book with shiny pages. Vans of all shapes and sizes.

"Megan, can you look through these pictures for me? I want you to show me the van that looks the most like the one you saw, okay?"

Megan began to turn the pages. There didn't seem to be any vans the same shade of blue as the one she saw.

Just then there was a lot of commotion down the hall.

A woman was yelling.

Her parents heard it, too. Everyone did.

It was Elise Lovett.

She had just come through the big thick door and was being led to a little office with windows for walls.

"What do you mean you don't know where she is?" she was yelling through her tears. She looked at the three officers who were with her, like she wanted each one of them to give her an answer. Then she looked past them, down the hall to where Megan sat with a notebook of photographs on her lap.

"Megan…" Elise said.

And then she ran to her.

"Megan, where's Jen?" Elise wailed, dropping to her knees in front of Megan. "Where is she? Who took her, Megan? Who took her?"

There was chaos in the hall as three policemen tried to subdue the distraught mother. Elise kept yelling. The policemen were saying things like, "This way, Mrs. Lovett," and "Please come with us, Mrs. Lovett." Trina was yelling, too.

"She doesn't know, Elise. She doesn't know!"

Even Megan was contributing.

"I want to go home! I want to go home!"

Finally, Elise let the policemen lead her to the little room, and the hall quieted down.

"Can we *please* take her home now?" Trina said, emotion thick in her voice.

"As soon as she's finished with that book," Detective Fuentes said, pointing to the notebook of photographs.

Megan turned the pages quickly, wanting nothing more than to escape to the safety of her home. On the last page of photos she saw a black van with the same little, tear-shaped rear windows she saw on the van that drove away with Jen inside.

"Like that," she said to Detective Fuentes. "Only blue."

"Good girl, Megan," he said. "What color blue?"

Megan did not hesitate.

"Ugly blue."

"So we can take her home now?" Gordy said.

"Yes," Detective Fuentes said. "But we'll need to talk to her again. And so will others. This is far from over. If there's any reason to suspect the child has been taken across state lines, the FBI will get involved. They'll want to talk to her, too."

Gordy nodded and motioned for his wife and daughter to come with him. Then he turned back to the detective.

"I don't want Megan's name released to the press," he said.

"They will not get her name from us," Detective Fuentes said to Gordy, and then he turned to Megan. "Goodbye, Megan. You were a very brave girl today."

Megan held up a hand in a tired wave.

As she rose from her chair, she noticed for the first time that Adele's chair was empty.

~~~

At first Megan was relieved to get home—away from the police station and its constant reminder that Jen had disappeared. But after only a few minutes in her own house, she realized there was no place she could go where she wouldn't be reminded of what had happened. The first reminder was the sight of her bike. It was on her porch leaning against a wall when she and Trina arrived home. One of the policemen had brought it back for her. Jen's was probably back at her own house.

A few minutes later, Gordy arrived with Michelle, who was miffed at having to spend the entire afternoon at the Wilsons' instead of just a few hours. She wanted to know what took so long. She wanted to know why Megan was crying. She wouldn't stop asking.

Megan ignored her sister, sauntered over to the family-room couch, and crawled onto it, resting her head on a cushioned arm.

"Maybe I should go get a pizza," Gordy said to Trina.

"Whatever, Gordy," she replied in a tired voice. "I don't have much of an appetite. I don't know if Megan will be able to eat either."

Michelle followed Megan into the family room and switched on the televisioin, plopping down on the floor in front of her sister.

Gordy grabbed his keys.

"Put a movie on for them," he said, nodding toward the girls. "I don't want them coming across a newscast about what happened this afternoon."

Trina nodded and stepped into the family room as Gordy left. Megan's tear-stained face was expressionless. It scared her. She felt in her pocket for the child psychologist's business card that Detective Fuentes had given her. Tomorrow she would call her. First thing.

"Where's Adele?" Megan suddenly said, staring straight ahead.

"Who?" Trina said softly, trying to make eye contact with her daughter.

"Adele."

Adele Springer. The older woman in the pink dress. Trina had all but forgotten about the woman who had stepped in for her at her daughter's dark hour. She had barely said anything to Adele at the station. One minute she was there; the next she was gone.

"I think she went home, honey," Trina said, coming to her daughter, sitting down by her, and stroking her head.

Megan said nothing.

"Maybe we could go see her sometime," Trina said, watching Megan's vacant eyes for her response. She could detect nothing. "Would you like that, Meg?"

Megan nodded once.

Trina felt fresh tears springing to her eyes, and she willed them away. *Help us get her through this*, she prayed silently. *Help us get her through this day.*

She tried not to let the terrifying thoughts that had begun to plague her at the police station re-enter her mind, those thoughts that affirmed she had been right all along. That Megan's befriending Jen had been a mistake. A huge mistake. *Look what has happened. Just look what has happened!* She shook her head as if to physically shake those thoughts from her mind. There was no use dwelling on what might have been. Or what *should* not have been.

As Michelle began to surf through the TV channels with the remote, Trina was roused from her thoughts.

She rose from the couch and walked over to the video cabinet to find a movie where everyone lived happily ever after.

9

Summer was winding down. Adele could feel it in the air. Not in the temperature, of course, but in the air around her neighborhood. Cars were appearing here and there on her street as teachers began returning to their still-quiet classrooms. From her kitchen window she could see desks stacked atop one another on the shaded outdoor corridors as janitors waxed class-room floors. A new school year was about to begin.

And for the most part, it felt like any other year. Adele had lived in her house by the elementary school for a quarter century, and most of the time, the back-to-school atmosphere was pre-dictable and ordinary.

This year was a little different, though.

A little shrine of messages, balloons, flowers, and pictures still hung from the chain-link fence near the spot where Jen Lovett had been abducted. Adele wondered if school officials were struggling with whether to leave it or remove it. It was painfully noticeable.

The school hadn't been responsible for what happened, of course; the kidnapping had taken place on the street. But it took place so close to the school, and it was now common knowledge that Jen had been a student there.

Yes, the start of school would be different this year.

Adele sat down with her third cup of coffee and waited for her arthritis medication to take effect so she could wrestle with the wing-back chair she was working on. She massaged her fingers. Arthritis was a curse, but as soon as she thought this, she was reminded that aching joints couldn't possibly be as bad as the pain of losing a child. She had lost several, all miscarriages, and they had hurt to her very core, but Jen Lovett's parents had to be hurting far worse than that.

Adele had never met Jen Lovett's parents, but she had seen them on television and in the newspaper. They looked like this was killing them. To have their daughter vanish without a trace, with no ransom note, no phone call, not even a body, had to be an unfathomable torture.

Adele had followed the case from Day One but consistently declined to be interviewed. The moment Megan Diamond's parents arrived at the police station that day, she had withdrawn from the horrendous inner circle. The police had taken her statement, and then she asked to be driven home. The last she saw of little Megan, she was poring over a book of black-and-white mug shots.

TV crews had been on her street when Adele arrived back at her house, but she politely told them she would talk to no one about what she saw and what she didn't see.

She watched the news that night, saw the reporters trying to put together a story with just the little bit police told them. The bikes were still on the ground surrounded by yellow police tape when the first reporters arrived. The six o'clock news coverage of the abduction ended with late-afternoon footage of Jen Lovett's bike and the bike of an unnamed playmate lying a few yards away. A number flashed on the screen for people to call with any information.

By ten o'clock that night, reporters had won the trust of Nate and Elise Lovett. The Lovetts appeared in front of their home with their son, Charlie, between them. Elise held an 8 x 10 framed photo of a beautiful young girl with golden hair and an easy smile. In the glare of camera lights, the Lovetts begged for the safe return of their daughter. They pleaded with the kidnappers, hoping they were watching, to bring their Jen back to them.

But days stretched into weeks, and there was no sign of Jen Lovett.

In a few days it would be September. The start of another new month. Adele wondered what it was like to begin another month not knowing where your daughter was.

Her thoughts were interrupted by the sound of her doorbell. She rose to answer it.

On her doorstep stood Megan Diamond and her mother.

Adele opened the door wide.

"Megan! How wonderful to see you!" she said. "Hello, Mrs. Diamond. Please, come in."

Megan said nothing, but Adele could see she had a hopeful look on her face.

"Thank you," Trina said as they stepped inside.

"Please sit down," Adele said as she motioned them into her living room.

Trina sat down first, and Megan sat down next to her.

"Can I get you a cup of coffee, Mrs. Diamond?"

"No, thank you, and please call me Trina," Megan's mother said.

"If you will call me Adele," Adele said with a smile. She sat down in the chair that had been Chet's favorite and turned to the little girl. "Megan, I'm so glad to see you. I've been thinking about you so much."

The corners of Megan's mouth rose but she said nothing.

"Megan's been thinking about you a lot, too, Adele," Trina said, looking at her daughter. "She's…she's been wanting to come see you for a while. But it's been a little difficult…"

Trina's voice trailed off.

"All that matters is you're here now," Adele said. "And I'm so glad you are."

Megan glanced at Adele and then quickly resumed staring at her hands.

Trina nervously commented on the beautiful furniture in Adele's living room.

"I saw your little sign out front. You did all the upholstery work yourself?"

"Yes," Adele said. "Chet helped me with these pieces, but I do the work by myself now. Chet died almost a year ago. He was my husband."

"Oh," Trina said. "I am so sorry."

"Thank you," Adele said. "It's getting easier. But I still miss him."

Adele stopped, wondering if she had said too much. Megan looked like she was about ready to bolt.

"Megan, I'm so glad you came to see me today," Adele repeated gently.

More silence. The two women did not know who should fill it.

"I just…I just wanted to thank you for…helping me when… that day," Megan said suddenly, only looking at Adele when she said the word *me*.

"You don't need to thank me, Megan," Adele said. "I think I was meant to help you. I had forgotten to water my flowers until that afternoon. If I had watered them in the morning like I usually do, I wouldn't have heard you. I think God put me on my porch when He knew you would need me."

Adele could see Trina visibly relax when she said this. Adele sometimes wondered how people would react to her open relationship with God. Trina seemed to welcome it.

"I'm just so glad you were there," Megan whispered.

"Come here, precious," Adele said, opening her arms.

Megan went to her, and Adele folded her into her chest.

"I will always be here for you, Megan," she said. "You come and see me anytime. Anytime at all."

Trina watched from the kitchen window as Megan rode off to school, to third grade. To third grade where there would be no Jen.

Megan didn't want to be driven to school the first day back. She wanted to ride her bike.

"Are you sure that's what you want to do?" Trina said. "Megan, you don't have to prove anything to anybody."

"Trina…" Gordy said as he poured coffee into his travel mug for his morning commute.

"Well, she doesn't!" Trina said.

"Let her ride her bike," he said, throwing a granola bar in his briefcase.

"Come home right after school, then," Trina said as she turned back to Megan.

"I want to stop and say hi to Adele."

"You just saw her yesterday, Megan," Trina said. "And the day before."

"I told her I would stop by," Megan replied, with little emotion.

"Let her go, Trina," Gordy said, not looking up from his mug.

Trina saw the look in Megan's eyes and said, "Just for a few minutes, and then you come right home."

Megan nodded and left the kitchen to brush her teeth.

Gordy then headed for the door that led to the garage.

"She's got to deal with it her own way, Trina. And you have to let her." And then he left.

Trina sighed as Megan pedaled out of sight.

It wasn't that she minded that Megan was back on her bike again. It was probably a sign that Megan was healing. Candace, the child psychologist Megan had been seeing, said it might be many months before Megan would feel comfortable riding her bike alone. Or at all. It had only been six weeks since Jen's abduction. Megan was ahead of that schedule by leaps and bounds.

But maybe that wasn't so good. Maybe it was too soon. Maybe she should call Candace and ask her.

And then there was Megan's daily desire to spend time with Adele. What was she supposed to make of that? Was that a good thing or a bad thing? Maybe she should ask Candace about that, too.

And while she was on the phone with Candace, she may as well ask about the nightmares. Megan wasn't having them as frequently as before, but when she did have one, it took both Trina and Gordy half an hour to calm her down. And they still awoke many mornings to find Megan curled up on the floor by their bed. Trina found this a little odd because she had invited Megan to sleep with them every night since the kidnapping, but Megan always declined.

Except for the first night when no one slept anyway, so that night didn't count.

She walked over to the phone and dialed.

~ ~ ~

Megan eased her bike down Adele's driveway to her double garage. A sign stuck into a wooden barrel by a side-door entrance and surrounded by petunias read Loving Touch Upholstery and Furniture Refinishing. It swung on a black wrought-iron bracket, making a little squeaking noise. Music filtered out the garage's open side door. It sounded like violins. Like heaven. Megan leaned her bike against the exterior wall and peeked in. Adele was on her knees, pinning fabric to a chair bottom.

"Hey there!" Adele said when she saw Megan framed in the doorway. "Come on in."

Megan stepped into the garage. The music came from a dusty boom box sitting half on and half off a stepladder. Odd pieces of furniture lay scattered about. A huge sewing machine sat on a large table in the middle of the cement floor next to a long wooden table that was covered with long bolts of pretty fabric. There was a peculiar smell in the garage. Megan had noticed it yesterday when she saw Adele's upholstery shop for the first time. It was the smell of old things mixed with new.

"You want to help me pin this, precious?" Adele said.

Megan walked over to Adele and knelt down beside her.

"Here," Adele said, handing Megan an enormous pincushion. "You can hold this for me. Then when we're done with this, we can have some tea and snickerdoodles."

Megan smiled and took the pincushion.

The two worked in comfortable silence for a while.

"How was your first day of school?" Adele asked, pulling the fabric taut.

"Okay."

"So, how do you like Mr. Wyndam? I hear he's a terrific third-grade teacher."

"He's nice," Megan replied with little inflection in her voice. They continued working silently.

"Adele, can I come tomorrow, too?" Megan suddenly interjected.

"Of course," Adele said, not taking her eyes off the chair. "You can come whenever you want."

Vivaldi's *Four Seasons* hovered over the young girl and the not-so-young woman as they quietly beautified a once-forsaken Queen Anne chair.

*M*egan was blushing as she left Adele's on a late September afternoon, and she knew why. Her face was hot with shame. She had lied to Adele. She told Adele she couldn't visit with her that afternoon because she had to get home. Adele had smiled and said, "Another time, then, precious."

But it wasn't true. Megan wasn't going home. There was something she needed to do. Something she had to do.

Megan got on her bike and eased onto the asphalt by Adele's driveway. She looked up and down the street to make sure all the kids from her school were gone.

Then she began pedaling toward Jen's house.

She hadn't been there since the day Jen disappeared. Elise had been to see her once, to drop off the swimming suit she had left at Jen's. It was a very awkward visit. No one knew what to say.

She didn't want to see Elise.

She didn't want to see anybody. She just wanted to see the house.

Megan pedaled faster, eager and apprehensive at the same time.

She turned on Jen's street and eased up on her speed in case any of the Lovetts were in the front yard.

But none were.

She parked her bike across the street and stood by a lamp-post trying to decide what to do next. She looked behind her, studying the house that sat across from Jen's. It appeared quiet, and the shades were drawn. Megan hoped that meant no one was home. She eased herself onto the landscaping that bordered the lawn, picking a spot between two prolific lilies of the Nile.

She sat for many long minutes just looking at the house, a warm, late-afternoon sun on her back.

Then the Lovetts' front door opened, and Charlie stepped out.

Megan froze. He looked straight at her.

She tried to hide among the tallest blooms, but she knew it was no use. He had opened the door because he had already seen her.

Megan stood up quickly and walked to her bike, not daring to look at him.

"Megan!" Charlie yelled. "Megan!"

She grabbed the handlebars, wishing she were in the safe confines of Adele's garage. Wishing she was anywhere but here.

"Megan!"

He was running over to her.

She turned the bike around.

"Megan, wait!"

She looked up. She saw his face.

She knew the look on his face. She had seen it before when he was threatening to go into the canyon and she was afraid for him. She had asked him not to. He looked at her then the same way he was looking at her now.

"Wait," he said. "Don't go."

"I have to get home," Megan whispered.

"Megan," he said. "She doesn't blame you."

"What?" Megan said, and she was at once aware that tears were running down her cheeks.

"She doesn't blame you, Megan." Charlie said. "My mom doesn't blame you. And I don't either."

~~~

On that first day with Charlie, Megan could not bring herself to go into the house. She sat with him on the stone steps that led to the Lovetts' front door. Elise and Nate were not home or she would not have stayed at all.

"They're never home now," Charlie said in a way that made it seem like he didn't really care.

She stayed for half an hour or so, long enough to know the person she disliked the most had instantly become the one person with whom she now had the most in common. And Charlie seemed different. He seemed older.

He showed her Jen's bike with the sparkly violet seat and chain guard. The police had brought it back.

"Mom still sets a place for her at the table," Charlie said absently.

They stood for several silent moments in the Lovett's garage.

"I have to go," Megan finally said.

Charlie looked at her with that familiar look on his face.

"See you around," he said.

Three days later she went back. This time she went into Jen's room. She touched Jen's Mexican money. Smelled the clothes in her closet. Ate Oreos with Charlie at the breakfast bar.

As she was walking past the living room, she noticed the statue of the lady with her hands lifted to heaven was gone.

Charlie noticed her looking at the blank spot on the coffee table.

"She broke it," he said.

Megan winced at the words and said nothing.

"Do you think God has a magic wand?" Megan asked.

Charlie looked at the spot on the coffee table for a moment, and then at something else across the room, but Megan couldn't tell what it was. Perhaps it was the place where the statuette had burst into pieces after having been thrown.

"I want to show you something," he said, and he walked over to the French doors that led to the patio. He opened one of the doors and stepped out. Megan followed him.

Charlie walked across the sloping lawn, past the pool, to the corner of the yard. He reached the gate and put his hand on the latch.

Megan froze beside him.

"Charlie, what are you doing?" she said, eyes wide.

"I want to show you something," he said again as he opened the gate

"But I'm not allowed in the canyon!" Megan exclaimed.

"I'm not either," Charlie said. He stepped through.

"Charlie!" Megan said, lunging toward him but stopping at the gate's opening.

"Come on," he said, as if it were the most natural thing in the world to go for a stroll in the canyon. He started walking away from her.

"But I can't!" Megan said.

"Suit yourself," he said, and then he began walking away.

Megan looked back at the house, wishing Elise would suddenly appear, but she didn't. She looked back at Charlie. He was now several yards away. He was not looking back. Megan took one more useless look at the empty Lovett house, and then turned to face the retreating form of Charlie Lovett.

She stepped through the gate.

Megan's first impression of being in the canyon was not that she was being sneaky but rather that she was suddenly terribly exposed. There were no trees on the sides of the canyon, just tumbleweeds, chalky-white boulders, and wild mustard plants. It seemed every house that bordered the canyon had an excellent view of the two young explorers. She imagined a mother in every house looking out on the canyon and then dialing her own mother. *"Did you know your daughter is in the canyon?!"*

Every noise, every stone she kicked, every rustle in the bushes made her jump, but Charlie just walked steadily down the side of the canyon to the ravine below.

At the bottom of the ravine, Charlie led Megan to a small copse of pepper trees and stepped into its shade. There was a dirt clearing in the circle of trees, as well as an old chair, several tires, and a dozen or so dusty, broken beer bottles.

"Teenagers used to come here," Charlie said, breaking the silence. "But they don't come here anymore. Just me."

"You've been here before?" Megan said, still surveying the scene with trepidation.

"Lots of times," Charlie said, but not like he was proud of it. He was just stating a truth.

"Why?"

Charlie plopped down in one of the tires, leaning his back against a pepper tree.

"I like it here. It's quiet."

"But you're not supposed to be here," Megan said walking over to him.

"They looked for Jen in here, you know," he said.

"In *here?*" Megan said, incredulous.

"Here. In the canyon."

"Why would they do that?" Megan said. "Jen would never come in here."

"They brought dogs and everything."

"Dogs?"

"Sniffing dogs. The cops went into her room and got her pajamas. They let the dogs sniff them, and then they came out here to see if the dogs could pick up her scent."

Megan was still confused.

"They stayed out here way past dark," Charlie continued. "You could see their flashlights all over the canyon. They were calling her name."

Megan looked out past the trees, trying to imagine Jen hiding in the canyon. It was unthinkable.

"They didn't find her," Charlie said, absently.

"Do you really think she could be here in the canyon, Charlie?" Megan said.

"She's not in the canyon," Charlie replied.

"How do you know?" Megan countered, sitting down in a tire next to him.

" 'Cause I looked for her, too," he said. "She's not here."

11

y late October, Megan had settled into the lifestyle she
had known in the days before Jen. She kept to herself
and avoided friendships. She did not engage in social activities
unless forced to. But Megan didn't mind. It was a familiar routine.
The only other student she would seek out from time to time was
Charlie. Their paths didn't cross often at school since he was in
fifth grade. She saw him more often out of school, on those days
when she would find a way to sneak over to his house.

One day, Charlie cornered Megan at school by the library.

"Can you come over today?" he whispered to her. "I found
something."

"What is it?" Megan whispered back.

"An earring."

"Is it Jen's?"

"Maybe. You need to come look at it."

Megan considered this. She wasn't going to Adele's today.
She was supposed to go straight home. Somehow she knew her
mother wouldn't like the idea of her going over to the Lovetts to
see Charlie. That's why she hadn't told her parents about the

times she had been there already. And she certainly had not said anything about having been in the canyon.

"I'll try," she told Charlie.

~ ~ ~

Trina couldn't explain why she was so worried as Megan got back on her bike after school and headed over to the Lovetts'. Something didn't seem right. Why on earth would Megan want to be with Charlie? Megan couldn't stand Charlie. At least that's how it was before Jen was taken from them.

But Megan had just told her only moments before that Charlie wasn't mean to her anymore. That he was nice to her. That he felt better about Jen's being gone when they could talk about it. And so did she.

What about Elise? Trina had wanted to ask, but she couldn't bring herself to say it.

"Will Elise be there?" she said instead, like her only concern was whether or not there would be adult supervision.

"Maybe," Megan said. "I didn't ask."

And Trina didn't want to call.

"Let me take you over there," Trina said.

"I want to ride my bike," Megan said, and then quickly added, "Please?"

Trina rubbed her forehead.

"All right," she finally said. "But only for an hour, Megan. I want you home before dark."

Megan nodded and left.

Trina stood there for a few moments after Megan's departure, unaware at first that Michelle was standing next to her and asking for help getting the Play-Doh down.

"Sure, sweetie," she finally said to her other daughter, grabbing the phone as she reached for the kitchen cabinet where she kept the Play-Doh and cookie cutters.

She dialed Candace, hoping the psychologist wasn't with another patient.

~~~

"It looks too old to be hers, Charlie," Megan said as she sat with him under the trees in the canyon. "Did you ask your mom?"

"I can't do that!" he said. "She'll know I've been in here."

"But you could tell her you found it in the backyard,' Megan said.

"So?" Charlie said. "What's so weird about finding Jen's earring in our own backyard?"

"Oh, yeah. You're right," Megan said, feeling rather foolish. She fingered the little silver hoop that Charlie had found. "So, where did you find it?"

"Just below our house—right near the boulder that looks like a giant tooth."

Megan frowned.

"I'm not sure if it's hers, Charlie."

"I'm keeping it anyway," he said.

Charlie took the earring from Megan and slipped it into his pocket.

They sat in tires side by side, their backs against the same pepper tree.

"I stayed out here past dark yesterday," he said to her after a few moments of silence.

"Why?"

"I'm not afraid," he said, like she had asked him an entirely different question. But Megan could tell he had been afraid and guessed that was why he had done it.

"It was easy," Charlie added.

"But, Charlie, if your parents had come home—"

"But they didn't!" Charlie interrupted. "It was fun, Megan."

Megan didn't know what to say to this. She had to admit she liked being in the canyon. But she was still afraid of it.

"Let's go for a walk," Charlie said, and he got up quickly.

"But it's getting late," Megan protested.

"Come on," Charlie said, ignoring her.

Charlie led Megan through the bottom of the canyon like a tour guide. It was obvious he knew exactly where he was going. He walked fast. She was out of breath when he finally stopped by a collection of boulders that looked milky white in the afternoon's fading light.

Megan leaned against one of the large rocks to catch her breath and noticed the sun setting off to her right.

"Charlie! I have to get home. It's almost dark!" she wailed. It would take a good twenty minutes to walk back through the canyon to the Lovetts' side. Then another ten minutes or so to ride her bike home. She would be late. Her mother would be furious. She probably wouldn't let her go over to the Lovetts again.

"I'll never make it home in time," she moaned.

Charlie took a few steps away from the boulders and scanned the canyon's sloping wall.

"Look!' he said to Megan. "That's your street right up there. You can be there in no time."

Megan peered in the direction where Charlie pointed. Off in the distance she could see the gray guardrails that marked the end of her street.

"But my bike!" she said.

"I'll ride it over to your house after it gets dark. I'll put it by the fence to your backyard."

"But what if my mom is watching for me and sees me walking home without it?"

"You worry too much," Charlie smirked.

"What if she does?"

"Tell her it has a flat tire. Tell her you left it at my house."

"I don't know, Charlie."

The light was fading.

"You'd better go, Megan," Charlie said as he started to walk back in the direction of his own house.

Megan's heart was pounding. She had never been alone in the canyon. She had always been with Charlie. And it had always been in broad daylight. Charlie stopped and looked back at her.

"Go!" he said. "You can make it!"

She wanted to ask Charlie to walk her to her street, but then he would have to walk the entire length alone to get back to his house. In the dark. She couldn't ask him.

"Go on, Megan!" Charlie said and his voice sounded far away.

She took one more look at him, and then began to head toward the gray guardrails. She walked toward them as fast as she could, willing them to close the distance between her and safety.

Megan was halfway there and starting to climb the canyon's sloping wall when she heard the unmistakable sound of a rattle.

Charlie was nowhere in sight. The sun was on the edge of the horizon.

She heard it again.

Megan had never seen a rattlesnake in the wild and had actually never heard one either. But she knew a rattlesnake was making that noise.

In that instant Megan knew everything she had been told about the canyon was true. It was a dangerous place. And she was alone in it.

"Jesus, save me!" she whispered.

The rattle sound was closer.

Run!

She took off, scrambling up the side of the canyon, her heart racing. A thunderous rushing sound filled her ears.

"Jesus, save me! Jesus, save me!" she kept saying. Or maybe she was just thinking it. When she thought about it later, she really wasn't quite sure.

Megan's side ached, and she had a long scratch on her arm from a dry branch she had scampered too close to, but she finally reached the gray guardrails that beckoned to her like escorts to a haven of rest. She stepped over them to the protection of her street and doubled over to catch her breath. Everything around her was utterly silent except for the sound of her labored breathing. Megan was amazed at how she felt as she stood there gasping for air. It was a very strange feeling. It was not fear that she felt. It was something else. Something like victory. Like exhilaration. This was a new, strange feeling.

The canyon lay before her quiet and serene in the orange light of sunset. Megan straightened her body as oxygen filled her lungs, and she looked out over the depth and breadth of what suddenly seemed like the valley of all her fears—and even her hopes. The canyon—the forbidden, terrifying, amazing, astounding place—had at that very moment become for her a window to the world. She would not be able to explain it in so many words, not for several years, but the canyon was suddenly a picture of all she knew about life. It was like she now understood something about the world God made that she desperately needed to know: Life could be both remarkable and menacing. She lived in a world that was both good and bad, just like the canyon was both beautiful and dangerous. She felt strangely strengthened. She felt like at last she could imagine living without Jen. She had conquered the canyon. She could conquer her dread of a life without Jen.

Megan felt immediately empowered, but she was too young to know the word—too young to know she had crossed a great divide.

She barely noticed the blood on her arm. Nor the sound of her mother's frantic cries as Trina drew near to her.

$\sim\sim\sim$

Trina looked up the street to where she expected to see Megan pedaling home on her bike. But she wasn't there.

"I shouldn't have let her go," Trina mumbled to herself, wondering if she should get her car keys and begin driving toward the Lovetts'.

The streetlights flickered on, and Trina turned to the lamppost behind her as light fell all around her. When she did, her eyes caught sight of a lone figure at the end of the dead-end street.

The figure was a child with her arms raised over the canyon as if she were conducting an orchestra.

"What in the world... " Trina started to say and then stopped. It was Megan.

She was standing on the edge of the canyon, facing it like she owned it. It was her daughter Megan, stretching her arms above the darkening gorge of tumbleweeds, rocks, and forbidden shadows.

It was Megan, perched on the periphery of danger, seeming to be inviting it into her embrace.

"God Almighty!" Trina cried, and it was both an exclamation and a supplication.

Trina took off down the street, crying out her daughter's name. It seemed her feet could not get her there fast enough. Trina somehow knew that Megan had not walked down the street to stand at the canyon's edge. She knew Megan had climbed up out of the canyon itself.

The very thought weakened Trina's legs as she sprinted down the street toward her daughter. She called Megan's name as she ran, but her daughter did not turn in response.

"Megan!" she cried out, as she reached her daughter and threw her arms around her.

Startled, Megan gasped, as if Trina had suddenly pulled her up from deep, frigid waters, and forgotten air was now filling the girl's lungs.

Trina gasped, too.

And then Trina yanked Megan away from the canyon's edge, hard and fast, like one might snatch something away from the jaws of evil.

PART THREE

Fall 1996

12

Megan shifted her weight off the leg she had tucked under her on her stool and dipped a paintbrush in the sand-colored shade she had created on her palette. It wasn't the exact color of dirt she wanted, but it was close enough, and it would do.

She could sense that Mr. Fine, her high-school art teacher, was coming near her as he made his rounds through the rows in her third-period art class. Megan braced herself for criticism.

"Megan," he said from behind her. "That's an interesting start you have there, but where is your photograph?"

Twenty-one sets of eyes turned her way. It was hard not to notice that everyone else in her class had a photograph of a landscape taped to the top left-hand corner of their canvases. Megan did not.

"I don't have a photograph of this place, Mr. Fine," Megan said quietly, swirling the head of her brush in the dirt-colored paint.

"What was that?" Mr. Fine said, leaning in.

"I said, I don't have a photograph of this place," Megan repeated, holding her brush still.

"Then why are you painting it?" Mr. Fine asked, not in an unkind way.

"Because I like this place," Megan answered, daring herself to turn to him.

"I might like it, too, Megan. But the assignment was to paint a landscape from a photograph."

Megan looked back at her canvas as one or two students went back to work. The rest continued to stare—and to see who would win.

"I know, but I don't have a photograph of it."

"Well, can you get one, Megan?" Mr. Fine said. "Maybe in a book or a magazine somewhere?"

"No, I can't...It doesn't exist anymore," she said in a softer voice still.

"What?" Mr. Fine said, squinting his eyes like that would make him hear her better.

"It's a golf course now." Megan said as she turned back to him. "It used to be a canyon by my house, but it's a golf course now."

"Well, there are other canyons, Megan. I'm sure if you were to look in the library, you would find lots of pictures of other canyons in this part of the state," Mr. Fine said as he started to walk away.

"There isn't another one like this one," Megan said quietly, but defiantly.

"Find a photograph, Megan," Mr. Fine said curtly. "That's the assignment."

Megan watched him walk away. There wasn't a sound from the other students in the class as they, too, watched him walk away. Then they turned back to their taped photographs and nearly blank canvasses. But not before they glanced her way.

Megan raised the brush and held it in midair for a moment. Then she lowered the bristles to the taut, white surface and began to paint the floor of her canyon.

∾ ∾ ∾

She sat alone as usual at lunchtime. Her economics book, open to the end of the third chapter, lay before her on the table. The first test of the school year for the advanced-placement class was scheduled for the next day. She didn't really need to study for it, but there was nothing else to do as she ate her yogurt.

It was highly probable Megan would ace the economics test even though she was a sophomore in a class primarily made up of seniors. She had a near-perfect grade point average. That it wasn't a perfect 4.0 didn't bother her very much. Megan had no desire to be a standout student. She actually didn't mind an occasional B+. When she graduated in two years, she wanted there to be no chance of being named valedictorian.

So, she really didn't care about what had happened in art that day. If Mr. Fine gave her an F on her first project, so what?

Megan decided to head to chemistry early. She threw out the remains of her lunch and began walking across the grassy commons toward the science building. Ahead she could see a collection of cheerleaders and pep-band members painting signs on a long stretch of concrete between the buildings. She quickened her steps, kept her head down, and avoided, as much as possible, any eye contact. But, uncharacteristically, she was noticed.

"Hi, Megan!" one of the cheerleaders said in an overly cheerful voice. A couple of the others laughed.

Megan looked her way. Charlie's girlfriend. For this week.

"Hi, Brynne," she answered but kept walking.

"Look at this sign!" Brynne continued. "It says, 'We Lovett!' Isn't that clever! Dana thought of it."

Megan stopped and looked at the sign that bore Charlie's last name and his football jersey number. Charlie was the star receiver for the Rancho Hills High School Eagles. Everybody loved him. He was expected to graduate in June with his choice of football scholarships. But nobody called him Charlie anymore. He was now known as Chaz. Chaz Lovett. Number 82. The All-American boy. But to her, he was still Charlie, though she never called him this to his face.

"Look at mine!" Brynne was saying.

Brynne tossed her long blonde hair back with a shake of her head and held up her sign. It read, "All That Chaz!"

"Very witty, Brynne," Megan said, managing a smile. She resumed her pace.

"Why do you even bother with her?" she heard one of the other cheerleaders say as she walked away.

She didn't hear Brynne's answer.

Megan kept her head down and her pace steady as she finished the distance between the commons and the science building. Despite her attempt to convince herself that it didn't matter what those girls thought of her, she knew the words had cut through to her soul. She hated the familiar feeling of warm weakness washing over her. Megan ducked into the girls' restroom on the corner by the chemistry classroom as her vulnerability assailed her.

She leaned over a sink with her hands on the cool, porcelain sides, and slowly raised her head to study her reflection in the mirror. She saw her plain face, her short brown hair, the smattering of freckles, expressionless eyes. Her clothes were nondescript. Featureless khaki pants, plain yellow T-shirt, denim jacket. No makeup. No jewelry. No perfume. There was nothing about her that said, "Look at me." And that was just the way she liked it.

But then why did she suddenly feel so exposed when those girls laughed at her? When they talked about her like she wasn't there?

Why do you even bother with her?

It was the word *even* that got her the most. It implied hopelessness. Like she was a useless waste of atoms.

She could feel anger welling up inside where the hurt was festering. She was glad she wasn't pretty. Pretty girls like Brynne didn't have a clue. Brynne was five and a half feet of brainless beauty. Charlie liked her because she looked good. That's all. He had liked the last girlfriend he had because she looked good. And the one before that. And the one before that. They had meant nothing to him. The absence of loveliness wasn't something to pine over. Doing so only caused trouble and heartache.

On the dark days when Megan still thought about Jen—even after seven years she still did—she reminded herself that Jen had been taken because she was pretty. There were two girls on the sidewalk that day. The kidnappers had their pick. They chose Jen. They chose the pretty one. Nothing good could come from being nice to look at.

From inside the bathroom, Megan heard the bell for her class. She splashed water on her face and shook her short, cropped hair so it looked a little less styled. She grabbed her book bag and headed to class.

〜〜〜

Adele was smoothing a long length of brocade fabric on her cutting table when Megan walked in that afternoon after school.

Adele had moved her business from her garage to a corner shop in a busy strip mall a mile away. Megan worked for her four days a week after school and every other Saturday. Most of the big refinishing jobs were still done in Adele's garage where the ventilation was better, but all the upholstery work was done in her new little shop. Adele also sold pieces she had picked up mangled and managed to revamp.

"Hey, Megan!" Adele said as Megan stepped inside.

"Hey," Megan replied back. "Sorry I'm late. The chain on my bike broke. I had to leave it at school and take the bus."

"Oh, that's too bad," Adele said. "Can it be fixed?"

Megan headed to the little refrigerator in the corner and pulled out a small bottle of apple juice.

"I suppose. But I get my license in December. After that I am *through* with bikes."

There was a momentary silence, as there often was between the two women when the conversation eerily sounded like a snippet of the past. The word *bikes* sometimes did that to their conversation.

Megan filled the silence.

"I'll finish that piano bench today."

"Great," said Adele, not missing a beat. "'Cause I've got another for you."

"Okay," Megan said, setting down her backpack and apple juice and kneeling before a half-upholstered piano bench.

"Say, Megan," Adele began as she walked over to Megan. "I hired that young man from my church I told you about. He starts on Saturday morning."

"Well, if you're sure we need somebody else," Megan said, shrugging her shoulders.

"The lifting is getting to be too much for me, Meg. And I can't keep asking your father to run over here to lift things you and I can't handle."

"But he doesn't mind," Megan said, stopping to look at her older friend.

"I know he doesn't," Adele said as she made her way back to the cutting table. "But I mind. Besides, David is a good kid, and he needs a job. He's the same age as you, you know. I think you'll like him."

"In what way?" Megan said suspiciously.

Adele smiled but didn't look up from the fabric as she cut it. "In no special way at all."

At five o'clock, Adele began shutting off lights and turning off equipment.

"Can I give you a lift home?" she asked as she switched on the answering machine.

"I think I'll walk, Adele. Thanks anyway," Megan said as she grabbed her book bag and threw her juice bottle in the trash. "See you tomorrow."

Megan stepped out and headed across the strip mall parking lot. It was a good two miles to her house, but she didn't mind. She liked being alone and yet not alone. Most of her walk home would be on busy roads, but she would likely not have to interact with anyone until she turned down her own street.

But just as she crossed the first of several intersections, a familiar voice called out to her.

"Megan!"

Charlie was sitting in his bright red Trans Am stopped at a red light two blocks from the upholstery shop.

"You walking home?" he called out. His hair was wet. He had probably just gotten out of football practice.

"Yeah," Megan said.

"Come on, I'll give you a ride."

Megan looked past Charlie to see if there was anyone else in the car with him.

"Brynne's not with me," he yelled.

Megan gave him an annoyed look and then ran to the passenger side of his car and got in. Charlie smelled nice. The air inside his car smelled of men's cologne.

The light turned green and Charlie took off.

"I wasn't looking for Brynne," Megan said coolly.

"Sure you weren't," Charlie said and laughed, as he braked suddenly to avoid the Toyota pickup that cut in front of him. A brief expletive followed.

"You know I don't like it when you swear," Megan said matter-of-factly as she kicked fast-food wrappers around on the floor by her feet. "Your car is a pigsty."

"Okay, no more swearing," he said with a grin. "And I clean my car every Friday."

"Too bad it's only Thursday," Megan continued, throwing Charlie's letterman jacket and several schoolbooks onto the back seat.

"Speaking of Friday," Charlie said sheepishly and looked Megan's way.

"What?" Megan said suspiciously.

"The test? Economics?"

"What about it?"

"C'mon, Megan. I need to pass it," Charlie said.

"I would suppose everybody taking it would like to pass it," she said.

"Megan, please? I promise this time I will not watch any sports programs while we study."

"You mean while I study and give you all the answers."

"Not this time, I promise."

Megan looked over at him.

"I suppose it has to be at your house?"

"Megan, your cat makes me sneeze."

"My mom thinks you don't like her."

"Get rid of that cat, and I'd be there all the time. Your mom's a good cook."

Megan couldn't help but smile. Charlie always seemed to know how to make sure his needs were met.

"You just want me to tell her that so she'll bake you cookies or something."

"Would she?!" Charlie said, his eyes twinkling.

The funny thing was, that's exactly what her mother would do. A few minutes later, Charlie turned on Megan's street and pulled into her driveway.

Megan yanked on her book bag and slung it over her shoulder.

"What time?" she said.

"Eight?"

"Seven. I don't want to get to bed at midnight."

"Okay," Charlie said.

Megan opened the door.

"Should I have my mom bring me?"

"I'll come for you," Charlie said, as he put his car in reverse. He drove off, honking twice.

Megan watched him drive away. She turned to go into her house but then stopped and cast a long look at the smoky gray guardrails at the end of her street. Though she couldn't see it from her driveway, she knew that directly below the rails lay a vast expanse of manicured grass, palm trees, and holes number ten and eleven.

What she had wanted to paint today—her marvelous window to the world —was nothing more than a memory.

Like so many other things.

~ ~ ~

Trina heard the front door open and wondered instantly why Megan hadn't come through the garage like she usually did.

She poked her head around the kitchen wall to the flagstone entry.

"Hi," she said. "You don't usually come in the front door."

"Chaz gave me a ride. The chain on my bike broke. Dad's going to have to go get it at school," Megan said, setting her book bag on a barstool.

"Oh, bummer," Trina said. "Maybe you two can go get it after supper? He's picking up Michelle from gymnastics today."

"I'm going to the Lovetts' at seven," Megan said, opening the fridge and pulling out a water jug. She took the cap off and drank from the jug.

"What's up at the Lovetts'? And maybe you could use a cup next time?" Trina said motioning with her head.

Megan swallowed and looked at the jug.

"No one drinks this stuff but me. You guys are all addicted to caffeine."

"Megan."

"Okay, okay," Megan said as she screwed on the lid and put the jug back in the fridge.

"So what's going on at the Lovetts'?" Trina tried again.

"We have a test in economics tomorrow. Chaz wants me to help him study for it."

"Well, I'm glad you're willing to help him, Meg, but it would still be nice if you asked first," Trina said.

"Asked what?"

"Asked first if you can go over there."

"May I go to Chaz's tonight?" Megan said quietly.

"Yes, Megan, you may," Trina said, smiling. "I'd be happy to take you over there."

"He's picking me up, Mom," Megan said as she walked past her mother headed down the hall to her bedroom.

"Megan," Trina said, and Megan stopped and turned back. "Charlie isn't...he isn't...I mean, you're not romantically involved with him in any way, are you? I mean I would understand if you liked him that way, but I just need to know if you do, Megan. I need to know if you're... involved with him romantically."

Trina held her breath. She had wanted to ask this for weeks.

"Mom," Megan said, "he *has* a girlfriend. Okay? He has one. I don't even *want* to be his girlfriend."

Trina nodded but wasn't satisfied.

"But you two have grown up together. You've been good friends for years. You were friends before you even knew the opposite sex existed, Megan. And now that you two are older, especially now that Charlie is older, I just think you should be careful."

"Careful of what?" Megan said, and Trina could tell her daughter was growing annoyed.

"Megan, I've seen the way he looks at you."

"Mom, you don't know what you're talking about," Megan said and started to walk away.

Trina followed her.

"Megan, I don't think you see what I see. He likes you. He really does."

Megan swiftly turned around.

"And I like him! But *not* that way! Not that way."

"But he might like *you* that way, Megan," Trina said. "You're smart and pretty, and you've been through so much together."

"Mom, you *really* don't get it," Megan said evenly.

"Maybe I don't, but—"

"That's right, you don't," Megan interrupted.

Trina decided to back off.

"I just want you to be careful," Trina said.

"I'm always careful," Megan said. "You insist on it. And I hear what you're saying. But you're wrong about Chaz."

Trina sighed, started to walk back toward the kitchen, then turned back to her daughter.

"It's your turn to set the table, Megan," she said.

13

When the doorbell rang a few minutes after seven, Michelle bounded off the couch to be the first one to answer it.

"Hey, Shelly," Charlie said, as twelve-year-old Michelle opened the door wide. "Want to go and get Meg for me?"

Michelle smirked and shouted down the hall.

"Megan! It's Chaz!"

Michelle looked back at him and grinned.

"Nice going and getting," Charlie said, tugging on her pony-tail as he stepped onto the flagstone entry.

"I saw you on TV last week," Michelle said, putting her hands into her pockets since she could find nothing else to do with them.

"Yeah, I saw you on TV last week, too," Charlie said.

Michelle's eyes widened, and her mouth formed a half-open O.

Then Charlie winked at her.

"You're lying!" she said.

The door to the garage opened then, and Gordy came through the kitchen just as Megan came out of her bedroom with her book bag.

"Hey, Chaz," Gordy said. "How's it going?"

"Not too bad," Charlie said, shaking Gordy's offered hand.

"Could you fix it, Dad?" Megan asked her father.

"I'm afraid I'll have to get a new chain from the bike shop in Mira Mesa, Meg. I can give you a lift to school tomorrow."

Megan sighed. "Thanks for trying, Dad," she said.

Trina came in from the garage at that moment carrying a bag of frozen cookies.

"Hi, Charlie…I mean, Chaz," she said.

"Hey, Trina."

"These will thaw in no time," Trina continued, handing the bag to him. "You and Megan might want a break later."

"Thanks," Charlie said as he took the bag.

"Say hello to your parents for us," Gordy said as Megan and Charlie stepped out of the door.

"Will do."

Trina stepped back into the kitchen. From the window above the sink, she watched Charlie and Megan drive away.

Gordy followed his wife into the kitchen and would have kept walking into the garage but Trina stopped him with nine unexpected words.

"Sometimes I think I've done it all wrong," she said.

"What do you mean?" Gordy said, turning from the garage door.

"Like I've blown it."

"Trina, you're going to have to clue me in a little," Gordy said, taking a couple of steps toward his wife.

"Every time there's a crucial moment, a teachable moment, with Megan, I manage to mangle it."

"I think you're being a little hard on yourself, Trina," Gordy said. "Did something happen today between you two?"

Trina shrugged her shoulders. "I asked her if she and Charlie are romantically interested in each other. She acted like I'd asked if she had a nice time on Mars. Like it was the strangest, stupidest thing in the world to ask."

"Well, maybe to her, it does seem strange. If they were interested in each other, don't you think we would have seen something by now? I mean, it's not like they would have any reason to hide it."

Trina ignored the question. She was already onto something else.

"You know, I told her she was pretty today, and she thought that was even *more* strange. Like I was totally out of my mind to suggest it. I think she thinks she's homely, Gordy. I think that's why she doesn't wear dresses or anything feminine or jewelry or even makeup. Gordy, I have Michelle *begging* me to wear mascara, and Megan wants nothing to do with any of it."

Gordy thought for a moment.

"That's not what a homely girl would do, Trina. I would think if a girl really thought she was ugly, she would try to improve her looks with all that stuff. I think maybe Megan may not want to draw attention to herself."

"Why not?"

"I don't know. Maybe because she likes it that way," Gordy said. "Give her some space."

"But Gordy, it doesn't seem right," Trina protested. "She has no one but Charlie and Adele. No girl friends. No boy friends. She doesn't even have close friends at church."

"She seems content with the way she is," Gordy said softly. "If you two aren't getting along, maybe it's because she can sense *you're* not content with the way she is."

"That's what I'm trying to tell you, Gordy! No matter what I do, it's the wrong thing! Every time I turn around, I do the canyon thing all over again."

"Trina, that was ages ago!" Gordy said. "Let it go, already. She probably doesn't even remember that day."

"She does," Trina said, folding her arms across her chest and gazing out the window.

"How do you know she does?"

"Because I do. I totally blew it that day. The things I said…" Trina broke off and her voice quavered.

Gordy went to his wife and took her in his arms.

"Trina, you were upset. And you were afraid for her. You didn't want anything to happen to her. Especially after what had just happened to Jen. And she *shouldn't* have been in the canyon. You were right about that."

"But all that time that I wouldn't let her see Charlie—"

"Trina, honestly, it's water under the bridge. It all worked out okay. They're now the best of friends. You did what you thought was best. We both did. I agreed to it, remember?"

Trina nodded and tried to let Gordy's comforting arms soothe her fears.

He was right about her having done what she thought was best.

But he was wrong about Megan's not remembering that day Trina found her poised on the edge of the canyon.

Megan remembered it.

Charlie stuck the bag of thawing cookies between the seats as he drove down Megan's street.

"You told her," he said to Megan with a grin.

"It slipped out during dinner."

"Yeah, right."

Megan looked down at her hands.

"I thought my mom could use the compliment. So I told her you said she was a good cook. That you especially liked her cookies. And *voilà*." Megan held up the bag.

"So why did she need the compliment?"

Megan suddenly wished she hadn't said that.

"We had a little disagreement. It was nothing."

"A disagreement about what?"

Megan fidgeted in her seat.

"Just girl talk. That's all. It wouldn't interest you."

Just then, they pulled into the Lovetts' driveway. Megan started to get out.

"Can you just wait here a minute?" Charlie said as he looked toward his house.

Megan turned to him but said nothing.

Charlie got out of the car, took several steps toward the front door, and stopped. He stood there for a moment or two, and then walked back.

"I'll move the car onto the street," he said. "We can shoot some hoops for a few minutes."

"What is it, Chaz?" Megan said, but she knew what it was.

"They're at it again," he said.

Charlie parked the car on the street and got out. Megan followed. She could hear raised voices as she set her book bag on the steps leading to the front door. Charlie appeared from the side entrance to the garage with a basketball. He threw it to her.

"One arm behind your back," Megan said, nodding to him.

Charlie gave her a humorous scowl but put his left arm behind his back. He crouched to block her from advancing to the basketball net attached to the garage roof.

"So why don't you like Brynne?" he said, waving his one arm.

"I didn't say I didn't like her," Megan said, pivoting as she dribbled the ball.

"But you don't," Charlie said, following through and trying to steal the ball between bounces.

"She doesn't like *me*," Megan said taking a few steps forward and eyeing the net.

"That's not true. She likes you," Charlie said, trying to bat the ball away with his free hand. "Why do you think she doesn't like you?"

Megan pivoted again and worked the outside of the imaginary key. She knew she'd have better luck shooting from the outside. At five-foot-six, she was no match for Charlie's six-foot-two frame on a layup.

"Why would she? I don't have anything in common with her," Megan said as she lobbed a shot. It hit the rim, and Charlie took the rebound.

She jumped in front of him and waved her arms wildly. It was the only defense she had against him. He skirted around her, nearly losing the ball.

"Maybe if you got to know her a little better, were a little *nicer* to her..." he said, taking advantage of an opening and lunging forward. He shot and the ball slipped through the open net. He caught it and threw it to Megan.

"Why should I be a little nicer to her?" Megan said, bouncing the ball but not taking a step. "Her friends are the most snooty, conceited...they all *hate* me."

She pivoted and used the shock of her last four words to try a shot. It sailed through the net. Charlie reached up and grabbed it with his one arm.

"They do not," he said, dribbling away with it.

"I don't care if they do," Megan said, darting up to him and reaching in to get the ball between bounces.

"No reaching!" Charlie said and pivoted quickly to his right.

"They don't hate you," he said again, working his way to the inside.

"I really don't care if they do," Megan said, trying to keep in front of him. "I'm not like them, and I'm fine with that. I don't care if they're all beauty queens and I'm not." She reached in, snagged the ball from him, turned, and shot. It hit the rim and bounced in. "I'd much rather have brains than looks." The ball fell into her hands.

"But you already have both," Charlie said, raising up both arms.

"Very funny. Put that arm back." She threw the ball to him.

"I'm serious," Charlie said. "I know all kinds of guys who'd like to ask you out."

"You always were a good liar," Megan said, resuming her wild arm waving in front of him.

He stood straight and held the ball to his torso.

"But I'm not lying."

She stopped waving her arms and crossed them in front of her.

"Then you're stupid. Because that can't possibly be true," she said.

"It *is* true. Guys like you because you're not a flirt, you don't need makeup to look great, and you don't take garbage from anybody."

Megan could think of nothing to say. She didn't like where the conversation was going.

"Brynne's brother, Ryan, wants to take you to the dance after the football game tomorrow night. I told him I'd ask you."

Megan felt funny inside. Exposed. Young.

"I don't even know him," she said.

"He's in your class," Charlie said.

"Chaz, there are four hundred sophomores in my class."

"But you know who he is," Charlie said, twirling the ball on an index finger.

Actually, Megan did. Ryan Talley was in her art class.

"Can I tell him you'll at least meet him there? You don't have to dance with him. Just talk to him."

Before Megan could answer, the garage door opened and Nate Lovett's newest BMW began backing out. Megan and Charlie stepped aside. Through the windshield, Megan could see that Nate looked angry. He didn't look at her, but he offered a weak wave to his son as he backed down the driveway. Then he threw the car into forward and took off down the street.

"Should be quiet enough to study now," Charlie said, without sentiment. He turned and entered the garage. Megan followed him, noticing that the corner where Elise had her kiln was dusty and empty, and she wondered how long the kiln had been gone.

Megan doodled on the cover of her notebook as she waited for the class period to end. She had been one of the first to finish the economics test, but she waited until half a dozen students had taken their papers up to the teacher before handing in her own.

She stole a glance over at Charlie. He had his face cupped in one hand while he wrote with the other. Charlie looked up then, saw her looking at him, and crossed his eyes. Megan hid her smile behind her hand. It was his own fault if the test was proving to be too much for him. They had only been studying thirty minutes the night before when Brynne called and he had spent the next forty-five minutes on the phone with her.

~~~

While he talked, Megan had busied herself in the Lovetts' kitchen, unloading the dishwasher, and putting away the remnants of what had obviously been Charlie's quickly eaten supper.

Elise emerged from somewhere in the house, looking somber and carrying an empty wine glass.

"Megan," she said softly when she came into the kitchen. "You don't have to do that."

"It gives me something to do," she said to Elise. "Chaz is on the phone with Brynne."

Elise nodded and set the glass down in the sink.

"I don't suppose Nate told you guys where he was going?" Elise said, not looking up from the sink.

"No, he didn't," Megan answered, not looking up either.

Elise rubbed her right temple for just a second, and then turned abruptly.

"You know what? It doesn't matter. I already know where he went."

Elise walked over to the kitchen table and grabbed a small, brown leather purse. She pulled some keys out and walked over to the door that led to the garage.

"Tell Chaz not to wait up," she said, forcing a smile.

The bell announcing the end of the class period roused Megan from the memory of last night's encounter with Elise. She stood up and gathered her books, as did everyone else. Charlie caught up with her in the covered hallway outside class.

"So can I tell him yes?" he asked.

"Tell who yes?" she said, but she knew who he meant.

"Ryan."

"Chaz, you know my parents won't let me date until I'm sixteen." Megan said, thankful she had that as an excuse.

"Which you will be in, what, two months?"

"Closer to three."

"Megan, he's not asking you out on a date. It's just a dance. At school."

They emerged into the sunshine, and Megan stopped by a cement planter heavy with the scent of jasmine.

"Chaz, why are you pushing me about this?" she asked.

"I'm not pushing you."

"Yes, you are."

Charlie looked beyond her, as if searching for what he wanted to say.

"Maybe it's because I'm worried about you. You need to get out more. Make some friends."

"I'm fine, Chaz." And she started to walk away.

He stopped her.

"That's what you say, but I don't believe it," he said.

"Even if I weren't fine, which I *am*, it wouldn't be your problem to fix," Megan said evenly.

"God, you're stubborn!"

"Yes, I am. And don't say God's name like that, Chaz, unless you mean it."

"Well, maybe I do mean it!"

Megan could bear just about anyone's rejection of her except Charlie's. She felt the warm, weak feeling that she loathed creep over her.

"Please, Chaz," she said. "I don't want to fight. Not with you. I just don't think I'm ready to have a relationship that's...like that."

"Like what?" he said.

"I'm not ready for a boyfriend."

"Meg, he just wants to get to know you. Maybe dance one dance with you."

Megan felt the weakness intensify. She knew exactly what was happening. Her carefully placed protective layers were being peeled away, and Charlie didn't even know he was doing it. She could keep her worst fears about the opposite sex buried only until something like this uncovered them, and then there was no stopping them.

Charlie studied her face, realizing something wasn't right. "Megan, what is it?"

She just shook her head and lowered her eyes.

"Megan," he said gently.

"Please, Charlie," she said, not much above a whisper. "Not here. Not now."

She hardly ever called him Charlie to his face anymore. She hadn't meant to then, either.

"I have to meet Brynne for lunch," he said, clearly unsure what to do next. "Are you going to be okay?"

"Yes." Megan said, but she wouldn't look at him. "Just stop talking. Go. Go have lunch."

He stood for a moment longer, took a step, and then turned back.

"Megan," he said, in as gentle a voice as Megan had ever heard. "Come to the dance. Just give it a try. Okay?"

Megan looked up and blinked the tears away.

"I'll think about it," and she turned and walked away from him.

Megan was glad she had asked for that afternoon off. Adele missed nothing. She would have sensed something hadn't gone right at school. And Megan didn't want to talk about it.

She rode the bus home, content to be unobserved and anonymous in the second seat from the driver.

After the ten minute ride, Megan stepped off the bus and walked the rest of the way home, deep in thought. She knew Charlie would want to know what had nearly brought her to tears. She wasn't sure she could explain it to him. She set her book bag on the lawn in front of her house and kept walking, needing a few minutes alone to come to terms with what was swirling inside her head and heart.

The warm weakness that had stayed with her throughout the day seemed to come to the brim of her entire being as she walked. She hadn't felt this vulnerable since the day Jen was taken from her. It was a brutal reminder of what it was like to be eight and have your world crumble around you.

It had been seven years since the kidnapping, and she still couldn't seem to get through a crisis without the past rearing its ugly head. Anytime life got difficult, she was reminded of that long-ago summer day when her life seemed to shatter. And then, suddenly, a thought occurred to her. The past didn't intensify the crisis. The past *caused* it. She knew it as surely as she knew anything. Her turmoil over a nondate with a guy she barely knew wasn't complicated by what happened seven years ago. What had happened was the *cause* of her turmoil.

It all made sense. She suddenly knew why the thought of being with a boy scared her stiff, why the whole dating scene petrified her. Guys eyeing girls. Guys wanting to kiss girls. Guys wanting to chase after girls. Guys wanting other things from girls. Guys with their hands on girls. Guys wanting…

Megan gasped and shook the thought from her head because she knew it would lead to Jen and what she couldn't stop thinking might have happened to her; what she might have suffered at the hands of a man…

She stopped at the end of her street, at the edge of the canyon that was now a green, grassy slope that led to two golf holes. The copse of pepper trees had been replaced by a sand trap. It was all lush and beautiful. But Megan knew that underneath the carefully laid sod was a wild, unforgiving place.

Years before, after her mother let her go over to Charlie's again, she would stand at the gate in the Lovetts' backyard on occasion and stare at the expanse that lay between her house and Charlie's. She never went into the canyon again. But for a long time she couldn't help thinking that Jen was in a place like that, somewhere. A forbidden place, a scary place.

When she had turned twelve, Megan began to understand the ways of men and women, and that was when she first began to wonder in terror if Jen had been abused in a way that transformed that sweet arrangement between lovers into a beastly crime. It was also the year the canyon had been bought by a developer.

So, while Megan agonized over Jen's fate and this newfound and awful possibility, bulldozers and earthmovers tore the canyon to pieces. It all felt like one and the same to her—the bulldozers, the earthmovers, the broken ground, her broken spirit, Jen's terror. It was all the same.

And now it all made sense.

She was afraid to let a boy, a man, look at her. Touch her. Love her.

She was afraid she might hate it.

She was more afraid she might like it.

Megan sat with her parents and Michelle at the football game that night and tried to act as though the day had been like any other. She noticed her mother looking at her from time to time, like she knew something was up. At dinner, Megan had asked her parents if she could go to the dance with Charlie and Brynne. She knew that just asking would raise her mother's eyebrows, which it did. Her dad thought it was a great idea. Her mom pretended like she did, too. And Michelle whined that she wished she were in high school so she could go to the dance.

"Are you coming home with them?" her father had asked.

Megan didn't think Brynne would appreciate that very much.

"Maybe you could come for me at eleven?" she said.

"Sure," Gordy had said, smiling and obviously glad his older daughter was volunteering to go to a typical, high school social event.

Her mother hadn't said much, and Megan was glad she wasn't pestering her with questions.

Even if she could have explained that the dance was like the canyon experience, her mother certainly wouldn't like that. Megan had decided that afternoon as she looked out over the canyon's rim that she would do what she had done that long-ago fall day when she braved the canyon's worst hazards. She would prove she was not afraid.

She would dance with Ryan Talley.

*E*ven standing in line to buy her ticket for the postgame dance bothered Megan. Kids were clustered about her in noisy groups. Ahead of her in line was a tangle of girls, heavily made up, smelling of half a dozen different perfumes. Directly behind her was a group of guys with their hands in their pockets, pretending like they didn't have a care in the world. One of them said something, and the rest laughed. The girls in front of her looked past her to the group of guys. The boys acted like they didn't notice. Megan could tell they did.

Once inside the gym, Megan gazed about in confusion. It was dark and the music was too loud. The kids who weren't dancing stood around, talking and laughing. Mr. Fine was in the corner of the gym talking to one of the football coaches—apparently chaperones, but it was clear they were more interested in talking about the game that had just ended than being at the dance. The game had been a good one, one of Charlie's best. Megan quickly realized it was ridiculous to think she would be able to see him or talk to him tonight. He was Number 82. Chaz Lovett. All that Chaz.

It was a stupid idea to come. What had she been thinking?

Megan wondered what her parents would think if she called and asked to have her dad come and get her now instead of an hour and half from now.

They would be disappointed. They would want to know why she didn't stay. They would want to talk about it.

No way.

Well, she would just go find a bleacher in a dark corner and sit there for the next ninety minutes. More than likely no one would notice her.

She started to walk toward the open bleachers, but then heard someone call her name.

Charlie was walking toward her with Brynne on his arm. Behind them was Ryan.

"Hey, you came!" Charlie said, clearly pleased. His hair was damp, and Megan could smell his cologne.

"Yep," she said for there was nothing else she could think of to say.

"Megan, you've met Brynne's brother, Ryan, before, right?" Charlie said, motioning to the young man behind him.

"Um, I'm not sure."

"Hi," Ryan said, stepping forward.

Ryan was close to Charlie's height, but not as athletically built as Charlie. He was brown haired, nice looking. Deep, brown eyes.

"Hello," Megan said politely.

"Let's dance," Brynne said to Charlie, leaning into him and practically planting the words on his cheek.

As Charlie turned to follow Brynne to the dance floor, he gave Megan a look that said, *Be nice!* Or maybe it was, *You can do this!*

"So, you want to dance?" Ryan asked.

He seemed nice. Even if he was Brynne's brother.

"I'm not sure I'm very good at it," she answered.

"I'm not either," he said as he took her arm.

Ryan led her to the open area where couples were dancing to a heavy rock beat.

"I'm not sure I can do this," Megan said, hating how young her voice sounded.

"We'll just wait for the next one," he said. "I think this song is about over."

"Okay," Megan said nervously.

Ryan was looking at her and smiling. What was he thinking? That she was stupid? That she was naive? That she was a lousy dancer? That she was hopeless?

The song ended, and Megan took a breath. The DJ said something into his microphone, but Megan couldn't hear him.

"What did he say?" Megan asked Ryan.

Ryan slipped his arm around her waist and offered her his other hand.

"He said, 'Here's a classic get-to-know-you-better tune.'"

Megan hesitated.

"C'mon," Ryan said, grinning. "I promise not to step on *all* of your toes."

Megan smiled nervously and took his hand.

Ryan tried to pull her closer to him. Megan stiffened.

"You're going to have to get a little closer if this is going to work," he said.

Megan tried to relax. That warm, weak feeling was starting to wash over her.

"I'm afraid I don't know how to dance this way," she said, trying to laugh it off.

"It's easy," Ryan said, as he gently brought her closer. "We just go around in circles. When we get too dizzy, we can reverse it and go the other way."

Megan was amazed at how easy this was for him. Too easy.

"See?" he said as he led for a few steps. "That's not so hard, is it?"

Megan relaxed a little and smiled.

"You're in my art class," he said as he led her in a slow, loopy circle.

"Yeah," Megan replied.

"That chalk drawing you did the first week of school was really good."

Megan blinked. Was he serious? Or was he just trying to flatter her?

"You must be confusing my drawing with someone else's," she said.

"No, it was yours," he said, smiling down at her. "A cat, right?"

"Yes. My cat."

"You must like art," he said. He rubbed her back with a thumb. It unnerved her.

"Um, no. No. Actually I don't." The room was beginning to spin.

"Me, neither. I'm only taking it for the fine-art credit," he said, then added, "You look a little dizzy. Must be time to switch."

Ryan spun her around and switched directions. He drew her in a little closer.

"Do you have your license yet?" he asked.

Megan swallowed. She looked for Charlie but couldn't see him.

"No. Not until December. I mean, I turn sixteen in December."

"It's great to finally have my own wheels," Ryan said. "I got my license the end of August. Maybe I can drive you home tonight?"

"Um. I don't know. My dad is coming and I…" she began and faltered.

"Hey, are you feeling okay?" he asked with concern.

"Maybe a little air would be good."

"Sure," Ryan said. He took her hand and led her to the entrance to the gym. They stepped out into the slight chill of a late September night.

"That better?" he asked.

Megan nodded. She hated the way she was feeling. *Hated it.* It made her feel stupid. Useless. Young. Eight.

Ryan led her to a cement bench a few yards from the entrance.

"Here, we can sit here for a few minutes."

After a few seconds, Ryan asked, "Feeling better?"

"I think so," Megan lied, attempting a smile.

"Great. 'Cause I'd like to kiss you," he said.

Megan opened her mouth to protest.

"I don't think—"

But he covered her words with his mouth.

It wasn't a long kiss. It wasn't even a passionate kiss. But it was a kiss. On her mouth. The kind of kiss a man gives a woman. His lips were soft and wet. Foreign. Unpleasant.

He backed away.

"I really like you, Megan," he was saying.

Megan was afraid she would throw up in his lap if she opened her mouth, so she said nothing.

"Wow. Now you really look pale," he said. "Are you sure you're feeling better?"

"No, I guess not," she whispered.

"Guess I shouldn't have kissed you, then!" he said nonchalantly.

That's right, you buffoon. You shouldn't have.

"I think I better call home," Megan said instead, rising unsteadily to her feet.

"I can take you home," Ryan said.

"No, no…" she started to say as she took a few steps.

Just then Charlie and Brynne appeared at the entrance to the gym.

"Everything okay?" Charlie asked, but Megan could tell he already knew everything was not.

"Megan thinks she might be coming down with something," Ryan offered, stroking Megan's back.

"I need to call home," Megan said as she began walking toward a set of pay phones on the other side of the entrance. She couldn't get away from him fast enough.

"I'll take you home," Charlie said, stopping Megan and looking deep into her eyes.

"Chaz!" Brynne said through her teeth.

"I already offered," Ryan said.

"It's okay," Megan said, looking at Charlie only. "I'll just call my dad."

"Brynne, it'll just take a couple of minutes," Charlie said with a wink. "I'll be back before the next slow dance."

"This is unbelievable," Brynne said, loud enough for everyone to hear.

"Let me just call my dad," Megan said to Charlie.

"Yes, let her!" Brynne said, throwing up an arm in Megan's direction.

"I'll be back in fifteen minutes," Charlie said, taking Megan's arm. "Ryan, don't let your sister dance with anyone until I get back!"

"Bye, Megan," Ryan said. "See you Monday?"

Megan turned and waved.

Charlie waited until they had closed the distance between the gym entrance and his car in the parking lot before he said anything.

"What happened?" he said as he unlocked his car.

"Nothing," Megan muttered, walking to the passenger side. They both got in, then Charlie started the engine and backed out of the parking space.

"It's not like you to lie to me," he said.

She sighed.

"It was all me. It wasn't him, okay? It was *me*," she said.

"*What* was you?" Charlie asked as he turned out of the school parking lot.

"I told you yesterday, Chaz. I told you I wasn't ready for this."

"Ready for what?!" he said, obviously frustrated. "It was just a dance, Meg. He didn't ask you to marry him, did he?"

"No," Megan said as she stared out her window, trying to regain her composure.

"Megan, this is my senior year. This time next year I won't be here."

"You think I don't know that?" she said angrily.

Chaz sighed and rubbed his forehead with one hand while he drove with the other.

"I know you know it," he said. "I just want you to make some friends. To open up. I don't want you spending your next two years of high school living like this."

"Like what?!" Megan said, turning to face Charlie.

"Like Jen disappeared just yesterday, Megan! It's been seven years!" Charlie said, raising his voice. "Megan, I know why you shut people out. I know why you pretend like you don't need anybody. But it's got to stop! Not everyone you befriend is going to disappear into thin air."

Megan's throat felt tight.

"Don't…" she said hoarsely.

They drove the rest of the way in silence. Once they were in Megan's neighborhood, Charlie pulled to the curb several doors away from her house and turned off the ignition.

"Look, I'm sorry I said that. Really I am. But I'm right, Megan. You've got to let her go."

Tears started to form at the edges of Megan's eyes.

"Megan."

She looked up at him. Charlie's eyes were wet, too. She had never seen him shed a tear before. Never.

"Don't think for a moment I don't know how hard it is," he said softly as he took her hand. "You know I do. Let her go."

"I don't know how," she whispered after a long pause.

He squeezed her hand.

"If you look for a way, you'll find it," he said.

The two of them sat for several long minutes in silence.

"Brynne will wonder where you are," Megan finally said.

"I'll make it up to her."

She put her hand on the car door handle, suggesting to Charlie she was going to walk the remainder of the way home.

"I can take you the rest of the way," Charlie said.

"No," Megan said softly. "No, you can't."

She squeezed his hand, then brought it to her lips and kissed it. It was the first time she had ever shown Charlie physical affection. It surprised them both.

Megan stepped out of the car and began walking toward home.

At breakfast the next day, Trina decided to again ask Megan if something happened at the dance. When Megan came into the house the night before, she had gone straight to her room, saying she wasn't feeling well. One look at Megan's face confirmed this, but there had to be more to it.

"Megan," Trina ventured. "Do you want to talk about what happened last night?"

Megan looked up from her English muffin. The look on her face suggested she was about to say, "Nothing happened last night." But then the look vanished, as if Megan had considered the contest and decided she didn't have the will to fight. That alone alarmed Trina.

"Not really," Megan said, picking up the muffin and taking a small bite.

Trina sat down next to her with a cup of coffee.

"Sometimes it helps to figure things out if you talk it over with someone," she said.

"I think I have to figure this out on my own, Mom," Megan said.

Trina fingered the handle on her mug.

"No, you don't," Trina said, feeling like she was taking a tremendous chance.

"What?" Megan said.

"You never *have* to figure something out on your own, Megan. That's a great line, but it's not true."

Megan just blinked at her and then looked down.

"I mean, I know you have to make decisions for yourself, and you alone have to live with those decisions, but you should never feel forced to figure out a problem all by yourself," Trina continued. "The smartest people in the world still talk things over with their hairstylists."

Megan looked up and smiled. It was a tiny smile, but a smile nonetheless.

"I'm here whenever you decide you want to talk," Trina said. "I promise to just listen and only give advice if you ask for it."

"Thanks, Mom," Megan said.

Gordy appeared in the doorway with his car keys in his hand. "You ready?"

Megan stood, wrapped her muffin in her napkin, and started toward her dad.

Trina grabbed Megan's free hand and squeezed it as she walked by.

Megan squeezed back.

～⁀～⁀～

Megan had forgotten Adele's new hire would be at work that day until she walked into the shop and saw a tall, slender teen with a mop of black curls on his head hoisting an end table over an overturned ottoman. Adele saw Megan come in and smiled.

"Megan," she said. "I'd like you to meet David Christopoulos. David, this is Megan Diamond."

The young man wiped his hands on his Levis. He had clear, olive-toned skin and the darkest brown eyes Megan had ever seen.

"It's a pleasure to meet you, Megan," he said, offering his hand.

"Same here," Megan said in response, shaking David's hand.

"David plays guitar at my church," Adele said. "He has five sisters!"

"I only have one," Megan said, walking over to the minifridge behind the counter and placing a container of yogurt inside.

There was a brief awkward silence, then Adele stepped over to her paper-strewn desk.

"Now, I have a list of things I'd like you two to get done today, and you may as well get started. It's going to be a busy day. David is letting us use his pickup, Megan. That'll be so much easier than using my old van. Now, let's see…this end table can go back to the Hollisters in Clairemont, and that dining-room chair is ready to go, too. You can take that to Pacific Beach. The address is on the tag. I have a bolt of fabric ready for me at Hancock; you can get that on the way back from PB. Then you can pick up a sofa in Tierrasanta. After lunch you can start on the buffet table back at my garage. There! We'll finally be able to get stuff done in a timely manner. Now, where are my scissors?"

"Sounds good, Adele," Megan said. "You want to give me that list so we don't forget anything?"

"Oh, of course. Here you go. I suppose you'll want to get going right away. Here. I'll hold the door if you want to get the chair, Megan. David, you grab the end table."

Megan lifted the chair and followed David out to the parking lot.

David's pickup was an older model Chevy showing signs of age. Megan recognized some of Adele's old blankets in the back, which she must have thrown in earlier. The two pieces of furniture were quickly secured.

As Megan approached the passenger side of the truck, David came alongside her. She looked at him quizzically. He didn't think *she* was going to drive, did he?

He gripped the handle of the passenger-side door and opened it. Then he stood there next to it.

"What...what are you doing?" Megan said.

David looked at the door and then back at her.

"I opened the door," he said.

"Because...?" Megan said and stopped.

"Because it would be hard to get in if it was closed."

Megan studied him. He waited.

She got in the truck and took the door from him.

David came around to the other side, got in, and started the engine.

"Um, for future reference, I can open my own door, David," she said.

"Of course you can," he said, looking over his shoulder to check for other cars as he backed out.

"I mean, I'd *prefer* to get my own door."

David put the car into drive and eased out of the parking lot.

"I don't think I can do that," he said.

"*What?*" said Megan, thoroughly baffled.

"I open doors for women. That's what I've been taught to do."

Megan squirmed in her seat. Was he serious?

"Well, if we're going to be working together, you might have to knock it off," she said coolly.

"Well, if we're going to be working together, you might have to get used to it," he countered.

She turned abruptly to look at him. He turned as well...and smiled.

"What else have you been taught to do that I should know about?"

He laughed. It was a nice laugh. But she wasn't ready to be friends quite yet.

"That's good!" he said.

"I'm serious," Megan said.

"Well," he said, stopping for a red light. "There's a good chance if I'm seated and you enter or leave a room, I'll stand up."

"You *do* know nobody does that anymore," Megan said.

"*I* do it. And my dad does, too."

"And what does your mom think about that?"

"She loves being treated like a princess," he answered.

"Well, *I* am not a princess," Megan said.

"No American *is*, Megan. I didn't say my mom loves being a princess. I said she loves being *treated* like one."

Megan squinted at David as if trying to see inside his mind.

"You are very odd," she said.

David shrugged. "Fair enough," he said. "But I'd rather be odd and polite than common and rude."

They rode in silence for a few blocks, and then David switched on the radio to a jazz station. He began to nod his head to the beat of the music.

"You like jazz?" he asked.

"It's all right," she said.

The music reminded her of Nate Lovett. And dancing under the Serengeti. A melancholy look must have crept over her face.

"You really *don't* like it. I can tell by the look on your face," David said.

"No, it's not that," Megan said. "It's just that a friend of mine, his dad likes jazz. My friend's sister and I used to dance in their living room to this kind of music."

"I don't see why that would make you sad. That sounds like a happy memory," David said.

"It is," Megan replied, staring out the windshield but not looking at anything in particular. "That little girl was my best friend. She was kidnapped when we were both eight. I was there when it happened."

Megan couldn't believe she had said so much in such a short amount of time. She had just met this guy, and she had practically told him the most important thing that had happened in her life in fifteen seconds. He must think she's nuts.

She stole a look at David. He was looking at her.

"Jennifer Lovett," he said, like he understood a great deal in the span of only seconds.

"We called her Jen," she said, turning away.

By the time they had picked up the sofa in Tierrasanta, it was nearly noon. As they tied down the couch, David announced he was hungry.

"Let's get some lunch," he said. "I know a great pizza place just on the other side of the freeway."

Megan didn't want to go to a great pizza place with a guy she had just met.

"I have some yogurt back at the shop," she said.

"Well, I don't have some yogurt back at the shop," David replied.

"Can't we just go to a drive through?"

"A drive through? I'm driving. How can I eat if I'm driving?"

"Fine. I'll wait in the truck," Megan said, starting for her door.

"You will wait in the truck for what?" David said, sprinting ahead of her.

"For you to eat!" Megan said crossly as David opened her door.

"Are you afraid to come into a restaurant with me? Are you thinking this would be like a date? Because this would *not* be a date. I don't date. I would be happy to buy you lunch if you have no money with you, but if you do, you can buy your own lunch."

"I have money with me," Megan said evenly as she got into the truck.

"Great! Pizza it is!" David said, shutting her door.

David's great little place turned out to be a busy, mom-and-pop establishment called Angelino's. Megan chose a table close to the door and handed David a five-dollar bill. He went up to the counter to order and came back with a tray, two large slices of pepperoni pizza, and a small pitcher of root beer.

David set the tray down, took a seat, and then audibly prayed over their meal. Megan looked around nervously. No one seemed to take any notice.

They ate for a few minutes without either saying anything.

"So, which school do you go to?" Megan said, not especially comfortable with the silence.

"I guess you could say I go to the school in my kitchen," David answered. "My mom homeschools my sisters and me."

"Oh."

"And you?"

"I go to Rancho Hills."

More silence followed. David didn't seem to be bothered by it.

"So, you don't date? Do your parents not let you?" Megan ventured, although the subject matter unnerved her some.

"I don't let me," David said, wiping his mouth with a napkin. "I plan to court the woman I marry, not date her. And since I'm too young to marry, there's no point in courting anyone at the moment."

Megan just stared at David. She couldn't decide if she liked him or was annoyed by him. Chivalry wasn't something she saw in guys her age. He was polite to a fault. But he also had a quick wit and a sarcastic edge. It was disconcerting. Worse, she had to go to the bathroom at that moment. And that meant she had to stand up.

"David," she said.

David looked at her.

"I'm going to stand up, walk to the back of this restaurant, and use the restroom. You are *not* to stand up, got it?" she said.

His eyes narrowed, and a huge grin spread across his face.

"I'll try not to," he said, eyes twinkling.

Megan stood and began walking away, looking back once to make sure he hadn't changed his mind.

She came back to find David chatting with the owner. She headed hastily for the front door, but David saw her, said goodbye to the owner, and zoomed ahead of her. He opened the door, and then stood holding the door for several other people who were coming into Angelino's. Megan took advantage of his preoccupation and began to walk quickly toward the pickup. She looked back and saw him glancing at her as the last person stepped inside the restaurant. She took off running, finding it impossible not to laugh as she heard him chase after her, wanting to get to the door ahead of her. Megan grabbed the handle and swung the door open just as David closed in on her. She jumped up onto the seat and grabbed the inside handle, slamming the door as he reached her. He slapped his hands on the closed window, laughing.

Megan was laughing, too.

"I see I'll have to wear my running shoes to work!" he yelled through the glass.

It had been a long time since Megan had laughed like that. She was suddenly very glad David didn't date. That meant she wouldn't have to worry being around him. It would be like being around Charlie, although she was certain she would never like David as a friend like she liked Charlie. He was too annoying. And thankfully there was no attraction to have to avoid or squelch or fear.

~~~

On Monday, Megan steered clear of Ryan Talley as much as she could, though in art class he came up to her and asked if she was feeling better. It was a difficult question to answer, so she just said yes and changed the subject.

Megan didn't see much of Charlie all that week or the next. She figured Brynne had been all over his case about his leaving her at the dance to take his annoying, unattractive neighbor home and that maybe he had to lay low for awhile to keep Brynne on speaking terms—or any other kind of terms—with him.

Two weeks later, on a Saturday, Megan and David were in Adele's garage, sanding a drop-leaf table that had been painted and repainted far too many times.

In between blasts of the motorized sander, Megan heard a voice. She looked up, pushing up her safety visor.

Charlie stood framed in the doorway of Adele's garage.

"Chaz!" Megan said. "Hi!"

"Adele told me I'd find you here," Charlie said taking a step inside and noticing David.

"Chaz, this is David Christopoulos," Megan said. "He works for Adele. David, this is my friend Chaz Lovett."

David removed a work glove and offered Charlie his hand. "Nice to meet you, Chaz," he said.

"Yeah," Charlie replied. Megan could tell Charlie was sizing David up, studying him.

"So, what are you up to?" Megan asked, setting her sander and visor down.

"I was wondering if you could take a break for a few minutes. I need to talk to you, Megan."

"Yeah, sure," Megan said as she turned to David.

"I'll be fine," David said. "Take all the time you need." He slipped his visor back down and switched his sander back on.

"Chaz, what is it?" Megan said.

Charlie looked toward his car parked at the end of Adele's driveway.

"Can I take you to my house for a few minutes?" he said.

"Sure," Megan answered and followed Charlie out to his Trans Am.

The ride to the Lovetts' house was a short one from Adele's. Charlie didn't say anything at first.

"I haven't seen you around," Megan said.

"It's been kind of crazy for me the past two weeks," he said looking straight ahead, then added, "Is David a decent guy?"

"David?" Megan said, surprised at the change in subject. "Yeah, he's decent. He's about as polite as they come. Chaz, what's wrong?"

"You'll see."

They turned down Charlie's street and within seconds were driving up to the Lovett house. Megan's eyes widened, and her heart seemed to skip a beat when the house came into view.

A For Sale sign was protruding from the Lovetts' front lawn.

The garage door was open, and the garage itself was completely empty.

"Charlie…" Megan said, but she couldn't finish her sentence.

Charlie stopped the car in the driveway, but neither one got out. Megan couldn't take her eyes off the hideous For Sale sign.

"They're getting a divorce, Megan. And selling the house."

Megan felt the familiar rush of powerlessness as she realized everything was about to change. Charlie was moving.

"But it's your senior year—" she began.

"I'll finish the school year at Rancho. I'll drive from Del Mar every day."

"Del Mar," Megan said, but her voice sounded weak.

"That's where my dad's girlfriend lives," Charlie continued in the glib tone he normally used to criticize bad referee calls. "Did I tell you he has a girlfriend? Her name's Caroline. We're moving in with her. Isn't that a kick? She's an heiress."

Megan could think of nothing to say.

"Get this, Megan. My mom has a boyfriend, too. She's had one for months. My parents were both sleeping around on each other and neither one knew it!" Charlie laughed. "So, when they finally had the Big Fight last week, they were, like, thrilled to realize neither one of them wanted to be married anymore to the other one. Now how convenient is that?"

"Charlie—" Megan began.

"Mom's moving to Mission Viejo to be with *Leo*," Charlie continued, in mock commentary. "The guy's name is Leo. He writes plays. You know what the really sad thing is, Meg? I kinda like Leo. Yep, I do."

Megan felt a chill. She began again. "Charlie, I'm—"

"The movers came yesterday for most of the furniture. There's a few things left. Stuff neither one of them wanted," Charlie continued, looking at the house, and then turning to Megan.

"There's something I found in my room, Megan, when I packed it up. And there's something my mom wants you to have. Come inside."

Megan followed Charlie into the house through the empty entryway. He stopped where the family room and living room met. There was nothing to distinguish one room from the other. The only thing in the living room was the oil painting of the Serengeti.

"My mom wants you to have that painting," Charlie said. "She knows how much you always liked it."

"I *couldn't*, Chaz—"

"You have to take it, Megan. She wants you to have it. Besides, she's already gone to Leo's with what she wanted to take."

Megan loved that painting, but the thought of having it as a result of Nate and Elise's breaking up depressed her. Charlie moved past her and started down the hall to the bedrooms. Megan followed him.

She paused for a moment outside the room that had been Jen's. For the past few years, the only thing that had remained in it of Jen's was the bedcover and one doll. Now even those were gone. The room was bare. It was like Jen had disappeared all over again. Nate and Elise had never declared their missing daughter dead. Not officially. But as Megan swept her eyes across the empty room, she sensed that at last they had. And now she felt a strange and unsettling urgency to do the same. Charlie said nothing as he waited for her outside the room that had been his. When Megan took a step away from Jen's old room, he walked into his own empty room and bent down to retrieve something that was inside a tiny plastic tray sitting on top of a sealed box.

"I found this yesterday, Megan, and when I did, I knew what I needed to do with it," he said to her. "Hold out your hand."

Megan stretched out her hand, palm up, and looked at Charlie.

He covered her hand with his and something small and slender passed from his palm to hers. He took his hand away.

Megan looked down at her hand. In the center of her palm was the tiny silver hoop earring that Charlie had found in the canyon a few weeks after Jen's kidnapping. Seeing it for the first time in seven years made Megan's breath catch in her throat.

"You told me you didn't know how to let her go," Charlie said softly. "I told you if you looked for a way, you would find it. Maybe you can use this to find a way." And he closed Megan's fist over the tiny earring.

It was all suddenly too much for Megan to handle. She threw her arms around Charlie.

"Don't go… don't go," she sobbed, but she couldn't tell who or what she wanted to stay. She wanted Jen. She wanted Charlie. She wanted this house. She wanted the canyon back. She wanted Time to give back what it had taken.

Charlie held Megan and said nothing as she cried. He didn't try to console her. He didn't tell her it would all be okay. In fact, he seemed to need the embrace as much as she did.

An aching need to feel safe filled Megan's heart and soul as her world was again falling apart all around her, much like it had seven years before. She wanted Charlie to stroke her hair and tell her God would take care of her, that He would watch over her, that He knew what had really happened to Jen, and that He loved them all very much. But she knew Charlie wasn't going to say any of those things.

He had long ago stopped believing in God.

It seemed like a long time before Megan broke away. But as her tears subsided and she realized she was in Charlie's arms, a strange uneasiness crept over her. She stepped back, wiping her eyes.

They stood there in silence.

"I'll see if I can fit the painting in the back of my car," Charlie said quietly and left the room.

Megan walked back down the hall to Jen's barren room. The airy openness felt strangely stifling. Megan closed her eyes and imagined Jen's Barbies, her dresser with the jar of Mexican money on top, her jewelry box of pierced earrings, her basket of hair ribbons. She imagined the two of them sitting on Jen's bed drawing pictures of cats, looking at horse magazines, and eating Sweet Tarts. She opened her eyes, and the void met her gaze.

Megan opened the hand that held the hoop earring. She stared at it, wondering how it could possibly help her let Jen go, as Charlie suggested. She took one more look at the empty room, and then closed her hand tightly around the earring. She stuffed it into her front pants pocket as she walked out of the room.

PART FOUR
Spring 1999

17

The familiar voice drifted into Megan's head, swirling, working its way into her dream. She was trying to get her graduation robe on, but the zipper was broken. She was late. They would be calling her name on the sunny football-field-turned-commencement-floor, but she wouldn't be there to get her diploma. Her mother was standing next to her in jeans and a sweatshirt.

"Why aren't you ready?" her mother was saying.

"Why aren't you?" Megan was replying.

"I'm going like this," her mother was saying, but then she coughed and when her mother spoke again, her voice sounded weird. "I came down for the wedding."

"What wedding?" Megan said aloud.

And then she was awake. The dream of being late for her own high school graduation slipped away.

"Yeah, they're getting married tomorrow."

The voice that had worked itself into her dream was real. It was coming from the living room, beyond her closed bedroom door.

It was Charlie.

163

Megan snapped her head around to look at her alarm clock. It was ten-thirty. She jumped out of bed, frantically wondering what Charlie was doing at her house unannounced. She hadn't seen him since last summer. He hadn't called. His last e-mail to her was in what, January? She picked up a pair of tattered jeans off the floor of her room and snagged open a dresser drawer, grabbing a black tank top.

Megan dressed quickly, afraid her mother was telling Charlie that Megan was still asleep and that he would leave.

Then she heard her mother's voice.

"She went to the prom last night and didn't get in until late, but I'll see if she's awake. I know she'll want to see you."

Then there was a light knock on her door.

"Megan?"

"You can open it, Mom. I'm up," Megan said, slipping on a pair of sandals.

"Charlie's here, Megan," Trina said, poking her head in the door.

"What for? I mean, did he say why he's in town?" Megan said, running her fingers through her hair. It felt sticky from the amount of hairspray Trina had used on her the night before.

Trina stepped in and picked up Megan's prom dress from off the floor. A corsage of tiny champagne-colored roses was still pinned to the filmy, midnight blue bodice. Trina slipped the corsage off the dress.

"His dad is getting married tomorrow," Trina said softly and then lifted the corsage. "I'll just put this in the fridge for you. You might want to keep it."

Megan walked past her mother and into the bathroom across the hall.

"It's okay to toss it, Mom," she said hastily. "They're already dead."

"Maybe I'll keep it then," Trina said.

"Tell him I'll be there in a sec," Megan said, closing the bathroom door.

After attending to her immediate needs, Megan washed her hands and then looked at her reflection in the mirror. She still wore makeup from the prom last night. It wasn't a lot, just mascara, some pale lavender eye shadow, and a little blush, but it was a different look for her. Trina had insisted she try a little makeup. It was her *prom*, after all. Megan had protested.

"Mom, it's not like I have to impress anyone," Megan had said. "David won't care. And I'm only going to the prom because *you* want me to. He only asked me because you begged him."

"You want your pictures to be nice, don't you?" Trina had replied, ignoring the inference to motherly meddling.

"We're not getting pictures," Megan had said.

"Why not?" Her mother had sounded very disappointed.

"Neither one of us wants them, Mom. David and I are just friends."

"What's wrong with *friends* having their picture taken?"

"Nothing," Megan sighed.

"Then get your picture taken, please? For me? I want one. *I'll* pay for it," Trina pleaded.

"Fine," Megan said and proceeded to let Trina gel and curl her short hair.

Now, looking in the mirror, Megan was a little unnerved by the sight of her made-up face. She had been too tired to wash it last night when she came home at three in the morning, and she didn't want to take the time to wash it now.

She wiped away a few mascara smudges and ran a brush through her still-curled hair. She calmed the curls down with a few sprays from Michelle's misting bottle, frowning at its flowery scent. She swished some mouthwash inside her mouth, spit it out in the sink, and wished for the tenth time in as many minutes that she had not slept in. She opened the bathroom door and walked down the hall to find Charlie sitting on the couch, chatting with her dad.

Megan hadn't seen Charlie since last August when he came to say goodbye. He was on his way back to USC for his sophomore year, had to be there early since football practice was beginning. He'd been offered a full scholarship the year before to play with the Trojans, and though he played very little his freshman year, he was always the first choice to play backup when an injury kept a first-string receiver on the bench. The first year Charlie was gone had been easier for Megan than she expected, partly because she had grown used to seeing less of Charlie after his move to Del Mar. By the time he graduated from Rancho Hills, he had been out of the neighborhood for seven months. Megan saw him only at school, and even then, things were different. It was like Charlie had left his old life behind when the house was sold and he and his father moved to Del Mar. Megan attributed it to Charlie's need to cleanse himself from all that remained of Jen. It hurt, but she understood it. She almost envied him.

Much to her surprise, David soon began to fill the void that Charlie left. At times, Megan felt compelled to thank God for providing David's friendship just as Charlie began to drift away, even though she knew she would never feel the same kind of bond with David that she did with Charlie. David was too practical, too predictable, too sure of things. Her parents liked David. More than once, she had overheard her mother comment to her father that David was "such a nice, godly young man." She never heard her mother say the opposite about Charlie, but she knew Trina felt that way. Even though it was no surprise when Trina politely pressured David into asking Megan to her prom, Megan had been a bit astounded that he agreed to it.

"You don't date," Megan said to him when he asked her.

"That's true. This wouldn't be a date, though," he said. "I would simply be your escort to your prom."

"Do you dance?" she said, in a rather challenging tone.

"My parents have taught me how to waltz," he replied, a tiny smile creasing his lower jaw.

"And so what are we going to do when the music doesn't lend itself to a waltz?" Megan had asked.

"We can stand around, drink punch, and find something about which to debate," he had replied.

In the end, Megan had a good time. David was fun to be around, didn't try to impress anyone, wasn't self-absorbed, was very attentive, and of course, opened all her doors for her.

As she stood there looking at her old friend, Charlie, she suddenly wondered how different it would have been to have gone to the prom with him.

The moment passed quickly, though. As soon as Charlie looked up and saw her, he stood, wide eyed.

"Megan," he said.

"Hey, Chaz," Megan said as she stepped over to him and gave him a quick hug.

She stepped back and saw that he still had a rather dazed look on his face.

"This is a surprise," Megan said as she ran a hand through her hair, still uncomfortable with having just awakened.

"Yeah, well…my dad and Caroline are getting married tomorrow, and I'm the best man, so…we had rehearsal last night…I drove down to Del Mar yesterday."

"So, you're the best man? Wow…" Megan said.

"Yeah, after two years, they've decided to make it legal," Charlie laughed nervously. Megan's parents smiled uneasily.

"Tell your dad congratulations for us," Gordy said, easing over the awkward moment.

"Yeah, sure," Charlie said. He turned back to Megan. "Can I take you out for breakfast? Or is it lunchtime yet?"

Megan smiled, relieved that Charlie had not forgotten how to tease her. Her parents laughed.

"I was out a little late last night," she said in her defense.

"So I hear. Big date, huh?"

"No, it was not a big date, and yes, you can take me out to breakfast," she said.

As they stepped outside, Megan noticed that Charlie had a new car, a sleek, silver BMW.

"New car?"

Charlie shrugged.

"Dad started his own business, and it's going really well. He doesn't need this one anymore now that he's driving a Lexus."

"It's nice," Megan said as she opened the passenger door, surprising herself by nearly waiting for Charlie to do it for her.

"So, what do you feel like having?" he said as he slipped in the driver's side, started the engine, and backed out of the driveway.

Megan felt funny in Charlie's new car. Charlie looked the same and was starting to sound the same after the initial stuttering a few minutes ago, but something felt different.

"I don't know," she said. "Maybe a bagel. And a latte."

"And a walk on the beach?" he said.

"Yeah, that sounds nice."

Charlie pulled into a bagel shop on their way to Interstate 15, and Megan selected a cranberry-orange bagel and a mocha. Charlie asked for a plain bagel and a Mountain Dew.

They ate as Charlie made his way to La Jolla Shores, a favorite beach for them both. The late morning traffic wasn't too bad, and soon they were atop La Jolla Village Drive and making their way down to the coast. On the way, Charlie told Megan about his new roommate, his classes at USC, and the plans the football coaches had to make him a starting receiver in the fall.

Then Charlie asked Megan what her plans were for the fall. Megan told him she hadn't decided.

"Sometimes I think maybe I should get away, you know? Go somewhere else. Like another state or something."

Charlie parked the car at that moment and was looking at her. Megan wondered if he had heard what she just said.

"Chaz?" she said.

"You're so beautiful and grown up," he said softly. "I can't believe how much you've changed, Megan."

"Don't…" was all she could say. She set her empty cup in the holder, noticing her hands were shaking.

"I'm serious. Megan, you look great."

"I just got up. I look a mess. Knock it off," Megan said, reaching for the car door handle and wrenching it open.

She heard Charlie's door open as well.

"What is it with you and compliments?" he said as he got out laughing, but Megan could tell he was serious.

"I don't need them," she said. "I don't want them."

"Who *doesn't* need a compliment now and then?" Charlie said, coming around to her side of the car. "I think you're kidding yourself, Meg. You can pretend you don't need them, but I don't believe you."

Megan shrugged her shoulders and began to walk toward the sound of the surf. The two of them slid over the waist-high cement wall at the end of the lot. They removed their shoes and set them side by side on the wall.

"Thanks for all those e-mails and phone calls this past year," Megan said sarcastically, elbowing Charlie as they trudged across the sand to where the surf caressed the beach.

"Oh, yeah. Sorry. You know, most men aren't very good about stuff like that," Charlie said. "I did think about you, though. A lot."

"In between girlfriends, maybe," Megan said cynically.

"I did!" Charlie laughed. "I just never did anything about it."

"So who's the latest? What's her name?" Megan said, stopping and bending down to pick up a shell in the wet sand.

"Well, I'm kind of not seeing anyone right now," he said.

"Chaz, that's like saying you're kind of dead. You either *are* seeing someone or you aren't."

"Okay. I'm not seeing anyone," he said, putting his hands in his pockets. "Are you?"

"Am I what?" Megan said, squinting up at him.

"Seeing anyone?"

Megan flicked the shell with her finger. It was broken. She stood up.

"Nope."

"So you and David aren't…" Charlie didn't finish.

"No, David and I *aren't*," Megan said. "He doesn't date. He plans to court the girl he's going to marry. He will only date *her*. Except it won't be dating, it will be *courting*."

"Courting?" Charlie said with a laugh.

"Yeah, Chaz, courting," Megan said as they resumed walking. "You know, build a relationship with someone, get to know that person as a friend, love as a friend, then fall in love, then get married."

"That's what dating is," Charlie said.

"No, dating is like trying on clothes at a department store. You just keep trying on stuff until something fits."

"That sounds pretty reasonable to me."

Megan stopped and looked at him. He stopped, too.

"And what about all those clothes lying on the floor that you didn't like? What about them?"

"Someone else will buy them," he said with a grin as he shrugged his shoulders.

"Not if they're lying in a heap on the floor," Megan said, punctuating each word.

"Point taken," Charlie said.

They kept walking.

"Has he ever kissed you?" Charlie said, smirking.

"No, Chaz. He has never kissed me. Courting means saving your kisses for the person you marry."

"Megan, have you ever kissed *anyone*?" he asked coyly.

Megan said nothing, but she could feel her face growing warm and red. She immediately thought of that night more than two years ago when Ryan Talley had kissed her without warning. And she had almost thrown up in his face. Charlie saw the deepening shade of red on her cheeks.

"You have!" he said, laughing and marveling at his discovery.

Megan looked away.

"Who was it? Anybody I know?"

"It was a long time ago."

"C'mon, Megan. Who was it?" Charlie said, putting an arm around her.

Megan took note of Charlie's muscular arm across her shoulder. It felt nice. In a scary kind of way.

"It was no one special, Chaz. I hardly knew him. And I didn't kiss him. He kissed me."

The smile on Charlie's face disappeared.

"So, he wasn't someone you cared about?" he said, looking at her intently.

Megan shook her head.

"It's different when it's with someone you care about," Charlie said gently, reaching up to tuck a stray hair behind her ear. His eyes were locked on hers, communicating something Megan was afraid to consider.

"I'll show you," he said softly.

Charlie pulled her close to him, leaned down, and kissed her softly and gently on her lips. It was nothing like that sloppy thing Ryan had forced on her. Charlie's kiss was tender and inviting. There was nothing remotely scary or perplexing about it. It was surprisingly lovely. Megan felt a tiny brick working its way loose in a fortress somewhere deep inside. She was suddenly aware of the faintest of notions that perhaps the embrace and kiss of a man was not a monstrous thing after all.

But she was also aware how powerful it was, to the point that it took her breath away. There was something incredibly right about it, and yet not right. It was like she was falling and had but one second to grab hold of something before it was too late. Megan broke away and took a step backward. Charlie's arms were still around her.

"I've wanted to do that for a long time," he said.

"No, you haven't," she whispered, closing her eyes, trying to get her bearings.

"Yes, I have," he said, leaning over and kissing her forehead.

Megan stepped away from him and sank to her knees in the sand. Charlie sat down beside her.

"Megan," he said. "You don't mind that I kissed you, do you?"

How on earth could she possibly explain what she felt? The feelings Charlie's kiss had awakened in her were startling, not awful, but she knew the moment she felt them that they were dangerous. Especially when it came to Charlie. She didn't want to have those kinds of feelings for Charlie. She *couldn't.*

"Megan?" Charlie tipped her chin toward him. Megan closed her eyes. She didn't want Charlie to see that they were brimming.

"Was it that bad?" he said with a laugh.

"It was wonderful," Megan whispered, opening her eyes. Charlie relaxed into an easy smile.

"See? I told you," he said. "It's different when it's someone you care about. And who cares about you."

"But I can't fall in love with you, Chaz," Megan said looking down at the sand.

"Fall in love with me? Megan, it was just a kiss," Charlie said, trying to make eye contact. "I mean, I wouldn't mind if it led to other things, but Megan, I'm not asking you to fall in love with me. Not yet anyway."

"But it wasn't just a kiss, Chaz. Not to me. It's hard to explain."

She hesitated. Charlie sat with his arms around his knees and waited.

"I'm afraid of what would happen to me if you kissed me again. You can't kiss me again."

He smiled, but it was a puzzled grin.

"What would be so bad about falling in love with me?" he said.

"You and I…we can't…we're too different. When it was over, we wouldn't be friends anymore."

"Who says?" Charlie said, stroking her back.

"Charlie," Megan said, not fully realizing she had called him that. "How many of your old girl friends are you still friends with? Are you going to look up Brynne while you're in town?"

"Brynne?" Charlie said, raising an eyebrow. "What has she got to do with…?"

"I would be just like all those other girls. In the end, we would find that we aren't compatible, and then I'd lose you forever. And I can't do that. You are all I have left of..."

"Of Jen," he said, and Megan nodded.

Charlie looked away and absently ran his fingers through the sand. Then he turned back to her.

"And why are we not compatible, Megan? We've been friends since we were kids."

She hesitated. What was it *really* that caused her to know that something huge and impassable lay between them, despite their close friendship? How did she know that the invisible barrier was as wide and deep as the canyon they had escaped into when they were young and searching for answers?

The thought of the canyon filled her with a sudden sense of insight that left her feeling sad as well as intuitive. She immediately saw herself as a scared eight-year-old, scrambling, breathless, up the side of the canyon with the name of Jesus on her lips, and she knew without a doubt why she and Charlie couldn't be more than just good friends. As a child, Charlie had viewed the world the canyon symbolized as one where life can turn on a dime and you simply can trust nothing. She had seen the same view of the canyon and had come to a wholly different conclusion. She had not thought about this in a long time, this difference between Charlie and her, not since the canyon disappeared and with it the tangible evidence that the difference existed: Charlie had seen their multiple escapes from the canyon's many curses as proof there is no God, while she had seen them as proof there is.

"You don't believe in God, Chaz." Megan said.

"I don't need a God."

"But I do."

"After all that's happened?" Charlie said.

"Especially after all that's happened."

Charlie squinted, looking out to sea. Megan sensed he was choosing his words carefully.

"If there is a God, Megan…" Charlie began.

Megan looked out on the huge expanse of undulating water in front of them. The sea, too, offered a view of the world with all its beauty and peril.

"I don't understand Him sometimes, either," she said. "But I keep coming back to Him, Chaz. The world's a tough place. I don't want to live in a world like this one without God."

A moment of silence passed between them.

"I don't know how to believe in God, Megan. I really don't," Charlie finally said.

Megan looked up at him and smiled.

"Someone once told me, 'If you look for a way, you'll find it,'" she said.

Charlie didn't say anything at first. Then a shimmer of recollection fell across his face. Megan could see that he remembered saying those same words to her on that long-ago night when Ryan had kissed her, the same night Charlie had begged her to let Jen go.

He turned to her with a half smile on his face.

"Aren't you the clever one," he said softly.

"I think it might be a little too late for me," he added quietly as he looked out across the ocean.

Megan took Charlie's hand and laced her fingers through it.

"It's never too late," she said.

They sat that way for a long while, each lost in separate but similar thoughts of letting go and hanging on and how sometimes they seem like the same thing.

"Will you come to the wedding with me?" Charlie finally said.

"I don't know if that's a good idea," Megan said. "Your dad is starting over. I'm afraid I'm too much a reminder of his old life."

"So am I," Charlie said quickly.

"But you're his son," Megan said.

"Please come," he asked again.

Megan hesitated.

"I'll come," she said.

18

*M*egan found it hard to concentrate on anything after Charlie dropped her off at home that afternoon. Her mother was eager to hear how Charlie was doing and how they enjoyed their visit together. But Megan didn't know how to describe their visit.

Eye-opening perhaps?

"He's asked me to come to the wedding tomorrow," Megan said, bypassing the question of their visit altogether as she poured a glass of water at the kitchen counter.

"Really?" Trina said, looking up from the grocery list she was making. "Are you going?"

Megan could tell her mother had the same concern she had, that Megan would be an unwelcome reminder of happier times. And sadder times.

"I told him I wasn't sure if I should," Megan replied. "But he pleaded. I think maybe he wants some moral support."

"I see," Trina said. And Megan thought she probably did see, but that she still wasn't convinced Megan should go.

"I'll try to keep a low profile, Mom. I'm only going because he needs me to."

Trina nodded. "How are things going for him at USC?" she asked after a pause.

"Okay, I guess. He's going to be on the starting lineup this fall."

"That's great!" Trina said, returning her eyes to her list. "Is he still dating that girl from Oregon?"

"No, he's not," Megan said as she quickly put her glass in the sink, feeling confused and bewildered. She could still feel Charlie's kiss on her lips. And the way he looked at her. She could feel herself blushing and she didn't want to. Didn't want to feel it and didn't want it to happen.

"I need to run over to Adele's," Megan suddenly said, grabbing her car keys.

"But I thought you asked for the day off," Trina said.

"I did…" Megan answered absently. "But I forgot to take care of something on Thursday."

"Well, can you take Michelle by Abbie's house? She wants a ride over there, and I told her I'd take her on my way to get groceries, but since you're going that way—"

"Sure," Megan said, anxious to be finished with this conversation.

"Megan can take you to Abbie's," Trina called down the hall to Michelle.

"I'm coming!" came a faint reply from behind a closed bedroom door.

"I'll be in the garage," Megan said, placing her hand on the doorknob and stepping into the semidark garage.

She pressed the button to open the garage door, and then got into the used, bronze-colored Toyota her parents had helped her buy the year before. Michelle came flying out the kitchen door and slid in on the passenger side, smelling heavily of perfume, her hair perfectly styled, and her makeup expertly applied. She wore a pair of tiny, ironed, stonewashed denim shorts, tan sandals, and a pale pink blouse. Her fingernails and toenails were painted a glittering opal color.

"I thought you were going to Abbie's," Megan said, putting the car in gear.

"I am," Michelle said, pulling out a pair of sunglasses from a small black leather purse on her shoulder. "And then her mom is taking us to the mall."

"All that for the mall?" Megan said motioning to her sister's attire.

"Somebody might *be* there!" Michelle said, laughing at Megan's apparent naiveté.

"Right," Megan said, shaking her head.

"So Chaz took you out for breakfast?!" Michelle said, popping a stick of gum into her mouth.

"Yeah," Megan replied.

"He is such a babe," Michelle said, letting the gum wrapper fall to the floor of the car.

"Do you mind?" Megan said, nodding to the wrapper.

"Sorry…" Michelle said, grabbing the wrapper, balling it up, and sticking it in the trash receptacle. "Too bad he's not a Christian. He's so cute!"

Megan said nothing.

"Do you think these earrings are too much?" Michelle continued, turning to Megan. She had inserted large, dangling earrings into her pierced ears.

"What if I did?" Megan said.

"I guess I'd wear them anyway," Michelle said, grinning.

Megan pulled up in front of Michelle's friend's house.

"Bye," Megan said, eager to be alone.

"See ya!" Michelle said cheerfully as she quickly got out of Megan's car.

Megan watched her sister nearly skip up the front steps to Abbie's house. The front door opened, and Michelle was welcomed by a fifteen-year-old mirror image except for the hair color and shade of pink on her blouse.

Megan pulled away from the curb and headed to Adele's. It had been a hastily contrived excuse to get out of the house. But now she thought it was exactly where she wanted to go.

~ ~ ~

Megan found Adele in her garage, applying a coat of stain to an old desk Megan and David had finished sanding down two days before.

"I thought we were all going to take the day off," Megan said, surprising Adele when she stepped into the garage.

"Oh, Megan! I didn't hear you drive up!" Adele said. She stuck the brush into the can of stain. "I'm almost finished here. It was just too nice a day not to do anything. And I get a little bored when you guys aren't around."

Megan came over to her and sat on a nearby stool.

"Did you and David have a nice time last night?" Adele said, pulling the brush out of the can and letting the excess drip off.

"Yeah, it was okay," Megan said, leaning down and pulling off a corner of newspaper that threatened to attach itself to a freshly stained leg of the desk. "The dancing part was ridiculous, though. Neither one of us can dance. We tried waltzing on one number—unsuccessfully."

Adele laughed. "Chet and I loved to dance," she said. "He was wonderful on a waltz."

"Yeah, well, I'm not sure my generation knows how to appreciate the waltz," Megan said.

"But you had fun anyway?" Adele said looking up.

"It was fun. And it made my mother happy."

Adele was grinning, but she had turned back to the desk.

"Your mom likes David a lot, doesn't she," she said.

"Dad too. He's so polite and *safe*. Just what she likes. He's not like Chaz."

"Chaz isn't safe?" Adele said, never taking her eyes off the desk.

"No, Adele. He's not."

"But you've known this for a long time, haven't you?"

Megan studied the intricate carving in the desk's edge and nodded.

"He kissed me today, Adele."

Adele stopped applying the stain and looked up.

"Chaz *kissed* you?"

Megan nodded.

"He's here in San Diego, then?"

"For a couple days. His dad is getting remarried."

"So, did you want him to? Kiss you?"

"No. Not at first. But it wasn't like I thought it was going to be…It took my breath away, Adele."

Adele smiled but said nothing.

"For a long time," Megan continued, "I was afraid of feeling any kind of attraction to a man because…of what I used to imagine had happened to Jen."

The smile on Adele's face faded, but she still said nothing.

"I was afraid…Jen had been…" Megan began but couldn't finish.

Adele laid down the paintbrush.

"You shouldn't imagine things that you haven't a shred of proof happened," Adele said softly. "Megan, physical love between a man and a woman is a wondrous thing, something

God created. It's not right that you should be robbed of this someday because of something evil someone may or may not have done to Jen."

"I know," Megan said softly. "It's going to take awhile. But I think I'm beginning to understand."

"That's good," Adele said, patting Megan's knee and picking up her brush again.

Adele focused on applying even strokes, then said, "So, why did he kiss you?"

"I don't know," Megan said, standing up and pacing a few steps. "I think he thought he was doing me a favor. He's also in between girlfriends."

"No, I don't think that's it," Adele said, dipping her brush in the can of stain. "I think Chaz has always cared for you in a way you're just now beginning to realize."

Megan stopped pacing and looked down at Adele.

"That can't be true, Adele. He's never been interested in me. He's had tons of different girlfriends. He's never acted like he liked me that way."

"You mean until now?"

"Yes."

"Maybe until now, he figured the one thing that separated you from each other was too big to breach."

"What 'one thing'?" Megan said. "That I reminded him of Jen?"

"No, I don't think you ever reminded him of Jen, Megan," Adele said matter-of-factly. "From what you've told me about Jen, you two were vastly different."

"Well, what, then?" Megan asked.

"Your faith, Megan. You've always depended on your faith to guide and sustain you, even those times when you haven't been aware of it," Adele said. "This is the heritage your parents have given you. It's what is second nature to you. I think Chaz knows this. It's what has always been the difference between you two."

"So…what has changed?" Megan asked.

"I think Chaz must surely see you as an adult now, for the first time. You're not a little-sister figure anymore. Maybe he was testing your faith, seeing if it was still there."

"He told me he doesn't know how to believe in God," Megan said.

"That's not so surprising, Megan. It takes faith to believe in God. And that's precisely what he doesn't have."

"And doesn't want."

"And he's been through so much," Adele sighed, shaking her head. "And without God to lean on."

"So, you think there's no hope for him?"

Adele snapped her head up.

"If there's no hope for him, there's no hope for any of us," she said. "Of *course* there's hope for him. But he must come to faith the way we all do, when he comes to the end of himself."

Megan nodded.

"*Did* he test your faith, Megan?" Adele asked, putting the brush down.

Megan thought back to the kiss. Relived it. She found she had already begun to memorize how it felt. How it seemed to pull at her.

"Maybe," she replied.

"And what came of it?"

Megan squirmed on the stool. She honestly wasn't sure what the test, if there had been one, had shown her. She knew somehow that to choose to love Charlie as more than a friend would certainly mean turning her back on God. She thought she had explained that to him well enough. She was fairly certain she had given him all the right answers. But was Charlie convinced the faith she had learned from her parents was now her own? Was she convinced of it? Did she really believe that God was her only sure foundation? That He was the only certain thing in an uncertain world?

At that moment Megan suddenly remembered sitting in her bedroom, playing dolls with Jen, and Jen's telling her that God should have used His magic wand to keep Jesus off the cross. She remembered how odd and uncomfortable it felt to have Jen say something like that. So foreign, so bizarre. Then she recalled vividly the time when her dad read the story about Eustace, the boy who had been turned into a dragon, who painfully peeled away his dragon scales but found he was still a dragon anyway. It wasn't a magic wand that made him a little boy again...

"Megan?"

Adele was looking at her, concern shadowing her face.

"I'm not sure, Adele," Megan said.

"What are you not sure of, precious?"

"I believe it. I believe all of it, everything my parents told me, everything I've read in the Bible, but..."

"But what?"

"But I'm not sure why I do," Megan said slowly.

"Then it's time for you to find out."

Adele said it so quickly that Megan knew Adele had known this about her for a long time.

"What should I do, Adele?"

"You should find out why you believe."

Megan was silent for a moment, then said, "I've been thinking about going away for college"

"Yes," Adele said, like she was expecting Megan to say it.

"*Far* away," Megan said, looking up at her older friend.

"Because you want to go on a quest. You want to find out why you believe what you believe. You want to find out what you were meant to do with your life," Adele said.

"Yes. I think so."

"You think there are too many painful memories here, too many ropes that bind you to your past. Too many obstacles to keep you from moving forward," Adele continued.

"Yes!" Megan said.

Adele stood up.

"You think if you leave this place and go far away, you'll be able to move past all that."

"Yes, Adele. I want to know who I am, who I'm supposed to be!"

Adele smiled, walked over to her, and took her hands.

"Megan," she said, kindly but firmly. "You already *are* who you're supposed to be. You just need to discover what you're supposed to do with the life God has given you. You don't need to go far away to figure that out."

Megan started to say something, but Adele went on.

"I'm not saying you should stay here, but you don't need to put thousands of miles between you and home. For one thing, the world can be a lonely place when you're on your own. For another, there are many people here who love you. You don't want to detach yourself from your roots, your family."

"No..." Megan agreed.

"Now I want you to think about something. Just think about it. My niece Cheryl...you remember her, don't you?"

Megan nodded.

"She and her husband, Adam, live in Phoenix. They're both doctors. They have a beautiful home and two terrific kids. They need a live-in babysitter, Megan. They had one the past couple of years, but that girl graduated from college last week and is moving away. You could move there after graduation and take care of the children during the summer. When school starts, you could start classes at the Christian university there. It's a nice college, Megan. And since you don't know what you want to do yet, you could try many things. When you're not in class, and Cheryl and Adam are at the hospital, you would watch over their home and their children. They have a beautiful little bedroom and bathroom set aside for this person. They will treat you like family. And it's only a day's drive away from San Diego."

Megan said nothing.

"Megan, Cheryl and Adam go to a wonderful church, they are very dedicated to their faith, and I know they would be the mentors you need right now. I've already told them about you."

Megan took a breath and studied Adele's face.

"How long have you been thinking about this?" Megan finally asked.

Adele couldn't keep a grin from spreading across her face. "Awhile."

"When were you going to tell me?" Megan said nervously.

Adele's grin widened into a smile.

"I've been waiting for the right opportunity, Megan. You showed up out of the blue today. And we're alone. It seemed to me like the right time," she said.

When Megan remained silent, Adele said, "They're wonderful people, Megan."

"It sounds like you're trying to get rid of me," Megan said, smiling uneasily.

Adele reached for her and hugged her.

"I'm trying to keep you close," she said. "I'm afraid you'll head off to New York or Europe and I'll never see you."

Adele pulled away and looked at Megan.

"And I'm afraid you might shake the dust off your sandals when you leave this place. And I don't want to see you do that to your family," she continued.

Megan nodded and wiped away a stray tear. "Can I let you know?" Megan said.

"Of course," Adele replied.

Megan smiled and returned Adele's hug.

"I think I'm going to go home now," Megan said as Adele held her close. "You'll come to my graduation party next Sunday afternoon?"

Adele stroked Megan's hair.

"Of course I will, precious. Of course I will."

19

*C*harlie came for Megan at three the next afternoon, although Nate and Caroline weren't getting married until five o'clock that evening. The ceremony was to take place on the beach at Del Mar, just a stone's throw from Caroline's beachfront home—a house Charlie described to Megan as a sprawling architectural monster of whitewashed timber and panes of glass.

"Did you tell your dad I'm coming?" Megan asked, as she slid into Charlie's BMW.

"Yep," Charlie said.

"And?" Megan, said, smoothing out the pale yellow dress she had kept on from church earlier in the day.

"And he's looking forward to seeing you."

"I'm sure that's what he said, Chaz. But did he mean it?"

"He's looking forward to seeing you," he said again as the engine roared to life.

Charlie looked exceptionally handsome in his black tuxedo. Megan had never seen him dressed in anything other than casual clothes or a football uniform. She decided it was best to pretend the kiss the day before had never occurred.

"You look nice," Megan said.

Charlie looked down at his suit, and then looked up at her and winked.

"Caroline doesn't know these can be rented. She *bought* this thing."

"You mean to *keep?*" Megan said.

"It's all mine," Charlie said.

"Maybe I should have worn something different…nicer," she said, more to herself than to Charlie.

"Why?" he said, looking over at her.

"Because I don't think I'm wearing something nice enough for this wedding. I forgot Caroline is …"

"Rich?" Charlie finished for her. "It's okay, Meg. She wears holey jeans sometimes. Besides, you got nothing to worry about. You look beautiful."

It wasn't exactly what she wanted to hear. Not from him. Not now. She decided to change the subject.

"Chaz, how did you decide on your major? I mean, how did you know a business degree is what you want?" Megan asked.

"I don't know, Meg. It just seemed to make the most sense," he said. "I'll probably join my dad's business when I finish. He's already got a department waiting for me; that is, if the NFL doesn't pick me up. His business is making tons of money, Meg. I could do worse."

"But…is it what you want to do?" she said.

"Do I want to make tons of money?" He turned to her. "Yes, I do, Megan. I do want to make tons of money."

"But do you really want to be in business? Is that what you feel you're good at?"

"Good at? That's what life is, Meg. It's all about business. It's about making things other people want and selling them so you can have what *you* want."

Megan thought how Charlie seemed to have become very much like his father.

"I don't know if that makes for a very satisfying life," she said.

"Of course it does," he said. "No matter what your career, you market something, Megan. Somebody buys what you provide, and that allows you to live the way you choose to live. Even the pastor of your church gets paid to deliver a sermon every Sunday."

"But it's what he *likes* to do," Megan said. "It's what he's good at. Don't you think it makes sense to find something you're good at and that you enjoy?"

"What are you getting at, Megan?" Charlie said, merging onto Interstate 5.

"I don't know what I should do with my life," she said.

"*Should* do? You should do whatever makes you happy—and rich," Charlie said.

"I'm not sure what makes me happy."

"Maybe you're thinking about it too much," Charlie said.

"David has known since he was ten that he wants to be a lawyer. He's been reading books about it since he was twelve. He's already taken a bunch of college courses, and he's only my age," she said. "He knows exactly what he wants to do."

"Well, next time I see him I'll have to congratulate him," Charlie said, with perhaps a twinge of jealousy in his voice.

"I just want to do something meaningful with my life," Megan said, looking out the window.

"Lawyers make tons of money, too, you know," Charlie added, like he hadn't heard the last thing she said.

Megan looked over at Charlie. His eyes were on the road ahead of him. Firm. Resolute.

"David's not too impressed with making *tons* of money," she said. "And he probably won't. He wants to be a prosecutor."

"Ah. So, he wants to make sure all the bad guys go to jail. Make the world a safer place and all that," Charlie said, grinning.

"I guess," Megan said.

"Too bad. He seems like a pretty smart guy," Charlie said, zipping past a van filled with kids. "Do you know how much my dad's corporate lawyers make?"

"Tons of money, no doubt," she said, wearily.

"*You're* the smart one," he said with a laugh.

～～～

None of the other guests had arrived when Charlie and Megan walked into Caroline's spacious house. Caterers were busy setting out the food, and several young women in flowing gowns were arranging flowers in nearly every corner of the main floor. Through a solid wall of glass, Megan saw a trio of violinists setting up their instruments on an outside deck. Beyond them was the sapphire blue expanse of the Pacific Ocean. Open windows carried the sound of the surf into the busy front room whose ceiling Megan judged to be thirty feet high.

Megan's heels clicked on the wide ceramic tiles that seemed to cover every inch of floor except for a spot in front of an enormous stone fireplace that was covered by a sheepskin rug. Every step seemed to announce she was there, making her want to take off her shoes and walk barefoot and unseen.

But before she could become invisible, Nate looked up from papers he had spread out on a wide, granite countertop that led to a huge, open kitchen.

"Megan," he said, calmly. Politely.

She hadn't spoken to Nate since a football game at the beginning of Charlie's high school senior year. Nate and Elise, still married then, had sat together on the bleachers a few yards away from her own parents.

Today Nate was wearing an expensive black tuxedo like Charlie's. He had a little more gray at the temples than she remembered, but his tanned face and obviously toned body gave evidence that Nate still loved the outdoors and physical exercise.

"How nice to see you," he said, moving toward Megan and extending his hand.

"It's great to see you, too," she said softly, taking his hand.

"You must meet Caroline," he said, stepping away and calling Caroline's name out an open window.

The bride-to-be appeared from behind the musicians on the deck where she had been helping them arrange their seating. She looked through the glass and smiled. Megan could see that Caroline—slim, tall, and brunette—was very beautiful.

Caroline was wearing a flowing, ivory, strapless dress that seemed to have a breeze of its own as she swept into the room from outside and came to where Megan and Charlie stood. She had a circlet of tiny white flowers in her upswept hair.

"You must be Megan," she said, also extending her hand. "I'm Caroline Pierre. At least I'm Caroline Pierre until five o'clock."

She offered a wide and cordial smile.

"It's a pleasure to meet you," Megan said. Caroline's perfume wafted delicately through the air around them.

"Make yourself at home, please. Chaz, why don't you show Megan around," she said as she turned to her fiancé. "Nate, darling, the musicians need an extension cord."

Caroline took Nate's arm, and the two of them left with Caroline's gauzy dress billowing out as she led Nate back outside.

"See?" Charlie whispered, like Megan had nothing to worry about. "C'mon. I'll show you the place."

Charlie showed Megan the downstairs rooms, including Nate's spacious study, which Megan noted was beautifully designed and offered not a scrap of evidence that any work was ever done in it. Several photographs in silver frames were arranged on a long, dark table. Charlie was in one of them. Nate and Elise were in several. There wasn't one of Jen.

The upstairs bedrooms all had ocean views, including Charlie's room.

"It's where I sleep when I'm home," he said, showing her inside and shrugging, like it really wasn't his room anymore. "I won't be here this summer, though. My roommate and I have a great apartment near the campus. We don't want to lose it."

Charlie's room was sparsely furnished and had the look of a room that's not used very often. His football trophies and medals were arranged on a large shelving unit that also held a row of books. Megan looked a little closer. The Bible she had given him for his high school graduation was sandwiched among them. She wondered if it had ever been opened. At least he had kept it.

Charlie had a few photographs in his room, too. Several large matted photos of him playing football hung on the walls. Smaller photographs of him and his mother, him and his father, and him with friends stood on a small table by the large plate-glass window. No photo of Jen.

"The view's not bad," he said as he led her out onto his room's balcony. The musicians had finished tuning their instruments and were playing a few measures of Debussy.

"It's very beautiful," Megan said. And it was. The house, though, made her sad in spite of its grandeur.

Neither said anything as they looked out over the Del Mar coastline and the music floated up to them.

"Caroline seems very nice," Megan finally said.

"Yes," Charlie said.

"Do you see much of your mother?"

"Oh, yeah," Charlie said quickly. "She and Leo have me down for dinner now and again. It's not much of a drive to their place. Under an hour when traffic is good."

"So did they get married?"

"No. I don't think my mother will ever get married again," Charlie said.

"Does she ever talk about…Jen?"

Charlie was quiet for a moment.

"Sometimes," he finally said. "Dad wanted to declare Jen dead ages ago, but Mom would never let him. She still won't," Charlie added.

"Do *you* think she's dead, Charlie?"

Charlie reached over to Megan and took her hand.

"Yeah, I do, Meg."

This didn't surprise Megan, but hearing it was harder than knowing it.

"Is that why there are no pictures of her here?"

Charlie stroked the back of Megan's hand and looked out over the ocean.

"This is Caroline's house. She never even knew Jen."

"But she doesn't seem like the kind of person who would mind…"

"Megan," Charlie interrupted her. "I haven't forgotten Jen, but I don't think about her much anymore. She's gone. I don't have a sister anymore. Ten years ago I did, but now I don't. I miss her and I always will, but she's dead. And I can't live my life wishing she wasn't. You can't either."

"Everything seems different now," she said, and Megan could tell Charlie wasn't sure what to make of her words.

"I don't know this house," Megan continued. "Your room is unknown to me. Your dad loves a woman named Caroline. You have dinner in Mission Viejo with your mom and a man named Leo I've never met. You have an apartment in Los Angeles and roommate I've never seen. You even have a new car. And there are no pictures of Jen in this house. It's all so different."

Charlie let go of her hand and turned her toward him.

"Megan, we've grown up. It's what happens. It's supposed to be this way," he said.

"Is it?" she said.

He put an arm around her.

She wanted to relax in his one-armed embrace, but she was afraid to. She wanted to rest her head on his chest and her heart in his companionship, but she knew she could not. He was right. They weren't children anymore. Everything was different. Everything had changed. All physical traces of Jen, the one grand passion she and Charlie shared, had disappeared from Megan's life, and Charlie was telling her that was normal.

All physical traces...except one.

Even as she remembered this, she knew it was probably the one thing that was keeping her locked into her childhood and that there was something she had to do if she wanted to grow up and say goodbye forever to Jen.

She knew doing it would be hard.

On Monday, the day after Nate Lovett's wedding, Megan found herself completely preoccupied with the task that lay before her. There were no more class assignments to worry about, for which she was thankful, and nearly all of Monday afternoon was spent mindlessly practicing step-pause-step-pause on the football field to an unremarkable recording of *Pomp & Circumstance*. She and the rest of her class would be graduating from high school Friday evening, just four days away.

But while the rest of her classmates droned on about how free they were going to be in four days, Megan's thoughts were far away from diplomas and tassels. She was yearning for freedom, too, but of a different kind. She thought perhaps she could wait to do what she wanted to do until after graduation, but by the end of the school day Monday, she knew it couldn't wait.

Megan walked slowly to her car in the school parking lot wondering where she should do it. When she had the place in mind and began to drive away, she decided it would be a good thing to have someone along with her, someone to remind her of this day if the time ever came when she needed to be reminded. Charlie was a likely choice. The best choice, really. But he had left for Los Angeles early that morning. Her mother would go with her if she asked, but Megan knew her mother wasn't really the right person. And Megan was a bit sorry about that.

Adele would understand. But Adele worked alone on Monday afternoons. Michelle was out of the question.

Then there was David. And the more she thought about it, the more she realized David was the only one she could ask. Next to Charlie, he was her closest friend. And despite his penchant for being a know-it-all, she knew he wouldn't tease her...or tell anyone what she had done.

She drove home first, went into her room, and grabbed a small envelope that was buried deep in her sock drawer. She left a hasty note for her parents saying that she would probably be home in time for supper.

Fifteen minutes later, she pulled up in front of David's large house on a rural North County lot. The Christopouloses' four dogs greeted her as she stepped out of her car. One of them, a Labrador mix, jumped on her, nearly sending her to ground. A voice called out.

"Nikki! Down, girl!"

Megan turned to see David's mother, Beth Christopoulos emerging from the garage. Megan didn't spend a lot of time at the Christopoulos home, but she liked and admired Beth. Beth was petite and fair-skinned, nothing like John Christopoulos, David's tall, Greek father. But she was strong and opinionated. Watching her talk and interact with people made it easy to see from where David got his self-confidence.

"Nikki, get over here!" Beth said again. "Megan! Sorry about that!"

"It's okay, Beth," Megan said, patting Nikki and the other dogs.

"Is David home?" Megan asked, as she reached down to pat a Border collie mix.

"Yes, but you two aren't working today, are you?"

"No, I just have a favor to ask of him," Megan said.

"Sure, come on in," Beth said, motioning Megan to follow her.

"School all done for the day?" Megan asked, walking into the Christopoulos kitchen. "I hope I haven't come at a bad time."

"No, you're fine. We're usually finished by two," Beth said.

Two of David's little sisters were sitting at the kitchen table having a snack. They put their heads together when Megan walked in, and then burst into giggles.

"Hi, Natasha. Hi, Sophie," Megan said to the two girls.

The girls looked at each other and giggled.

"Tasha, go tell David he has company," Beth said, ignoring the giggles. "Sophie, say hello to Megan."

"Hello!" the six-year-old said, but then covered her laughing face.

Beth gave Megan a look that let her know she had no idea why her girls were acting that way, and then offered her a cookie.

"Thanks," Megan said, taking one.

"Hey," David said a few moments later as he walked into the kitchen. "What's up?"

"Hi," Megan said, suddenly unsure if she had made the right choice. "You busy?"

"Nope. Just writing my congressman," he said, and Megan couldn't tell if he was joking or not. His eyes were twinkling...but they always did that.

Natasha whispered something to Sophie, and they both burst out laughing. David threw them a look as they covered their mouths. Their eyes, however, were dancing with delight.

"What has gotten into you two?" Beth said to her girls as she walked over to the kitchen sink.

"David, can I borrow you for a little while?" Megan said, looking at David.

David looked at her quizzically.

"Yeah, sure," he said, and he took several steps toward her.

"We won't be gone long," Megan said to Beth.

"Bye!" Beth replied.

The girls behind them offered another chorus of giggles as Megan and David left the kitchen and stepped into the garage.

When the door had closed, David motioned with his hand toward the giggling.

"They think we're engaged," he said plainly.

"What?!" Megan gasped.

"They think we're engaged," he said again.

"Why?!"

David shrugged.

"My mom got her pictures back from Friday night. You know, the prom? Me in a tux? You in an evening gown? And actually wearing jewelry?"

"You told them we're engaged?" Megan said, stopping in the garage and looking at him as if he were crazy.

"Of course not!" David said. "They came up with that on their own."

"Well, did you tell them we're *not*?!" Megan exclaimed.

"I certainly did. But they're little girls. They'll believe what they want to believe."

Megan shook her head in disbelief.

"Where are we going?" David asked calmly, abruptly changing the subject.

"I need to do something a little…crazy," she said. "And I want you to come with me."

"Crazy? You mean, like, illegal?" David's eyebrows lifted.

"No, not illegal. It's just…will you just come, please?"

He looked at her, looked into her—she could feel it.

"Is everything all right?" he asked.

"It will be," Megan said.

He studied her for another moment.

"I'd like to drive you to this crazy thing you must do."

Megan smiled.

"I can drive, David."

"I know you can," he said. "But I would like to take you there."

She hesitated.

"All right, but I need to get something from my car."

❧❧❧

Megan chose the same beach she and Charlie had walked only two days earlier. It seemed like the obvious choice. David said nothing as they walked from his pickup to the sandy shore. A few joggers were out, and a couple of surfers in wet suits were getting ready to head out into the late-afternoon waves.

They took off their sandals at the water's edge and left them in the dry sand. David rolled up his pant legs. Megan wordlessly stepped into calf-deep water, and David followed. She reached into her pocket and pulled out a tiny hoop earring.

She held it in her open palm and looked at it. The sunlight made it glisten in her hand. David looked at it, too, but made no comment. Without saying a word, Megan took several big steps forward, pulled the arm back, and hurled the earring into the foamy surf. David watched, wondering what was going on.

After a few moments, Megan stepped back to stand by him. A tear in each of Megan's eyes hovered in her bottom eyelids.

"I need to go home and write a letter to Chaz," she finally said. "And tell him what I've done."

David looked out toward the water.

"You're going to tell Chaz you threw an earring into the sea," he said plainly, with no hint of sarcasm, but there was a layer of bewilderment to his voice.

"Not just any earring," she said with a slight smile.

"Yours?" David asked.

"No. I don't know whose it was," she said.

David paused before speaking again.

"But it meant something to you, didn't it?" he said.

Megan looked to the sea, across its vastness, to where the sky met it, and there was no telling what lay beyond.

"Chaz found it in the canyon by our houses, when it was still a canyon. He found it a few weeks after Jen disappeared. We used to pretend it was hers."

"But it wasn't," David said quietly.

"No."

"And you've kept it all this time," David said.

"Chaz had it until just a couple of years ago. I think he had forgotten all about it. He found it when he was packing up his room at his old house, just before he and his dad moved to Del Mar."

"And he gave it to you?" David asked.

"He thought I'd be able to really let Jen go if I had something tangible to let go of," she said, looking at the water where she had finally done it.

"But you kept it," David said.

"I just couldn't let go of it," she said.

"Because that would mean she would never be coming back. And you still held out hope she would," David said, nodding his head.

Megan looked at him quizzically. How had he seen in a few minutes time what it had taken her a decade to realize?

"It's not that hard to figure out looking at it from my vantage point, Megan," David said, looking back at her.

She took a deep breath and let it out in a sigh.

"There…were other things, too. Things that I couldn't lay to rest until…just recently."

Megan thought of the pleasantness of Charlie's kiss.

"For the longest time I couldn't stop thinking that Jen had been…hurt by the people that took her. That they had…I was afraid to let anyone touch me or hold me or kiss me because I…couldn't stop thinking that maybe someone had…" but Megan couldn't finish.

David took a step closer and put an arm protectively around Megan's shoulders. Megan let him.

"That's why I've kept everyone at arm's length. Everyone. And nobody knew why. Not even me."

David said nothing for a few moments.

"Adele knew," he said, and Megan looked up.

"She did?"

"She didn't know everything you just told me, but she knew there were two victims the day of the kidnapping. One little girl was forever taken from view, but the other little girl, though she remained, was lost just the same. It was hard for people to understand that about the second little girl because they could still see her."

Megan processed this before saying, "Adele told you this?"

"Not in so many words," he said. "She told me once, when I expressed frustration over you, that Jen wasn't the only little girl whose life had been irreversibly changed that day, and to please try and exercise a little mercy."

Megan smiled at the thought of Adele getting after David for complaining about her often prickly exterior. Then the smile faded as she realized David had again hit the nail on the head.

She had been a victim, too.

"Why has it taken me so long to realize this?" she said.

"You had to grow up," David said. "You were a kid, Megan."

"But, David, sometimes I feel like I still *am* a kid," Megan said, clearly bothered. "Something will happen in my life, and I'm right back there. Right back. I feel powerless and weak. Like a kid."

David nodded.

"Megan, pardon me for saying this, but kids don't have a monopoly on powerlessness and weakness. Till the day we die, we're going to come up against stuff that hurts us to the core, and we're not going to be able to do anything about it."

Megan looked at him.

"Is this supposed to make me feel better?"

"No, it's supposed to make you see the truth. You take the steps you can to deal with what you can, and the rest you have to leave to God."

"But I don't feel like I'm taking any steps," Megan said.

"You just took several big ones, Megan. You threw the earring into the sea. You came to terms with being a victim. You now realize love and affection are different from crimes against the body. You've probably been taking steps all along, you just didn't realize it."

"Maybe I have..." she said, contemplating the notion for the first time.

"Of course you have," David said.

What David said made sense, but Megan thought if any steps had been taken, they were no doubt small and uneven. She wasn't where she was supposed to be at this stage in her life. And she knew why. She was walking into a headwind that constantly kept her from really making any progress. As long as she stayed right here where it all happened, she would never really get any-where—geographically or figuratively.

As she stood there, with the strong arm of a good friend around her, Megan realized she had the answer to her dilemma. She couldn't stay in San Diego after graduation. Throwing the earring into the ocean, experiencing Charlie's kiss, absorbing David's intuitive insights—all of it was pointing her in a new direction. She needed to find a life outside the childhood one that still threatened to keep her bound to fear. She needed to find a life beyond the sights of the one she shared with Jen. And she needed to be away from Charlie and the kiss she couldn't stop reliving.

And at the heart of it all, Megan needed to discover what she really believed about God. She had wanted Charlie not to let go of God, but she now recognized that her own hold on Him was as tenuous as that of a child holding on to a balloon. At any moment, it seemed like a strong gust could whisk it all away. And she would be able to do nothing but stand there and watch it float out of sight.

As the waves weaved in and out around her ankles, Megan found herself sure of these two things: She wanted a life free of the past and a God she knew at the center of that life. She couldn't picture obtaining either if she stayed. And the truth was, Megan didn't want to stay.

For the first time in her life, Megan felt like she had a purpose. She gazed at the spot where the earring had disappeared. Then she turned to David.

"I'm ready to go," she said.

21

Trina placed a stamp on the last of Megan's graduation announcements and pushed the stack of sealed envelopes to the center of the breakfast bar. Another task completed on her list. A slight smile spread across her face in spite of the gnawing ache in her heart and soul. This was the first time in her life she had a to-do list whose end she dreaded. When everything on the list was checked off, Megan would be through with high school, through with being a child. Trina could feel that a change was taking place between mother and daughter even though Megan still slept in her room down the hall. It was an alteration in their relationship Trina had certainly known was going to take place.

Trina wasn't quite sure what it was going to be like being the mother of an adult; wasn't sure what to expect or how hard or easy it was going to be. She quickly reminded herself that there had been a day eighteen years ago when she hadn't been sure what it was going to be like being the mother of a helpless infant, either. That long-ago December day when Megan was first placed in her arms seemed now but a mere turn of a page. Yet here they stood side by side at the edge of change. Though it seemed the journey had begun only yesterday, the task of raising her first-born was suddenly complete. And in spite of horrible moments in a childhood that should have been marred only by skinned knees and occasional acne, Megan had grown into a lovely, compassionate young woman. The milestone was bittersweet.

Trina knew part of her heightened unease was caused by Megan's quiet, almost brooding manner the past few days. Trina could tell something heavy weighed on Megan's mind, but she was afraid to ask what it was, and that was wholly unlike her. Gordy had often said she was overzealous in her attempts to draw out Megan's inner feelings, but not this time. Trina had the feeling Megan was contemplating a change in her plans. And that likely meant a change for her as well. It was easier to postpone knowing than to deal with the knowledge.

It had been Trina's idea that Megan attend San Diego State University—her and Gordy's alma mater. Megan had been unimpressed with her campus visit to SDSU, but then she had been unimpressed with her visit to Azusa Pacific University, too, which was Gordy's two-and-a-half-hour-away pick. Trina had worried needlessly that Megan would fall in love with Azusa the moment she saw it, that she would happily pack up her things in August and leave, coming home only on those weekends when there wasn't much to do.

Megan in fact didn't seem to have a strong attraction for any college campus she visited. She had been accepted at SDSU months ago, but Trina knew Megan had no keen interest in attending her parents' former college. It was just a place to mention when someone asked her, "So, what are your plans?" Megan never said as much, but Trina knew it was true nonetheless. It unnerved Trina that Megan didn't know what she wanted to do and that she didn't know where she should go to find out. It seemed to Trina that a good parent is one who can raise a child to have aspirations. She must have failed Megan somehow in that respect.

Because of that, Trina thought the best place for Megan to figure out her future was right here. At home. Where there were no other pressures or changes to distract. Gordy had been agreeable, although he was oddly more in favor of Megan's attending a college near to home, but not at home. Megan had been noncommittal for months on the issue.

It had been a mistake to mention that David was staying at home while he attended the University of San Diego. Megan had bristled at the comparison. It hadn't mattered to Megan that David was staying in San Diego and wasn't going off to some other city or state to go to college. Megan had thought it was silly to weigh her situation against his. David *knew* what he wanted to do with his life. She didn't. Trina had not mentioned it again.

For now at least, it was SDSU. That was enough for Trina. After Megan had a chance to try out a few new things, Trina was sure she would stumble across an idea, a career path that hadn't occurred to her before. And in the meantime, she could be at home where life was comfortable and predictable.

~ ~ ~

"She won't understand," Megan said as she pulled on the brocade fabric while David nailed it to the wooden back of a sofa frame.

"She might not at first, and she certainly won't if you just tell her you're leaving without telling her why," David said, firing another nail into the wood with his nail gun.

It was Wednesday afternoon, two days before Megan's gradu-ation and two days after Megan decided to take Adele's niece up on her offer. If all went as planned, next Wednesday would be her last day at Adele's. And her last day in San Diego. She shivered involuntarily.

"What?" David said, eyeing her.

"Nothing," she said, recovering. "I m just not looking forward to the next few days."

"Well, if it's any consolation, I think your dad will be okay with it," David offered, firing the nail gun.

"Yeah," Megan answered.

"And your mom will be, too, after she has had time to think about it," David continued. "I mean, you've had time to think about it, Megan. You weren't sure you wanted to go when Adele first told you, either. And now you are. Besides, you've prayed about it and feel it's what God is directing you to do, right?"

"Yes," Megan said, sighing.

"How can she argue with that? Give her some time, Megan. She'll come around."

Megan nodded and tightened her hold on the fabric as David nailed it down the sides.

"Do *you* think it's a good idea?" she said after a few more nails had been fired. "For me to go to Arizona, I mean."

David didn't look up, but Megan could tell he was thinking. He fired the nail gun.

"Actually Megan, the location is immaterial. It really doesn't matter much that you've chosen Arizona over any other place," he said. "What matters is why you're going and what you hope to find. If you want to discover what God has in mind for you, well, I imagine He could show you just about anywhere."

"So, you think it's a dumb idea," Megan said, trying to follow his reasoning.

"No, that's not what I think," he said, grinning. Then he put the nail gun down and looked at her. "I think if you're headed to a place where you want nothing more than to seek the face of God and His plan for your life, then you shouldn't let anything stop you from going."

"Thanks," Megan said after a lengthy pause. What David said made a lot of sense. It would give her the confidence she needed to tell her parents, and for that she was grateful. Megan realized with a start that she was going to miss David. She hadn't really thought about it until that moment.

"No problem," David replied, picking up the gun and leaning over the couch frame.

"You really think you and Adele can get along here without me?" Megan said after several minutes.

"Well, it will be different, that's for sure," David said. "And I likely won't have to wear my running shoes anymore."

David turned to her and winked.

"Adele lets me open all her doors," he said.

Trina was putting a load of clothes in the dryer in the garage when she heard a car pull up behind her in the driveway. She turned.

Megan was home.

Her daughter got out of the car and walked toward her, and it seemed to Trina there was purpose in her steps. Trina yanked off a dryer sheet and threw it in with the wet clothes. She closed the door, set the dial, and pressed the "start" button. Megan was right behind her.

"Hey there," Trina said, turning from the dryer.

Megan stood before her, tall and composed, even strangely confident.

"Hi, Mom," Megan said. "Are you busy?"

It was a loaded question. Loaded with the weight of all that makes mothers writhe in worry about their kids, Trina thought. Was she busy?

"Not really," Trina said, smiling weakly.

"Can we go for a walk?"

Trina's breath caught in her throat. Megan had asked the simplest of questions, and yet Trina felt her pulse quicken. She and Megan had shopped together, cooked together, cleaned together, and read together, but they had not taken a walk together in years.

"Sure," Trina said, tossing the dryer sheet box on a shelf.

She turned back to her daughter and followed her out the open garage door into the early June sunshine.

"Where do you want to go?" Trina said as she caught up with Megan.

"Just down to the end of the street," Megan said calmly.

The end of the street. Trina had not been alone with Megan at the end of the street in a decade. Not since an eight-year-old Megan had been in the canyon. The memory of it still haunted her.

The silence as they walked made Trina nervous. She asked about Megan's day. She asked how Adele was. She asked if they should have helium balloons for her party on Sunday.

By the time Megan told her balloons would be fine, they were standing at the guardrail, looking down to where a scrubby wall of wild mustard and sagebrush sloped down to the emerald green expanse of the golf course. A fountain in a pool of dark water spurted water into the air above it. Palm trees swayed in a light breeze. Two faraway men in plaid shorts were on the green, making their final attempts at hole number ten.

Trina was afraid to ask Megan why she had brought them there, so she said nothing.

"Mom, do you remember that day you found me here? That day I walked home from Charlie's house through the canyon?" Megan said, breaking the silence.

Trina could hardly believe Megan was asking her. *Remember it?* It was like asking her if she remembered the day Megan was born.

"Yes…I remember," Trina answered softly. "I remember it often."

Megan turned to her, surprise etched on her face.

"Why?" she said.

"Because I handled it so badly," Trina shrugged.

"No—" Megan started to say, but Trina interrupted her.

"Yes, I did, Megan," Trina said. "I totally blew it."

"You had a right to be angry, Mom," Megan said.

"It wasn't just about anger," Trina continued. "I was so scared, Megan. I was scared to death for you. And for me. I was afraid I was losing you somehow, just like Elise had lost Jen, only you were disappearing from me slowly, not all at once. You were having those horrible nightmares, you barely talked to Dad and me about anything you were feeling, you got back on your bike long before the psychologist said you would. And you were lying to me about where you were going after school. So when I saw you here with your arms outstretched over the canyon, like…like you were about to dive into it…"

Trina could not finish.

Both mother and daughter were picturing the long-ago scene when Trina had her hands on Megan's shoulders and was shaking her, screaming at her from the depths of her soul. "You will not do this to me! You will not! You will not!"

The memory was sketchy in Megan's mind, but it lived vividly in Trina's.

"I should have held you in my arms and kept my mouth shut," Trina said bitterly, stray tears slipping down her cheeks. "And I never should have kept you from seeing Charlie all that time."

Megan reached for her mother and put an arm around her.

"None of us knew how to handle what we had been dealt, Mom." Megan said. "We did the best we could. That's all we could do. And I shouldn't have been in the canyon that day. You were right about that. It was too dangerous."

"A mother always wants to protect her child..." Tina said.

"Yes, and I knew you loved me," Megan said. "But I don't think a child can ever really grasp how hard it is for a mother to watch helplessly. I can't imagine what it's like to watch your child suffer and be powerless to do anything about it."

"It was hell," Trina said, with no disrespect in her voice.

"You know, someone told me we must take the steps we can to deal with what we can, but the rest we have to leave to God."

"You sound like David," Trina said, smiling through her tears.

"That's because he said it," Megan said, and there was a moment of easy silence between them.

"You brought me here to tell me something, Megan," Trina said. It was not a question.

"Yes," Megan replied.

"Tell me," Trina said.

When Megan had finished telling her mother about Phoenix and her future home with Adele's niece, Trina could only stand at the rim of the canyon and stare down into it.

"I know it seems like an abrupt change of plans, Mom, but I've been thinking about doing something like this for months,"

Megan said. "You have Adele to thank that I'm not heading for the East Coast."

Trina was having a hard time picturing herself thanking Adele for this.

"Are you sure this is the right thing for you, Megan?" she finally said in response.

"I feel good about it, Mom. I think it's the right path for me."

Trina shifted her weight from one foot to the other.

"It…seems like you're running away from your past," Trina said, as gently as she could.

"I thought that at first, too," Megan said, looking out over the pristine floor of the canyon golf course. "But the more I think about it, the more I feel like I'm not looking to remove myself from my past as much as I'm looking to find myself in the present. I want to find out what I'm good at, what I'm supposed to do with the time I've been given. I don't think I'll find out if I stay here. It is too easy to look backward. And that's not where my future lies. That's why I brought you here, Mom. I need to step out, find my own way, even if from here the path looks a little dangerous."

They held on to the moment in silence.

"Can you leave the painting here?" Trina finally said.

"The painting?" Megan asked.

"The Serengeti," Trina replied. "If you leave it, I'll know you're coming back."

Megan smiled, rubbed her mother's shoulder, and let her arm fall to her side.

"Sure, Mom."

The deepening hues of the early-twilight sun bathed mother and daughter in amber light as they looked out over the canyon's breadth. Trina looked at Megan and saw the decade of change.

She saw a young girl with her arms stretched out over the canyon. And though Megan's arms were now at her sides, Trina imagined them, the long slender arms of her adult child, thrust out, beckoning the world that lay just beyond her fingertips.

PART FIVE

Summer 2004

The hum of the air conditioner and the steady clicking of a wall clock were the only sounds in the room as Megan rocked the hammock that held the child.

Megan wanted to hum a tune or perhaps tell the child a story but she knew either one would only aggravate seven-year-old Ian, not help him rest. Like the four other autistic children in the room, Ian was best calmed after a tense sensory activity by silence—and the punchy feel of the pillow that he gripped to his chest as the hammock swayed back and forth.

She used the silence instead to gather her thoughts. For some reason home had been much on her mind the past few days. Not home in Phoenix with Adam and Cheryl McDowell and their kids, but home in San Diego. Megan hadn't seen her family or Adele in nearly eight months, not since Christmas. Frequent phone calls and e-mails helped bridge the distance, but Megan was aware of an unfamiliar urge to head for home. Perhaps it was because she knew that's exactly where she would be in three weeks. Or perhaps it was because Adele wasn't in good health. Or maybe it was because her mother couldn't disguise the disappointment in her voice the last time Megan called home and told her parents she could only spare a week. Classes would be starting soon. She only had a semester left at Arizona State University West. Megan wanted to begin it with a clear head, and sometimes going home to San Diego only made things cloudy in her mind. Even after all these years, there were still echoes in places where unpleasant memories loitered.

Megan's thoughts were suddenly interrupted. A little boy named Cole, wrapped tightly in a blanket and sitting in a beanbag chair nearby, suddenly let out a high-pitched wail. Another worker in the room hurried over to him. Ian let go of his pillow and clamped his hands over his ears. He began thrashing his head back and forth. Megan retrieved the pillow from the floor. She gently took one of Ian's hands and placed it on the pillow.

"Here's your pillow, Ian," Megan said softly.

"Here's your pillow, Ian," Ian echoed, still thrashing his head back and forth.

"Now let's have your other hand," she continued, lifting Ian's other hand away from his ear and placing it on the pillow, which was now back on his chest.

"Here's your pillow, Ian," Ian said again. He stopped thrashing, eyes focused straight ahead.

"That's right," Megan said calmly, resuming the steady but slow swing of the hammock.

The other worker, Kelly, had managed to calm down Cole, too. She stood and looked over at Megan and smiled.

That had been an easy one.

Sometimes when one of the kids who came to the Pathways Developmental Center had an episode like that, it could send the whole room into chaos. All the children Megan worked with during her internship were living severly challenged lives because of autism. Sudden bursts of sound or light or movement often disrupted the quiet patterns of their ordered world, sending a ripple through the room from which the children could not always easily recover.

But those times didn't bother Megan. She didn't actually enjoy trying to settle a mentally agitated child, but she had empathy for a youngster who seemed lost in a big, perplexing world. She felt, in a small way, she could relate. It was why she had gone back to school after getting her bachelor's degree in sociology last year. She wanted to help children like Ian as a career.

And Cheryl and Adam were only too obliging, as were their children, Felicia and Kyle. After having Megan as part of the family for four years while she attended Grand Canyon University, they were unwilling to let her go.

"I can get an apartment," Megan had said when she announced to Cheryl shortly before she graduated with her bachelor's that she was going to ASU West to become certified in special education.

"An apartment? What for?" Cheryl had said. "You already have a home with us."

"I feel like I've worn out my welcome, Cheryl," Megan had said. "You were only expecting me to stay until I finished college."

"Well, you haven't finished college," Cheryl replied, laughing and leaving the room like the conversation was over.

"Yes, I have!" Megan said, laughing, too, and following her. "I already have a degree."

"But not the one you want," Cheryl said. "Stay with us, Megan. The kids aren't ready for you to go yet. And neither are Adam and I. Besides, with us you can concentrate on your studies and you won't have to go into debt. It makes the most sense and you know it."

Megan smiled at the memory as she rocked Ian. The truth was, she hadn't really wanted to leave Adam and Cheryl and the kids. She loved being a part of their family. And Adam and Cheryl paid her well to look after the kids and their home. She was even starting to love Phoenix, though she missed the ocean—more than she thought she would.

Megan sat back on the stool by Ian's hammock frame and looked out the window. At 108 degrees, the shimmering July heat was washing across the parking lot like a searchlight. Chrome and steel on every car glistened like liquid metal. Her car was going to be like an oven. Megan turned back to Ian, but with an eye on the clock. Their session would be over in a few minutes. The boys' mothers would come for them, and then the room would be empty; silent like it was right now, but empty. Megan dreaded the thought of getting into her car. She wouldn't have time to wait for the air conditioner to cool it down. She had to pick up Felicia and Kyle from swimming lessons in twenty-five minutes.

Five minutes later, Megan coaxed Ian out of the hammock.

"Shall we put your sandals back on?" Megan asked.

"Here's your pillow, Ian," he said, looking at nothing in particular.

"You like the hammock, don't you, Ian?" Megan said. "You can lie in the hammock next time you come. Now it's time to put your sandals back on."

Ian made no attempt to slip his bare feet back into his sandals.

Megan gently tapped his left foot.

"Okay, first this one," she said.

Ian slowly lifted his foot and placed it in the sandal.

"Good job. Now the other one, Ian," Megan said, looking at him.

Ian was looking at the ceiling.

"The other one, Ian," Megan said, resisting the urge to tap his other foot. She wanted him to do it without her help.

"The other foot, Ian," Megan said again.

Never taking his eyes off the ceiling, Ian slipped his other foot into the waiting sandal.

"Excellent," Megan said calmly.

The door to the classroom opened, and several mothers stepped inside.

"Mom's here," Megan said.

Ian's mother came to them. Ian continued to stare at the ceiling.

"Did you have a good day?" Ian's mother said, more to Megan than to her child.

"Ian did great today," Megan replied, wanting to touch Ian on the shoulder or ruffle his hair. She resisted the urge, knowing Ian wouldn't like it.

"Wonderful," Ian's mother said looking at her son, clearly pleased. "I think continuing these sessions with you during the summer is going to make all the difference in the world when school starts up. I can already see a difference at home."

"I'm so glad," Megan said.

"I know he doesn't let you know it, but he really likes you, Megan," the woman said. "Sometimes at home he'll say your name."

"I like him, too," Megan said.

She watched Ian go, and then helped another little boy leave behind the row of blocks he had created and go to his mother. When the last child had left, Megan and Kelly put away the vocabulary cards, the blocks, the exercise balls, and the cups from snack time.

"Have a good weekend," Kelly said, as she grabbed her car keys.

"Oh, yeah. You, too," Megan said, locking their classroom door behind them.

She had almost forgotten it was Friday. She also suddenly realized it wasn't just an ordinary Friday. It was the twenty-third of July. Tonight David would be having his wedding rehearsal somewhere in Seattle. Tomorrow he would be getting married.

Megan walked through the Center hallways, waved at a few familiar faces, and then headed outside to the heat and her car. She opened the car door and stood there, letting the air that had reached 120 degrees inside her car waft outside.

She had to admit she was a little surprised David hadn't sent her an invitation. Granted, she wouldn't have been able to go. His fiancée, Jamie, was from Seattle, and that's where the wedding ceremony was going to take place. And she knew from an e-mail from David ages ago—when he first told her he was getting married—that Jamie wanted a small, intimate ceremony. But still...

Megan got into her car, wincing at the feel of hot upholstery on the back of her legs. She removed the windshield visor from her dashboard and started the engine, throwing the switch on the air conditioner to full, even though only hot air surged past her face and arms at first.

As she drove to the community center and pool, Megan shook off the disappointment regarding David. She had a gift for David and Jamie—a beautiful piece of Navajo pottery that she planned to take with her when she went home in August. Hopefully David and Jamie hadn't changed their plans to stay in San Diego after their honeymoon. Megan wasn't sure. She hadn't heard from David in six months.

Within ten minutes, Megan arrived at the community center parking lot. She parked her car and turned off the engine, wishing there was a way she could leave it running while she went inside to fetch the kids. By the time she got back outside, it would again be blistering hot inside the car.

She found the kids still in the pool, even though the lessons were over, enjoying some free swim time with other children. Loud and happy voices echoed off the tile walls, and the sound of water hitting water was everywhere. Ten-year-old Felicia was in the deep end with three other girls, her reddish brown hair plastered against her scalp. Eight-year-old Kyle was doing handstands in the shallow end with the boy whose mother had brought them there.

"Watch this, Megan!" Felicia yelled to Megan when she saw her.

Felicia climbed out of the pool, climbed the ladder of the shorter of two high dives, and stepped onto the bouncing board.

Felicia raised her arms over her head until her hands met. She jumped on the edge of the board and bowed her body as it left the solid surface, easing into the water in a nicely executed dive.

Megan waited until Felicia's head broke the surface of the water and then applauded.

"Very nice!" Megan yelled.

"Watch me, Megan!" Kyle called out to her.

Megan turned to watch Kyle submerge himself, stand on his hands, and then proceed to walk across the bottom of the pool until his lessened body weight catapulted him off his palms. He came up for air grinning.

"You two are amazing," Megan said. "You want to stay and swim for a while?"

The kids yelled their approval, and Megan turned to find a deck chair to sit on.

As Megan watched Felicia and Kyle swim, she found herself amazed at how much the children had grown and changed in five years. Felicia had been five years old when Megan came to live with Adam and Cheryl the summer after high school graduation. Kyle was three and barely out of diapers back then.

She silently wondered if anyone could tell she had also changed or if she only imagined that she had matured in many ways. Adele had been right about Cheryl and Adam. They had been the perfect people to mentor her, walk her through her faith, and help her get her feet on solid ground as an adult. The many Bible studies they had in their home had probably helped her figure out the level of her commitment to God as much as anything. Many times those evenings would end with Megan in an intense conversation with one of Adam and Cheryl's friends on a deep, spiritual truth. They were the sorts of conversations her dad loved. She often e-mailed him immediately afterward to tell him what they had discussed.

But the best thing Adam and Cheryl had shared with her was how to simply live by faith in a world where you can explain just so much. It was the same life of trust her parents had modeled and taught her, but Megan had been right about the need to see it fleshed out beyond the four walls of her parents' house. She had come to Arizona asking why she believed everything her parents had told her about God. Five years later, she was now convinced there could be no other way *but* God's way. Only God promised a perfect life to follow this imperfect one. Only God could offer this kind of hope for the believer, even the hurting one. *Especially* the hurting one. On those occasions when she did make the eight-hour drive home—sometimes taking Felicia with her if it was during the summer—she could tell her father was glad she had gone to Phoenix. And her mother was just glad the painting of the Serengeti was still in San Diego.

At four o'clock, Megan called the kids out of the pool, and then went outside to start the car and cool down the interior.

During the twenty-minute drive home, Felicia and Kyle told her all about the kid who had thrown up on the slide.

"Let's change the subject," Megan said after Kyle decided she needed to hear the whole story again. "What shall we make for dinner?"

"Macaroni and cheese!" Kyle yelled.

"I was thinking more along the lines of halibut steaks on the grill. Your dad loves those," Megan said. "Should we stop and get some?"

"Yeah!" Felicia said. "And let's have Caesar salad. And lemon poppy seed muffins!"

"Why can't we have the fish with macaroni and cheese?" Kyle interjected.

"Well, I guess we could," Megan answered.

"Mac and cheese!" Kyle yelled.

The trio stopped at a grocery store a few miles from home and picked up the few things needed to make supper. Cooking for the McDowells was something Megan had grown to enjoy almost as much as being nanny to the kids. It had been a treat to have Cheryl's big kitchen to work in and state-of-the-art appliances to use. On weekends, Cheryl liked to claim the kitchen for herself.

"I don't want to forget how to boil water," Cheryl would say from time to time.

But most days Megan chose the menu, shopped, and prepared the evening meal. Felicia often helped her.

After getting the groceries, Megan and the kids got back into the car, and Megan drove the last few miles to home. She pulled into the gated community where Adam and Cheryl lived and made her way to the large, two-story stucco home she shared with them. She pressed the remote to one of three garage doors and was surprised to see Cheryl's Lexus in the next stall over.

"That's odd," Megan said to the kids. "Your mom's home. I thought she had patients all day today."

"Maybe she's sick," Felicia said.

"Yeah, maybe she threw up, too!" Kyle said.

"Gross!" Felicia exclaimed.

"Well, let's go find out," Megan said as they got out of the car and the garage door closed behind them.

Megan and the children walked into the laundry room that led from the garage and then into the tiled entryway of the main floor. The kids headed for the family room, Megan close behind.

"She's here," Kyle yelled back to her.

Megan heard Felicia ask her mother what was wrong. Concern was in her young voice.

Megan rounded the corner to find Cheryl putting a cordless phone back on its cradle.

"I was just going to try and call you," she said, looking up at Megan. Her face was laced with worry. "I wasn't sure where you were."

"We stayed a little longer at the pool, and then stopped at the grocery store. Cheryl, what is it?" Megan asked.

"What's wrong, Mommy?" Felicia asked again.

"It's my Auntie Adele, kids," she said, but she was looking at Megan. "She had another heart attack, and she's in the hospital."

"Is she going to be all right?" Megan said.

"My mom said it's too early to tell how badly her heart was damaged," Cheryl said, in uneven tones. "She and my father are taking the next flight from Albuquerque to be with her. They should get there sometime this evening."

The groceries suddenly felt very heavy in Megan's arms. Cheryl seemed to notice.

"Why don't we save whatever you bought for another time, Megan," she said. "Let's order out, okay?"

"Okay," Megan said numbly.

"Kids, why don't you go hang up your wet things and then go play," Cheryl said to the children. Then she turned to Megan. "I'm going to call Adam. I think we may need to change our plans for next week. Can you get away from work if we need to go to San Diego?"

"Of course," Megan said softly.

"Here, I'll take these," Cheryl said, reaching for the grocery bags. "Your mail is there on the dining table, Megan. Why don't you take it into your room and relax for a few minutes?"

Megan appreciated Cheryl's motherly instincts and murmured her thanks.

She walked over to the dining table, picked up three envelopes and headed for her room just off the main entrance to the house.

Megan closed her door and stood for several minutes in the middle of her room before sinking into an armchair by a multi-paned window. The room was cool, and Megan left the light off to add to the feeling of rest. Outside the window, a lizard ran up a large saguaro cactus that was part of the McDowells' land-scaping, and then ran back down, disappearing into the rocks below the cactus.

"Don't let her die," she whispered to God. "Don't let her die."

Megan closed her eyes, knowing the inevitable couldn't be postponed forever. Adele had not been well, especially after her first heart attack eighteen months ago. She was only seventy-six, but the last time Megan saw her, she could tell Adele's body was slowing down at a brisk pace. Even before she sold her uphol-stery business four years ago, it had been evident. At Christmas, Adele had told Megan that all she really wanted was to go home to Jesus and dance waltzes in heaven with Chet.

"Don't let her suffer," Megan said, changing her plea.

She sat there for a while, losing all track of time, thinking back over the years she had known Adele, wondering how different her life would have been if Adele hadn't been on her porch that long-ago July day.

Her mail fell from her lap as she sat there thinking. Megan roused herself from the past and reached down to retrieve it. She turned over the first envelope as she set the envelopes back on her lap. It was a letter from the University about her class schedule next fall. The next one was an invitation from the leader of the singles group at church. An indoor rock-climbing party was being planned for next Friday night. The last one was a thick envelope from her mother. Megan tore it open.

Inside was a magazine article from an early July issue of *Time* magazine with a sticky note attached to it:

> *Hey, Meg: Just thought you would enjoy reading this article about Nate and Chaz. Guess they really hit the big time. Wish I had time for a longer note, but now that I'm working again, I'm finding out I'm not as organized as I thought. Gotta run. Can't wait to see you next month.*
>
> XOXO Mom

Megan unfolded the article. A large color photo of Nate and Charlie in dark blue business suits met her eyes. Father and son were leaning against a boardroom table made of glass in an office with windows for walls. A huge headline read, "Making It Crystal Clear." A smaller subhead read, "Nate Lovett's data-management software designs are clearly one step ahead of the competition." The article went on to describe Nate's San Diego–based company, Crystal Clear Management Systems, and how effective the company's software designs were at making data management and retrieval "crystal clear." Nothing ever got lost, apparently.

Hundreds of companies had contracted Crystal Clear to build and install data-management software, which had boosted the company's revenue into the millions in just four years. "Chaz Lovett," the article said, "the CEO's son and savvy vice president of marketing, has been a key player in the company's terrific ride up Wall Street."

Megan read the article twice. The story almost seemed to be about people she didn't even know. She hadn't seen Nate since his wedding to Caroline five years earlier. She hadn't seen Charlie in two years. It was just after Nate and Caroline moved into a new home in Rancho Santa Fe two summers ago. Charlie was living in their old house and getting his feet wet in his dad's growing company, since a knee injury in his senior year precluded any aspirations of an NFL career. Megan had the impression Charlie was glad he didn't have to choose. He e-mailed now and then, but Megan couldn't remember the last time they had communicated. Had it been over a year?

She folded the article and tossed it onto her desk, staring at it and thinking the polite thing to do would be to e-mail Charlie and tell him congratulations.

But she didn't feel like it.

She rose from her chair to see if Cheryl wanted her to run down to the nearest Chinese take-out place and pick up dinner.

⁓ ⌣ ⁓

When the phone rang at one in the morning, Megan pried her eyes open from sleep, knowing instantly what the call was about. Calls at one o'clock in the morning never brought good news. There was only one ring. Adam or Cheryl had answered right away. She waited for the knock at her door. Within five minutes it came.

"Megan," Cheryl said softly from outside her closed door.

"I'm awake, Cheryl," Megan said.

The door opened, and Cheryl stood framed in moonlight from the skylight above her head.

Megan waited.

"She's gone, Megan." Cheryl said, coming into Megan's room and leaving the pearly moonlight behind her. "Adele is gone."

23

*M*egan studied the faces of the people who stopped at the podium where she stood overseeing the guest book. The people smiled at her as they signed, but no doubt wondered who she was. It was odd, really. None of Adele's little family knew the people who attended Adele's church or the many customers whose furniture had been made beautiful by her hands. And Adele's church family and customers didn't know Adam or Cheryl or the kids. They didn't know Cheryl's parents; didn't know the petite woman in gray with damp eyes was Cheryl's mother—Adele's younger sister. Didn't know Adele's nephew Gavin and his family.

The little crowd of guests and the smaller group of family were united in grief but remained strangers to one another. Yet they had all loved Adele.

Megan looked for David's parents among the small groups of people, wondering if they would come to Adele's funeral even though John Christopoulos had moved his construction business and his family to Ramona a few years back and the family no longer attended Adele's church. She didn't see them. Megan wasn't sure if Adele had been good friends of all the Christopouloses or if it was just David she had been close to. Megan was certain David wouldn't be among the guests. He was likely still on his honeymoon.

Adele's minister walked up to her as the last of the guests was being seated.

"The family is coming," he said softly. "They want you to walk with them. And sit with them."

"Oh, I couldn't," Megan whispered.

"But they really want you to," he said kindly.

Behind the minister the family suddenly appeared. Felicia was looking for her, Megan could tell. She smiled at her, and Felicia smiled back. Relief was in her tiny grin.

"Just a minute," she mouthed to Felicia and then she slipped into the sanctuary to the last pew where Trina was sitting, waiting for her.

"Mom, they want me to sit with them. The family wants me to sit with them," Megan whispered.

Megan could tell her mother was a bit taken aback. Then she seemed to relax.

"Go ahead, Megan. I know how much Adele loved you," Trina whispered. "It's okay."

Megan stepped back into the foyer where a highly polished casket waited. Yellow and pink roses lay atop it like a giant bridal bouquet. Ready to guide it into the church were Cheryl and Adam, Cheryl's parents, and Cheryl's brother, Gavin, and his wife. Behind the adults were the children: Felicia, Kyle, and Gavin's six-year-old son, William. Megan took her place with the children. Felicia grabbed one of her hands and Kyle the other. Not wanting William to feel left out, Megan whispered to Felicia to take William's hand, hoping the aisle was wide enough for the four of them to walk abreast.

The casket began to move on its rollers as a pianist began to play "Shout to the Lord."

As they began to follow behind the adults, Megan could see they would not fit, but she didn't want to let go of either hand. Nor did she want Felicia to let go of young William.

"Don't let go of William," she whispered to Felicia, "Just gently pull him along behind you."

"Okay," Felicia whispered back.

The guests smiled at each other as the chain of four made their way down the aisle. It eased the sorrow somewhat.

～～～

Later that day, in Adele's living room, the family gathered to talk over Adele's estate. Megan had not wanted to come, but Cheryl told her she was mentioned in the will, and it would be best if she could be present.

"But I don't have a car," Megan said, as if the chore of someone's having to take her back to her parents' house afterward was too much of a bother. Her car was still in Phoenix. Adam had driven them all out to San Diego.

"You can use Adele's car while you're here," Cheryl said.

Megan now sat at the edge of the living room, wanting to be as inconspicuous as possible. But Cheryl drew her in from the beginning.

"Megan, Adele wants you to have the furniture in this room," Cheryl said, referring to a sheaf of papers in her hand. "She also wanted you to be able to live here or stay here if that's what you desire for all or part of the next eight years. She has left the house to Felicia, Kyle, and William, but with stipulations that the house not be sold until the last one turns eighteen. That's in twelve years. She wants you to have the right to live here rent-free until Felicia turns eighteen. At that time, Felicia can choose to live here if she wants, and if you still want to, and it's agreeable to both, you can live with her."

"But, I'm living in Phoenix now," Megan said, barely above a whisper. "And I couldn't possibly take this furniture. Adele and Chet…they worked on all this furniture together. It should go to the family."

Cheryl laid down the papers and walked over to Megan and took her hands.

"First of all, Megan," Cheryl said. "You *were* family to her. And you are family to us. Besides, it's what Adele wanted. And second, you don't *have* to live here. She just wanted you to be able to if that's what you wanted. We can rent this place if you don't want to or until you change your mind."

Megan looked over to Gwen, Adele's sister, who simply nodded and smiled at her. None of this seemed to surprise anyone in the room except Megan. Cheryl squeezed her hands and then let go.

The rest of the afternoon was a bit of a blur. Megan mentally faded in and out of the conversation as Adele's survivors discussed the remainder of her estate.

Finally at four o'clock, Adam left to take Gavin and his family to the airport for their flight home to Denver.

"We'll stay until tomorrow, but then we have to get back to the hospital," Cheryl told Megan as she prepared to head to her parents' house. "If you want some alone time, Megan, think about staying here. In fact, stay in the house as long as you want. Use Adele's car. Do things with your family. Look up some old friends. When you're ready to come back to Phoenix—if you decide you want to come back—we can contact a property-management firm to find a renter. You can drive Adele's car back, and we can sell it in Phoenix. Or if you like it, you can keep it and sell your old one."

Megan was feeling numb.

"I'll have to think about it," she said. "Are you leaving in the morning?"

"My mom has an appointment first thing in the morning to settle some estate matters, and then we're taking them to the airport. We want to be out of here before noon."

"I'll stop by before you leave," Megan said, reaching for Cheryl and giving her a hug.

"Sounds good," Cheryl said, returning the embrace.

Megan said goodbye to the kids, and then went out to Adele's driveway carrying an unfamiliar key ring. Adele's Bonneville sat in the late-afternoon sun. Megan got in and noted with a grimace a nearly empty cup of coffee in the cup holder. A kiss of lipstick was on the rim. Adele's shade.

She started the car, put it in gear, and drove to her parents' house.

Megan left the car at the curb rather than parking in the driveway of her old house so that her parents could still get into the garage. Both her parents were still at work. Trina had only stayed for the memorial service, and then had headed back to the local library where she worked as a children's librarian.

Michelle's car was there, however.

Megan walked into the kitchen to find her sister, home from her sophomore year at Biola University, making a fruit smoothie.

"Megan!" Michelle said. "Someone just called here for you. She's called twice already."

"Who was it?" Megan asked, wondering who knew she was in San Diego.

"Some lady."

"She didn't leave a message?"

"I asked her if she wanted to, and she said she'd call back."

"Is that it?" Megan asked.

"Yep. She also wanted to know when you would be home. I told her I didn't think it would be too much longer. You've been gone the whole day."

"All right," Megan said, thoroughly perplexed. Only a handful of people in Phoenix knew she was here. And any of those people would have left a message. She walked down the hall to the bathroom, opened the medicine cabinet, and took out the bottle of Tylenol. After swallowing two capsules, she went to her old room and stretched out on her bed. Not many minutes later the warm hues of the Serengeti on the wall across from her lulled her to sleep.

Megan didn't know how long she slept. She was just suddenly aware of Michelle standing at her doorway with the phone in her hand. It couldn't have been too long—it was still light out.

"Phone's for you," Michelle said, handing her the handset.

Megan sat up and ran a hand through her hair. She cleared her throat and reached for the phone.

"Hello?" she said.

There was a momentary pause.

"Megan?" said a woman's voice on the other end.

"Yes," Megan answered, becoming more alert.

Another pause followed.

"Hello?" Megan said.

"Megan, I …" but the voice didn't continue.

"Who is this?" Megan asked.

"Are you alone? Is anyone with you?"

Megan's pulse began to quicken. Something wasn't right.

"Who *is* this?" she said for the second time and without the inflection of a question. It was more like a demand.

"Please don't hang up!" the woman said, desperation evident in her voice.

"Tell me who you are," Megan said.

"Please don't tell anyone yet," the woman pleaded. "Promise me."

"Look, I don't even know who I'm talking to," Megan said evenly, trying to disguise the rising fear coupled with annoyance. "I think you have the wrong number."

"Megan! For God's sake, don't hang up!"

Another pause.

"Tell me who you are," Megan said again.

Seconds of silence.

"Megan, it's *me*," the woman said. "It's Jen."

If Megan had not been sitting on the edge of her bed, she might have collapsed. As it was, the wave of anxiety and nausea that swept over her made her sway as if she might anyway. Megan was suddenly aware of her heart wildly beating. It sounded like it was in her ears. In her brain.

"Megan, *please* don't hang up," the woman said again.

"This can't be happening," Megan said, but not to the woman on the phone. To herself.

"I know how hard it must be, Megan. I *know* it. It's why I've waited so long to call you," the woman said.

"Why are you doing this?" Megan suddenly found her voice. She was shaking. Someone was playing a horrible trick on her. Someone who knew that Adele had died, and that Adele had been the woman who was there the day of the kidnapping. Someone who knew Megan had come home for the funeral.

"Megan, if you'll just listen…"

Megan stood up and began to pace her room.

"Look, I don't know who you are or what you want, but I'm going to call the police and report you!" she said, fear and anger making her voice do funny things.

"Megan! Please don't call the police yet!" the woman exclaimed. "I swear to God I'm Jen. I swear to God. And I don't want anything but your help. *Please?* That's all I want."

"You read about Adele's funeral in the paper, huh? Is that how you knew?" Megan said, her voice breaking in odd places. "Is that why you're doing this?"

Then Megan suddenly remembered there had been no funeral notice in the paper. Cheryl and Adam had made arrangements to publish Adele's obituary in next Sunday's issue of the *Union Tribune*. That was still five days away.

"What?" the woman said. "Who is Adele? Megan, I don't know what you're talking about!"

"What do you want?" Megan asked, still unconvinced.

"I need help, Megan," the woman said. "I need someone to *help* me. I need someone I can trust."

Megan found no words.

"Megan?"

"You are dead," Megan finally whispered into the phone, nearly choking on the words.

"I…know that's what people must think, Megan," the woman said. "But I'm not dead."

Megan paused to catch her breath, gather her thoughts.

"Where have you been *all this time?*" Megan said in a tone punctuated with a mixture of frustration and awe.

"I will tell you everything, I promise, but not on the phone," the woman said. "Can you meet me tomorrow?"

Megan stalled, searching for a response to make.

"Please, Megan?"

"Where are you calling me from?" Megan said, closing her eyes.

"I'm staying with some…friends in Chula Vista."

The words sounded utterly foreign to Megan. The idea that Jen was staying *anywhere* with friends was incomprehensible. Megan always pictured Jen in one of two ways after her abduction: in bondage or dead.

"You're in Chula Vista," Megan repeated, surprised at the underlying tone of anger in her voice.

"Yes, I've been here for a couple of days, Megan. I've been living in Texas the last few years, but I'm…back now," said the woman.

Megan could think of nothing else to say. All those years she had imagined, prayed, and anticipated Jen's return home, and now she could think of nothing to say.

"Megan, can you meet me tomorrow? Please?"

Megan rubbed her pounding forehead. This woman could not be Jen. How could she be? She'd be twenty-three if she were alive. How could anyone be missing for fifteen years and then suddenly show up "staying with some friends in Chula Vista"? It made no sense.

And yet Megan knew there was that faint chance this woman could be telling the truth. A body was never found. There had never been a ransom note. If Jen could vanish in the blink of an eye, could she not also reappear the same way?

"Megan?"

Megan swallowed. "Where?" she said, barely above a whisper.

"You pick the place. Just not your house."

The voice of reason thundered in her ears. Was she actually considering making arrangements to meet this person? What if it was a trap of some kind? On the other hand, what if it really was Jen? After all these years, *what if it was?*

It would have to be a very public place. Somewhere where there were lots of people in case anything went wrong.

"Do you know where the Horton Plaza mall is?" Megan said, wiping her eyes with a balled up tissue.

"I can ask someone," the woman said.

"Meet me by the clock on the first level. At noon."

"Noon," the woman said. "I'll be there. And could you please come alone, Megan?"

"Are *you* coming alone?" Megan replied, fear still creeping into her voice, and she knew the woman could sense it.

"Yes, I'll be alone," the woman said. "Megan, I am *begging* you not to call the cops. Please? Maybe later. But not yet. Please don't tell *anyone* yet. Can you promise me that?"

It seemed like a very foolish thing to do, but Megan promised she would not.

"Thank you, Megan. I knew I could count on you."

Megan let the compliment slip away. She did not feel like embracing it.

"How did you know I would be here today?" Megan said instead.

"What?" the woman said, like she hadn't understood the question.

"How did you know I would be in San Diego *today*."

"Don't you live in San Diego anymore?" the woman said.

"No, I don't," Megan said. "So how did you know?"

"I didn't," the woman said. "I mean, I just remembered your dad's name is Gordon. I looked the number up in the phone book. I didn't stop to think maybe I wouldn't find you there."

Megan was ready for the conversation to end. Her mind was awash in confusion.

"I'm going to hang up now," Megan said. "I'll...see you tomorrow."

"Bye, Megan," the woman said. "I can't wait to see you."

Oh yes, you can, Megan wanted to say as she clicked the phone off. *You've no idea how long you can wait if you have no other choice.*

She stood suspended in a daze of thoughts. Finally, she stepped out into the hall, wondering if Michelle had heard any part of the conversation. But Michelle was gone and so was her car. It was just a few minutes before five-thirty. Megan was alone in the house.

What to do? What to do? she said to herself as she paced the kitchen. She needed advice. She didn't want to break any promises, but she felt she needed one other person to tell her she wasn't crazy for agreeing to meet this woman. She needed someone with a cool, clear head, who wouldn't fly off the handle, who knew how to handle the legal matters if this really was Jen.

David.

Megan sighed. David had just been married four days ago. If only she knew how long he would be gone. How long were people gone on honeymoons? A week? Two weeks? Maybe David and Jamie only took a short one. Honeymoons were expensive after all, and David had joked that his school loans would keep him in the workforce until he was eighty. Maybe they were getting home soon. She had to try.

Megan headed to the cabinet in the kitchen where her mother kept the phone books. She opened the most current issue and found the listing for John Christopoulos in Ramona. Beth would surely know when David and Jamie were expected back. And Megan wouldn't have to tell Beth anything about the phone call from Jen. She could just tell her she had a gift for the David and Jamie.

She dialed the number. Beth answered it on the third ring.

"Hi, Beth. It's Megan."

"Megan, how wonderful to hear from you," Beth said. "Are you home for a visit?"

"Well, yes and no. I came home for a funeral, Beth. Had you heard that Adele passed away?"

"Oh, no! Oh, that's so sad, Megan. No, we hadn't heard," Beth sounded genuinely saddened. "When is the funeral?"

"Well, it was today, actually," Megan said.

"Oh, I wish we had known. I would have liked to come. I know David would have too."

"But…isn't he still on his honeymoon?" Megan asked.

"Honeymoon?" Beth said. "Oh, Megan. You didn't know? David and Jamie called off the wedding three months ago."

"They did?" Megan said. It was turning out to be a day riddled with surprises.

"He didn't phone you or e-mail you?"

"No, he didn't," Megan said, trying to absorb this new information as quickly as she could.

"Well, I'm sure he was planning on it," Beth said. "It was a hard thing for him. It was hard for all of us actually. We really liked Jamie."

"Can I ask what happened?" Megan said.

"Well, in a nutshell, Jamie rekindled a relationship with a guy she dated in high school. She broke off the engagement with David. As far as I know, she's planning to marry her old boyfriend now."

"Oh, Beth," Megan said. "How sad."

"Well, yes, it was," Beth said. "But at least it came about *before* they got married and not after. That would have been a million times worse."

"Yes, I suppose you're right," Megan said. "So, is David around then?"

"Well, he and another law student share an apartment in Mission Valley," Beth said. "And he's working for the county at the downtown office. In the appellate courts department, I think. You should be able to find him at one place or the other. He's only taking one class this summer because he's working nearly full time. You want his home phone number?"

Megan knew her parents would be coming home any minute. She didn't want to have a conversation with David about Jen that might be overheard.

"Well, maybe you could give me his work phone, too, and I'll call him tomorrow," Megan said. "Maybe I can buy him a cup of coffee or something and break the news to him about Adele."

"That's a good idea, Megan. I'm sure hearing it from you would be better than from me," Beth said.

Megan jotted down the numbers and said goodbye to Beth. When she hung up, she called Adele's number and was glad Cheryl answered.

"Cheryl, I'm not going to be able to see you off tomorrow," Megan said. "I'm going to see David instead. He ended up not getting married after all, so he's here in San Diego. He doesn't know about Adele, and I think I should be the one to tell him."

"Of course, Megan," Cheryl said. "Are you doing okay? You sound exhausted."

Megan rubbed her temple with her free hand, wanting to tell Cheryl the unbelievable news but hearing the promise she made to the woman echoing in her ears.

"I'll be okay, Cheryl," Megan said. "It's just been a lot to deal with."

"I'm leaving a few things in the fridge here for you, okay? And I'll call you this weekend."

"Okay. Bye, Cheryl."

Megan replaced the phone and wondered if it was too soon to take more Tylenol. Her head felt like it was about to explode, and her parents would be home within the hour. She hoped the stress of Adele's funeral and then having been named in Adele's will would explain her befuddled manner to her parents. If they pressed her on it, she knew she would cave in and blurt out the whole thing. If it really was Jen, she didn't want to break the promise not to tell anyone.

It was going to be impossible to sleep tonight. Megan both dreaded and anticipated ending the day.

As she had guessed, sleep eluded her until well after two o'clock in the morning. Her eyes kept drifting to the shadows on the Serengeti—cast by the moonlight that, after all these years, still danced across her bed at night.

The morning rush hour was long over by the time Megan pulled up to an available parking meter by the county's main offices downtown. It was just a little after nine-thirty. Megan hoped David would be able to get away for a cup of coffee. She had a lot to tell him. She hoped he could spare more than just a couple of minutes.

As she walked toward the entrance, she wondered for the third time if she should have called first.

"It's a little late for that now," she said under her breath.

Megan stepped inside and headed to a directory of the building. She found the location of the appellate court offices and said a prayer as she walked to them. Megan was about to break the promise she had made not to tell anyone. She was going to tell David. She prayed it was the right thing to do.

She was about to put her hand on the door to David's department when it opened in front of her.

David stood there with a stack of files in his hand, utter surprise on his face. He was wearing dark blue dress slacks, a cream-colored shirt, and a striped tie. Megan had rarely seen David in a tie. His black hair was still intensely curly, but he wore it shorter than the last time she had seen him.

"Megan!" he said. His face broke into a wide smile. "Don't tell me this is just a coincidence!"

He reached out to her and embraced her as best he could with the files in his hands.

"Hi, David," Megan said, hugging him back. "No, it's not a coincidence. Your mom told me I'd find you here."

He backed away.

"This is great! Wow, what a surprise! You don't usually come home until August," he said.

"Yeah, something happened to change that," she said, and then she couldn't keep the words back. "David, I really need to talk to you."

"Of course! You want to go get a cappuccino or something?" he said, concern replacing the surprise on his face.

"If you can get away for a little bit."

"Sure, sure," he said. "Let me just put these back on my desk. I'll be back in a sec."

David disappeared behind the door and reappeared less than a minute later without the files.

"There's a coffee shop around the corner," he said, as he ushered her back outside, holding the door open for her as she left the building first.

"Is everything okay at home?" he said as they stepped into the sunshine and began walking toward the coffee shop.

"Everything's fine at home, David," she said. "It's something else. There are two things, actually."

"Megan, are you sick?" David said, stopping her in midstep and taking her arm.

"No, David." Megan said. "It's not about me."

"Maybe I'd better get the cappuccinos first," he said, worry lining his face.

"Can we sit outside?" Megan asked, motioning to a few sidewalk tables outside the coffee shop.

"Sure. I'll be right back."

Megan pulled out a metal chair and sat down at a glass-topped table under a striped awning. She had only a few moments to pray for strength and wisdom.

David returned with two frothy cappuccinos. He set one down before her, and then took the chair opposite her.

He said nothing.

Megan put her hands around her cup as if to warm them though her hands weren't cold.

"So, when were you going to tell me?" she said.

David looked surprised for the second time that day.

"What?"

"I thought you'd be on your honeymoon today."

"Oh, that," he said.

"Yeah, *that*," Megan replied.

He shrugged.

"I figured you'd be home this summer and I'd tell you then. It wasn't like I wanted to send a mass e-mail telling all my out-of-state friends that my fiancée had dumped me," he said, and then took a sip from his cup. "I hadn't heard from you in a while. I thought maybe you were busy."

"I wasn't too busy to read an e-mail or talk on the phone," Megan said, taking a sip herself.

"Then why didn't you e-mail me or phone me?" he asked.

"Because *you* were getting married!" Megan replied. "I didn't think Jamie would appreciate your getting e-mails and phone calls from another woman."

He sighed.

"It wouldn't have mattered anyway," David said. "I don't think she was ever really over that guy. I think I believed I could woo her out of it. But I couldn't."

"I'm sorry, David," Megan said.

"Yeah," he said, as he took another sip.

"I wish you would have called me," Megan said.

"I probably should have," David replied, looking up at her and then down at his cup. "But I was embarrassed. And hurt."

"Are you doing okay?" Megan asked.

He looked up again and there was a weak smile on his face, but a smile nonetheless. "Every day it gets better," he replied. "And actually the romantic feelings I had for Jamie kind of died when she told me she didn't want to marry me, that she wanted to marry someone else. The affection I had for her as a friend is taking a little longer to shake. But I'm getting there."

"So the courtship thing didn't really work after all, did it?" Megan said as she raised her cup to her mouth.

"Are you kidding? It worked great," David said, looking straight at her. "Just think if Jamie and I had gone straight into marriage without a courtship first. I'd be married to a woman who didn't really love me. Besides, I have to believe this is what God wanted for me all along, that there is someone else for me."

Megan nodded in agreement.

"Megan," David said, changing the subject. "Those two things. Tell me."

Megan took a breath.

"Well, the first thing, David, is that Adele passed away," she said, watching David as realization crept over him. "She had a bad heart attack last Friday afternoon and another one later that same night. I didn't know you were in town or I would have called you. I thought you were on your honeymoon. The funeral was yesterday."

David's eyes had filled with tears, but he did not look away from her until she stopped talking. Then he looked beyond her to nothing in particular—into his own thoughts.

"I'm really sorry you didn't know," Megan continued. "If I had known…"

But David put up a hand to silence her.

"It's not your fault," he said.

David took a deep breath, trying to regain his composure.

"I should have been by to see her more often," David finally said. "I knew she wasn't doing well. I knew that house was getting to be too much for her."

"I know what you mean," Megan said. "I wish I had called her more often, too."

"Was it a nice homegoing?" David said.

"It was beautiful," Megan said.

David nodded.

"She left me all the furniture in the living room, the stuff she and Chet worked on together," Megan continued. "And she kind of left me the house for right now."

"The house?" David said, slightly stunned.

"Well, not really. She left it to her grand niece and nephews, but she wanted me to know I could live in it until they become adults."

"Really?" David said. "Are you thinking of coming back to San Diego?"

Megan shrugged. "I hadn't thought about it. I still have a semester to complete at ASU. I don't know what I'll do after that."

David nodded.

"Thanks for telling me in person about Adele," he said, then after a brief pause, he began again. "So, what's this other thing?"

"I'm not quite sure how to tell you," she said.

"Has someone else died?"

A faint smile crept across Megan's face.

"No...it's quite the opposite," she said, knowing her words made no sense to David whatsoever.

"*What's* quite the opposite?" he said.

Megan was suddenly filled with apprehension. What if David insisted on calling the police? What if he called her parents? What if he physically stopped her from going to meet Jen?

"David, will you promise me you will hear me out? Will you promise not to go nuts on me?" she said.

"Go nuts? *Me?*" David said.

"Promise me," she said.

"What exactly am I promising?" he asked.

"You are promising not to tell anyone or call anyone or *go nuts*," Megan said.

"Okay, I promise."

"You have to *mean* it," Megan said, agitated.

"Megan, I promise not to go nuts. And I won't tell anyone unless I think you're in some kind of danger."

"That's not the same thing!" Megan exclaimed.

"That's the best I can do. Sorry," he said.

Megan closed her eyes and sighed.

"Megan," he said, and his voice and eyes were kind. He reached for her hand and held it. "*Tell me.*"

"David, I got a call yesterday."

David waited for her to continue.

"From who?" he said when she didn't.

"I'm afraid you'll think I'm crazy," Megan said softly, wiping her eyes with her free hand.

"I will *not* think you're crazy, Megan. I promise," David said.

Megan looked at David and then down at her hand held in his.

"David, it was Jen," she said, barely above a whisper. "It was a lady who said she's Jen."

There. It was out. But she couldn't look at David.

"Megan, look at me."

Megan raised her head. David looked angry. Afraid.

"What did this person ask of you?" he said.

Megan could barely speak. A lady at a table next to them was staring at her.

"Megan," David said.

"She asked for my help."

"What kind of help?"

Megan shook her head.

"I don't know what kind. I'm to meet her today at noon."

David leaned over the table.

"Megan, you didn't actually agree to meet with this person, did you?" he said. Was that anger in his voice or fear?

"Yes, David, I did. I—"

But David cut her off.

"Megan, are you crazy?!" he said, half under his breath.

Megan snatched her hand away from his.

"You told me you wouldn't think I was crazy!" Megan said angrily but as softly as she could so the woman next to them wouldn't turn back around.

David looked down at the table.

"I'm sorry," he said. Then he raised his eyes to her. "I don't think you're crazy, Megan. But do you realize how dangerous it could be?"

Megan wiped her eyes. The woman at the other table got up and left. *Thank God,* Megan thought.

"Of course I do," she said. "If I thought it was a simple thing, do you think I would have come down here to tell *you* about it first?!"

"Megan, please don't do this," he said. "If it is her, we should call the police. If it's not her, we should call the police. Can't you see that?"

"I promised I wouldn't," Megan said, reaching a shaking hand for her cappuccino. It was getting cold.

"You promised you wouldn't call the police? She made you promise that?" David said, incredulous.

"Yes."

"Megan, when someone begs you not to call the cops, that's usually a huge clue that you should!"

"Don't talk to me like I'm a child," Megan said evenly. This was turning out to be a disaster.

"That's not what I meant," he said. "But just think about it, Megan. If it *is* Jen, why wouldn't she want you to call the police? She was kidnapped! She's been missing for what, fifteen years?"

"She asked me not to call the police *yet*, David. She didn't ask me to never do it. She just said *not yet*."

Why? For what possible purpose?"

"I don't know!" Megan replied.

"Okay. So where has she been for the past fifteen years? Huh? Where has she been?" David said pointedly, leaning back in his chair.

"She told me she would tell me everything today," Megan said.

"Megan, you *do* know it might not be her, right? You do know that?"

Megan looked down at her cup. She said nothing.

"You know it could be someone who knows the story, who knows what happened to Jen Lovett, who knows you were the little girl who saw it all, that you were Jen's best friend. Tell me you know it could be someone who has figured out if Jen Lovett were alive, she'd be worth millions. That if Jen Lovett were alive, she'd be the daughter of one of the richest men in America. Tell me you know this!"

Megan raised her eyes to him.

"I know it. I know maybe she's not really Jen."

"Then why have you agreed to meet this woman!?" David exclaimed.

Megan held his eyes.

"Because maybe she is."

David stared at her. She could tell he was willing her to change her mind. She didn't take her eyes off his.

"I'm going with you," he said.

"No, you're not."

"Oh, yes I am!"

"No, you're not! I told her I would come alone."

David leaned across the table again, nearly spilling his half-empty cup.

"Can't you see it? Megan. She wants you to come alone. *Alone!* Why would she say that?"

"Because she doesn't trust people right now. She told me she knew she could trust me."

David was silent. Megan could see his chest rising and falling. She had never seen him so aggravated.

"I am coming with you Megan. I *am.*"

Megan knew she would not win this one. And maybe it was best if he did come.

"All right," she said. "But you mustn't let her know you're there. I'm meeting her beneath the clock at Horton Plaza. I picked a very public place, David. You can stand on one of the levels overlooking the clock, but you can't stare at us! You have to promise me you will stay hidden until she leaves. Okay?"

"You promise not to leave with her?"

Megan nodded. "I promise."

David pulled a mechanical pencil out of his shirt pocket and handed it to her.

"The second you feel like something is wrong, you drop this, okay? Then stay put. I'll be there in a heartbeat."

Megan put her hand around the pencil as her other hand took David's.

"Thank you, David."

He looked at his watch.

"I've got to get back," he said as he stood up.

"Come back to my office at a quarter to twelve. I want us to get there at the same time," he said. "Then I'll disappear."

Megan nodded and watched him as he turned the corner and then was gone.

25

*T*hough it was a Wednesday, the noon hour crowd at Horton Plaza was as Megan had hoped. A cruise ship had docked at the harbor earlier that morning, and passengers enjoying a day on shore in downtown San Diego added to the sizeable crowd on a typical July weekday.

Megan and David approached the Jessop Jewelers clock carefully, staying back from its sunny location as they stood near the sheltered glass front of a department store. A vendor selling sunglasses out of a brightly colored kiosk partially hid their view of the area around the clock. A customer looking at the sunglasses moved at that moment, and it was then Megan saw her.

She was there.

On a bench near the clock sat a young woman with shoulder-length blonde hair. She was dressed in faded jeans and an equally faded, peach tank top. A dusty black backpack lay at her feet. She was picking at a hole in the fabric of her jeans by her left knee. In her other hand she held a lit cigarette. Megan could not see her eyes. The woman was looking down, and she and David were too far away.

"David…" Megan whispered.

David took a step forward.

"Is that her?" he said.

Megan put a hand on his chest and pushed him back.

"Yes," Megan said softly. "I mean, it looks like it *could* be her."

David tried to look past the kiosk from his new position behind Megan.

"I can't see anything from here," he said.

Megan looked above their heads to the second level.

"Go up there and find a spot," she instructed him. "But don't stand at the railing, and don't stare at us. You go first. I want to know where you are."

David pointed to the pencil clipped on the cloth handle of Megan's purse.

"The minute something doesn't seem right—" he began.

"I promise, I'll drop it," she finished for him. "Go."

David ran up a nearby escalator, and then disappeared for a few moments. Then he reappeared and Megan watched him secure a place above the bench where the woman sat. He looked over to Megan and gave her a thumbs-up.

"God help me," Megan whispered as she began walking toward the woman.

When she was within only a few feet, the woman raised her head. Two things stopped Megan in her tracks. The first was the sight of Nate Lovett's eyes looking back at her. The second was the pair of tiny silver hoop earrings the woman was wearing. Both nearly sent Megan to the pavement.

The woman smiled and threw down her cigarette, crushing it out with a worn sandal. She stood up.

"Megan!" the woman said, and she brought a hand to her mouth, like people do when they don't want to let out a scream.

The woman was terribly skinny.

Megan willed herself to close the distance between them. She could tell the woman wanted to embrace her. She let her.

"I can't believe it's you!" the woman said as they parted.

That would be my line, Megan thought as she reached for the back of the bench. She had to sit down.

"Megan, you look wonderful! You still have your freckles!" the woman said.

Megan could only stare.

The woman seemed to sense that Megan's astonishment was rendering her speechless.

"I know how much of a shock this must be for you," the woman with Nate's eyes said. "I can't tell you how grateful I am that you came." She was smiling widely.

Megan hardly knew how to begin.

"Shock doesn't even begin to describe how this is for me," Megan finally said, and the woman's smile faded. "The little girl who was my best friend has been missing for fifteen years. She's been thought to be dead for most of those years. Then suddenly you call me and tell me you're that little girl. That you're Jen."

"I can explain it, Megan," the woman said quickly. "I know it seems incredible right now, but it won't seem so strange after I tell you."

"Then, please, tell me," Megan said.

The woman licked her lips, and then rummaged in her backpack for another cigarette. Just as quickly, she put it back. She looked up at Megan.

"The thing is, there's quite a bit I don't remember," she said.

Megan waited.

"I remember all of it," Megan finally said. "You were kidnapped in front of my eyes. I never saw you again. No one did."

"Yes, I know. But what happened is...I became the child of this other couple. The people who took me told me I was really someone else. And the man who grabbed me…well, he and his wife told me I was really *their* daughter. They took me to Oklahoma and they raised me there. They told me my name was Sara."

Megan was again speechless.

"They told me their daughter, Sara, was born in Los Angeles and Jen Lovett was born in Los Angeles and there was a switch. A mistake at the hospital. The baby they came home with was really Jennifer Lovett. Only she had a heart condition. She died when she was four. When I was little, Rudy told me that that's when they knew that baby couldn't be theirs, and so they went looking for their real daughter. Me. It took four years to find me, but they finally did. And so they took me."

"And you *believed* them?" Megan said.

"Megan, I was eight! What was I supposed to do?"

"Well, how about try to escape? Call the police. Anything."

"I don't remember ever being near a phone once we got to Oklahoma. I remember being very afraid, and then I remember not being afraid at all. They were nice to me, Megan. They hugged me and bought me clothes and told me stories about what it was like the day I was born. They showed me pictures. They started calling me Sara."

"So you just…just fell for it," Megan said with resentment in her voice.

The woman looked at her blankly, trying to take in what Megan had said.

"What did you believe happened to me?" the woman said.

Megan felt fury rising up inside her.

"You wouldn't believe the awful things I believed happened to you," she replied, and she felt her eyes filling with tears.

"But those things didn't happen," the woman said. "So you fell for stuff that wasn't true, too."

When Megan didn't speak, the woman continued.

"I was just a kid, Megan. You can tell a kid something long enough and she'll believe it. I really did come to believe I was their daughter, Sara. So when we began living in populated places where I could have called the police, I didn't. I didn't see the need. I was Sara Curran. Rudy and Beanie were my parents."

"Rudy and Beanie," Megan said softly but crossly. "So Beanie was the woman at the wheel of the van?"

"No, actually, that was her sister, Ruthie. There's more, Megan."

The woman sighed and continued.

"Rudy knew all along I wasn't really Sara. He knew their real daughter really did have a heart condition, that it killed her. But he loved Beanie so much, and when they lost Sara, Beanie kind of went…crazy. She tried to commit suicide. Several times. Every year it got worse. Ruthie and Rudy came up with the plan to kidnap a child who would look like Sara four years later. They chose San Diego because they wanted to escape through Mexico. Rudy told me Sara had been born in LA, like me, but she hadn't. She was born in Amarillo, Texas. That's where they buried her. Well, anyway, they took me, told Beanie they had found Sara, and brought me to her."

"So you're telling me this Rudy guy and his sister-in-law decided, out of the blue, to become criminals and steal a child, all out of love for Beanie?" Megan said the two names with contempt in her voice.

"I didn't say they decided to become criminals," the woman said, looking down.

"How can you say they weren't criminals! They stole a child!" Megan said, trying to keep her voice down, but anger was making it difficult.

"I didn't say that, either!" the woman shot back. "They already *were* criminals when they kidnapped me, Megan. All three of them. They were all already wanted in three states for all kinds of offenses—bad checks, extortion, insurance fraud—it really wasn't that hard for them to steal a child when they had already learned how easy it was to steal something. And yes, they did it because they loved Beanie!"

Megan looked away. She couldn't see how love had anything to do with this. She didn't want to see it.

"Megan, I know what they did was wrong. But they never laid a hand on me. They were good to me. They took care of me. I was happy with them. After a while, I forgot about my old life."

Megan winced. "Did you forget about me?" she said.

The woman blinked.

"For a while, yes."

Megan put her hands to her face to calm them.

"I wanted to forget and couldn't," Megan said.

"Megan, I'm sorry about that; I am," the woman said.

Megan dropped her hands to her lap. "So, when did you figure out you had been lied to all these years?" she said.

The woman paused before answering.

"A year and a half ago, Mom—Beanie—died. Ruthie had run off some years before that, and Rudy and I didn't know where she was. So it was just Rudy and me. Last winter Rudy told me the truth. He was in all kinds of trouble and didn't want me to get caught up in it. He cried when he told me. Rudy told me I deserved a better life, and he told me what my real name is. I had sort of forgotten. He told me I should go find my real parents, that they probably were still missing me very much."

"You forgot your name?" Megan said, incredulous.

"When he told me the truth, I started to remember little things. I remembered you, Megan."

"You've known this since last winter?" Megan said.

"I didn't know what to do," the woman said. "I wasn't sure how to come back. Then, I remembered you, Megan, and I thought maybe you could help me."

"Where is he?" Megan said, abruptly moving the conversation on.

"What?" the woman said.

"Where is this Rudy?"

The woman leaned back on the bench.

"I don't know," she said.

"This is why you didn't want me to call the police, isn't it?" Megan said evenly. "You know they'll arrest him."

The woman looked down.

"He's the only father I can remember, Megan. And I know the police are going to have to be told. But yes, I don't want to see him arrested. And I really don't know where he is. He said it would be better for me if I didn't."

Megan looked at the woman, studied her face, and caught a glimpse of those eyes that were so much like Nate's. She looked away.

"You said you needed my help," Megan said, looking down at her feet.

"I want to see my family," the woman said. "I want to see my parents. My brother."

"How does that involve me?" Megan said, whipping her head up. "Why don't you just call Nate Lovett up? You do know who he is, don't you? Just one of the richest men in America."

"You've got it all wrong," the woman said.

"I hope I do," Megan replied, watching her.

"I know my father is rich. But I honestly can't help that. I don't have anyone right now, Megan. I want my family back."

Megan still studied her. "Who are these friends of yours in Chula Vista?"

"They're not even my friends. They're AJ's friends."

"Who's AJ?"

The woman sighed. "Just some guy I met in San Antonio. He drove me out to California on his motorcycle."

"Is he your boyfriend?"

"Not really," the woman answered.

"Does *he* know who Nate Lovett is?"

The woman looked up, her familiar eyes filling with tears for the first time since Megan sat down with her.

"I know what you're thinking, and you're wrong," she said, her voice breaking. "I don't care about the money. I just want my family back. I want my life back! And I need your help! I need you to believe me, Megan."

Megan sat and stared at the crying woman in front of her. Something kept her from embracing her, from calling her by name, from believing her.

"I'd like to believe you," Megan said, feeling fresh tears spring to her eyes.

The woman looked up, her Nate-like eyes beseeching Megan.

"What can I do to convince you?" the woman said.

Megan wanted desperately to be convinced. She felt like she was teetering on the edge of two worlds: the one she'd had to live in without Jen and the one she would have lived in had Jen never been kidnapped. She only knew what one of them was like. Everything about the life she had been forced to live the past fifteen years was now turning on a dime if what this woman said was true. All the nightmares, the anxious thoughts, the unanswered prayers, the terrors of the canyon, the fear of physical intimacy, the careful hedge she kept around her heart—it all meant nothing if the woman on the bench next to her was really Jen Lovett, safe and sound. Alive.

As she sat there with those familiar eyes upon her, Megan suddenly grew very bitter. She had been tricked. Either way, she had been tricked. She felt gullible and stupid. Outraged. The woman sensed something had changed, and her eyes widened.

"Megan?" the woman said.

"What was the name of my cat?" Megan said, boring her eyes into the eyes of the woman across from her.

"What?" the woman said.

"What was the name of my cat?" Megan repeated, drawing a strange kind of strength from her indignation.

"I can't remember," the woman said.

"What was the color of my bike?" Megan asked pointedly.

The woman looked flustered.

"I don't...I only remember bits and pieces like—"

But Megan cut her off.

"Who was our first-grade teacher?" she said.

"Megan, please, if you would just—"

"Where did we go on your seventh birthday?"

The woman was thoroughly perplexed, and Megan felt a queer and sick sense of victory. The woman could not answer any of these questions. Megan wanted to grin. She wanted to weep.

Then the woman's expression suddenly changed, like she had suddenly found the mother lode in a dark, lonely mine.

The woman stood up and scanned the stores around them, above them. Megan could sense movement above her. David was backing up away from the railing.

The woman's eyes stopped scanning, and then she looked back down to Megan.

"Would you please wait here? Please?"

Megan didn't know what to say.

"Please, Megan," the woman was pleading. "I'll be right back. Don't go, please?"

The woman started to walk away.

"Where are you going?" Megan called out to her.

"I'll be right back!" the woman, as and she began to run toward the department store.

When she was out of sight, Megan could see that David was leaning over the railing.

"What?" he mouthed, thoroughly confused.

"Just wait!" Megan mouthed up to him.

Megan watched him throw up his hands and begin to pace.

Five minutes went by.

David was back at the railing.

"Well?" he mouthed.

Megan waved him back with a frown.

"Wait!" she mouthed back.

A few minutes later, the woman returned, smiling, breathless, and with a little white Mervyn's bag in her hand.

She sat down next to Megan. As she lowered herself to the bench, Megan glanced up to make sure David had hidden himself again.

"Megan," the woman said. "I swear before God that I am Jen Lovett. I will take any kind of test to prove it. Any lie detector test. Any DNA test. Anything. But I want you to believe me."

Megan said nothing at first.

"What's in the bag?" Megan finally said.

"My old life," the woman said. "And hopefully my new life."

And then the woman reached inside the bag and pulled out a small package wrapped in plastic.

Inside the wrapping was a pair of little girl's socks—white, edged in lace, and dotted with tiny rosebuds.

Megan could feel her heart racing, her pulse quickening. The familiar feeling of weakness that she had grown to hate was creeping over her. But there was something different about it this time. There was no crushing weight to the fear. It was as intense as it had ever been, but it felt wild and unfettered.

She was aware that Jen was still sitting next to her on a bench in the middle of a shopping mall and that there were tourists walking by. She was aware that in her hand she held a pair of little girls' socks. And though her eyes were open and tears were falling freely from them, she didn't see the shoppers. She saw instead a young girl of eight watching in horror as an ugly blue van sped past her.

"Jen," the little girl said.

And the words came from her own mouth.

"Megan," said Jen, and suddenly Jen's slender arms were around her and the anguish of five thousand days began to slowly slip away.

"All this time," Megan whispered. "All this time you were alive."

Jen held her close, saying the words, "I'm sorry, I'm sorry," over and over.

After several minutes, Megan became aware that they had drawn attention to themselves, and she hastily wiped her eyes. Jen laughed and did the same. Above Jen's head, Megan could see David leaning forward on the railing, his face showing surprise yet puzzlement. While Jen bent down to grab a tissue out of her backpack, Megan motioned for David to come.

"Jen," Megan said, marveling for a second at the joy of saying it. "I have a good friend here who can help us. He's here…at the mall."

"Who is it? Does he know?" Jen said right away. "Did you tell him?"

"Jen, he's the only person I told. And I trust him completely. Next to Charlie, he's the closest friend I have."

"Charlie?" Jen said, forgetting for the moment that Megan had told someone she had returned. "You're friends with Charlie?"

Megan smiled and nodded. "Charlie got me through some pretty tough times, Jen. And I suppose perhaps I did the same for him. He was the only friend I had for many years."

"So, you can call him! You can talk to him," Jen said. "He'll believe you."

"Yes, Jen," Megan said. "I can talk to him. But it's probably going to be very hard for him. He's believed you've been dead for many years."

"But you will tell him, won't you? You'll convince him! I'll take any test. Any test!"

Megan took Jen's hands to calm them.

"Let's just take this one step at a time, Jen," she said gently.

David came up from behind them. He looked at Megan.

Megan reached for him, and he stepped closer to her, eyeing Jen, obviously unsettled.

"Jen," Megan said, "this is David Christopoulos."

"It's a pleasure to meet you," he said, polite as ever, reaching out with his right hand, but Megan could sense the undertone of doubt in his voice.

Jen shook his hand.

"Hi," she said, taking his hand. Doubt was thick in her voice as well.

Jen looked back to Megan. The expression on her face was obvious. *Why is he here?* it said.

"Jen, David is a law student. He's very smart and very kind," Megan said. "We are going to need his help. And I trust him. I want you to trust him, too."

Jen looked back to David and then to Megan.

"All right," she said.

Megan realized she was very hungry. She wondered if Jen was hungry, too.

"Jen, have you had lunch yet? Megan said.

"No," Jen said uneasily.

Something in the way she said it made Megan ask her if she'd had anything at all to eat that day.

"I had some lunch yesterday," Jen said, stuffing her tissue in the front pocket of her backpack.

Megan looked up at David.

"David, do you think you can join us for lunch, or do you have to get back to work?"

"I have plenty of time," he said cheerfully, looking at Megan and letting her know he had no intention of leaving her alone with this woman.

They made their way to the food court on the top tier, and David told them he wanted to treat them to Asian food. While Megan and Jen sat at an outside table, David ordered three teriyaki rice bowls and three iced teas. When he returned, he set them before the two women and took a seat opposite them.

"Seems like a great time to offer a prayer of thanksgiving," he said, looking at Jen and then at Megan. Megan suspected he wanted very much to be alone with her to quiz her and make sure she hadn't been duped.

"Yes, it is," Megan said, looking back at him with the same intensity in her own eyes.

David bowed his head and prayed over their lunch, adding a few lines of gratitude for God's goodness and provision in bringing Jen safely home to the people who loved her.

"Thanks," Jen said softly, looking at David with less skepticism than she had ten minutes earlier.

It was hard to make small talk when there was so much "big talk" that needed to take place. While they ate, Megan quietly told David what had happened to Jen. She told him about Rudy and Beanie and Ruthie, about the little girl named Sara Curran, and about the life Jen had led the past fifteen years. Then Megan asked David what Jen should do first.

"You'll have to go to the police, Jen," he said. "Maybe not today, but tomorrow or the next day. You can't reclaim your identity without notifying the police."

Jen nodded and looked down at her nearly empty rice bowl. "Okay," she said.

"If they find Rudy Curran, there will be charges. You'll likely have to testify against him," David said.

"I don't want to do that!" Jen said.

"You'll be subpoenaed. You won't have a choice."

"He didn't mean any harm," Jen said.

"Kidnapping is a federal offense. It doesn't matter how well he treated you," David said.

There was silence around the table.

"I suppose there's no other way," Jen said softly, a moment later.

"Not if you want to go back to being Jen Lovett," David replied.

Megan looked hard at David, but he didn't look at her. He seemed to be a little harsh with Jen, a little too brutal with the truth.

"I need to use a restroom," Jen said.

"There's one right over there," Megan said, motioning with her hand.

"I'll be right back," Jen said, rising.

Megan started to rise, too, but she suddenly felt David's hand firmly on her knee.

"You want me to come with you?" Megan said to Jen, brushing it off.

"No, I can manage," Jen said with a tired smile.

As soon as she was gone, Megan turned to face David.

"What was all that?" she said.

"All *that* was precisely what that woman needs to know if she is Jen Lovett," David said. "It's also precisely what she needs to know if she's an imposter."

"But she's not an imposter, David," Megan said. "She *is* Jen. I wasn't sure at first, either. She doesn't remember as much as I do. But she remembered that the first day we met, we both had on the same socks. Socks like these, David!"

Megan reached into her purse and pulled out the rose-dotted socks Jen had bought less than an hour before.

"No one knew about these but Jen and me," Megan continued. "No one could have gotten that from some old news article. Adele didn't even know it."

David sighed. "So you're sure?" he said.

"I'm positive," Megan said. "She said she would take any kind of test. Lie detector, DNA—"

"She may have to," David interjected.

From across the court, the ladies-restroom door opened, and Jen stepped out into the sunshine. She rejoined them at the table.

"Are you okay?" Megan asked.

"Yeah, it's just been awhile since I've eaten so much all at once," Jen said.

"Jen, is someone picking you up? Did you borrow a car to come here today?" Megan asked.

Jen shifted in her chair.

"Well, actually...I took a bus," Jen said.

Megan waited.

Jen said nothing else.

"Jen, do you need a place to stay tonight?" Megan asked. She was slightly aware of David tapping his foot.

"AJ's friends kind of scare me," she said with a nervous laugh. "And AJ seems different when he's around them."

"Why don't you stay with me tonight?" Megan said.

Jen looked down at her hands.

"AJ might wonder where I am."

"We'll call him."

"I don't know if there's a phone at that house," Jen said.

"Jen," Megan said. "Come home with me."

"Okay," she said, looking up.

"Can you come over for dinner tonight, David?" Megan said, turning to David.

"Of course," he said.

～～～

After dropping David off at the county building, Megan began the twenty-five minute drive to her parents' North County neighborhood, the neighborhood she and Jen had shared.

"This isn't the kind of car I pictured you in," Jen said, surveying the dark blue interior of Adele's sedan.

"It's not my car, actually." Megan said. "It belonged to a very good friend. She died last week. Her name was Adele Springer. She lived three houses away from where you were abducted, Jen. She heard me screaming that day. She came out to help. But of course there was nothing she could do."

Jen was silent.

"She came to the police station with me, though. Stayed with me until my parents got there. Watched over me then and every day afterward while I grew up."

"I can barely remember that day," Jen said.

Megan drove. It was her turn to be silent.

"Tell me what happened, Megan. I can hardly remember anything. I just remember it was hot. And I remember a bicycle with a purple seat. Was that one yours?"

How could Jen not remember? *You are so lucky*, Megan thought, remembering words Jen had said to her ages ago, when the world was beautiful.

"The one with the purple seat was yours, Jen," Megan began.

It took only a few minutes to tell Jen what that day had been like. It was impossible to tell her what every day after that had been like. Megan didn't even try.

"I couldn't find my parents' number in the phone book," Jen said nervously as Megan took an exit off Interstate 15.

It occurred to Megan for the first time that Jen didn't know her parents had divorced, that she didn't know the house across the canyon didn't belong to the Lovetts anymore.

"Jen," Megan began, "there are some things you need to know."

Jen slowly turned to her, anxiety etched across her face.

"I'm going to drive to the house, your house, but we're not going to get out of the car, okay? I'm going to stop the car and then tell you."

Jen nodded. She didn't take her eyes off the neighborhood streets. It was like she was trying to absorb it all at once—the houses, the street signs, the swaying palms.

"Do you remember any of it?" Megan asked.

Jen shook her head.

"It *has* changed a lot, Jen," Megan said.

Megan turned onto the street that had been the Lovetts'. She eased to a stop in front of the house whose landscaping Megan had hidden in that day Charlie found her watching the Lovett house. She turned the ignition off.

Beside her, Jen drew in a breath.

"It's that one!" Jen said, pointing across the street.

The basketball hoop was gone. The trees were taller. The garage door and shutters had a new coat of paint. The rest was the same.

"Yes," Megan said.

"But my parents don't live there anymore, do they?" Jen said.

Megan shook her head. She took a breath. Jen was looking at her.

"Jen, losing you was really hard on everyone," Megan said. "But…but it was especially hard on your parents," Megan said, trying to look at Jen, but she couldn't. She said the rest of the words to the steering wheel in front of her. "I think they tried to get past it, but it was too much. They both started seeing other people. When Charlie was a senior in high school, they got a divorce. They sold this house."

Jen didn't say anything. Megan stole a look at her. Jen's Nate-like eyes were glassy with tears.

"Charlie went to live with your dad and his girlfriend in Del Mar. That's not too far from here. The girlfriend's name is Caroline. Your dad and Caroline got married a few years after that. Charlie was the best man. I went to the wedding. Caroline is very nice. Charlie lives in that house now."

"Where is my mother?" Jen said, saying each word carefully.

"Your mom moved to Mission Viejo. It's about an hour and a half drive from here, Jen. She moved in with a man who writes plays. I've never met him. His name is Leo."

"Is she happy?"

"I haven't seen her in eight years, Jen. But Charlie says she's doing well. He went to college in Los Angeles, so he saw her a lot when he was a student. But he's been back in San Diego for a couple of years. I don't know how often he sees her now."

"She didn't marry this man?" Jen said.

"No, she didn't."

"Is Charlie married?"

"No, he's not. And actually he hasn't been called Charlie in a decade. He goes by the name Chaz now."

"Chaz," Jen said absently.

Megan said nothing as she allowed her friend to take in the news.

After a few minutes, Jen sat up straight and wiped her eyes.

"I want to go now," she said.

Megan nodded, started the car, and drove away.

Within five minutes they were pulling into the driveway of Megan's own childhood home. She could see her mother's car inside the garage. It was a little after three o'clock. Wednesdays were her mother's half day at the library.

Jen got out of the car, studying the house as she did. She walked to the end of the driveway, looked up and down the street, and then back at the house. She turned toward the silvery gray guardrails at the far end of the street.

"The canyon," she said softly.

Megan smiled.

"It's a golf course now," Megan explained. "You want to go inside the house?"

Megan went ahead of Jen, stepping into the cool shadows of the garage and entering the house through the kitchen door. She hoped her mother was alone, not on the phone, and not in a hurry.

Trina was unloading the dishwasher. She smiled as Megan stepped in, and Megan could sense the moment her mother noticed there was a young woman behind her.

Megan smiled back and said nothing as she walked into the kitchen. Her mother's ready smile for Megan's unexpected guest only lasted a second. When Trina saw the young woman's face in full, her face became awash in astonishment.

"Oh, dear God!" Trina said, her eyes wide. She dropped the clean coffee mug she was holding in her hand. It fell to the floor with a thud and shattered.

It was after four in the afternoon before the next round of tears and storytelling ended. Trina made tea halfway through, after her initial shock wore off, and then insisted they all have a seat in the family room. She also insisted Jen call the police.

"I will, I promise," Jen said. "I just want to see my family first."

"Where are you staying?" Trina asked.

"She's staying with us," Megan said, finishing the last of her tea.

"Do you have any other belongings, Jen?" Trina asked, looking at the dirty, black backpack at Jen's feet.

Jen looked down at it, too.

"None that I cared to bring with me," she said.

"I bet you'd like a nice, soothing shower and some clean clothes," Trina said. "Megan, why don't you and Jen go see what Michelle has in her closet. Jen looks about her size. Take whatever you need, Jen. Michelle has way more clothes than she needs. And I know she won't mind."

"That would be really wonderful," she said.

Megan guessed it had been a long time since anyone had mothered Jen. She flashed her mom a look that said "thank you."

"I'll start dinner so we can eat early," Trina continued, rising from the sofa and gathering the mugs from the tea.

"Here, I'll show you where everything is," Megan said, and Jen rose to follow her.

Megan had already passed the door to her old room and was saying "here we are" at the front of Michelle's room when she noticed Jen had stopped following her. She turned back. Jen was standing at the entrance to Megan's room, staring into it.

Megan walked back to her.

"Jen?" she said.

"That painting…" Jen said, hardly more than a whisper. She was looking at the Serengeti hanging across from Megan's bed.

"Do you remember it?" Megan said.

"Yes…" Jen said, not taking her eyes off it.

Megan looked at the painting's warm, inviting colors, its fierce magnificence.

"It used to hang in your house," Megan said softly. "We liked to dance under it. Your mother gave it to me when the house was sold."

The two stood looking at the picture, not saying a word.

"Ready for that shower?" Megan finally said.

"Yes," Jen answered, peeling her eyes away.

~ ~ ~

While Jen showered, Megan helped her mother in the kitchen.

"You knew in an instant," Megan said to Trina as she placed plates on the table.

Trina turned from the salad she was making.

"Didn't you?" she said.

Megan placed the last plate. "I was almost afraid to believe it," she said.

"That's not so surprising, Megan," Trina said, tearing a leaf of romaine.

"How did *you* know, Mom?" Megan said, turning to her mother. "Jen was my best friend, not yours."

"Those eyes," she said, like there was no other explanation. "They haven't changed. She looks just like Nate. She always did."

Megan nodded and headed back down the hall. Jen was just finishing in the bathroom. She looked even more slender with just a towel wrapped around her.

"Megan, I don't have any makeup or a blow-dryer or anything…" she began.

"Just use whatever you want, Jen," Megan said. "Michelle and I won't care."

Most of the makeup in the bathroom was Michelle's; Megan only wore a little blush and mascara most days, but Megan was confident Michelle wouldn't put up too much of a fuss.

"Thanks," Jen said. Then she reached out to Megan and hugged her. "Thanks for everything."

Megan was surprised at how light Jen felt in her arms.

"Megan, can we call Charlie or my dad tonight?" Jen asked as they parted. "I don't think I can wait another day."

"Sure," Megan said.

Megan left so Jen could get dressed. She went into her parents' room where it was quiet, called David's apartment, and left a message on his answering machine telling him dinner would be early. She hung up, and then sat on her parents' bed and stared at the phone. Overcoming her hesitation, she picked up the handset and dialed Charlie's number, hoping it hadn't changed. It had been a year since she had spoken on the phone with him.

Charlie's phone was also picked up by an answering machine.

"Hi, you've reached Chaz and Emily. We're not able to take your call right now, but you know what to do. Catch you later!"

Megan waited for the beep and cleared her throat, wondering who Emily was.

"Hey, Chaz, it's Megan. I'm in town, and it's pretty important that I talk to you tonight. So, can you call me at my parents' house as soon as you get this? It's really, really important, okay? It's about four-thirty. Call me right away."

Megan could hear the whir of the blow-dryer—the normal, commonplace sound of a woman getting ready to go out or have friends in or go to work. It was so ordinary. But nothing about this day was ordinary.

Her dad would be coming home from work shortly; Michelle would, too, and the story would have to be told a third time. Then with any luck, Charlie would call. And Megan would tell it again. How many more times would she have to tell it?

Though she hadn't done so in years, Megan laid across her parents' bed, her thoughts leaping in a dozen directions.

Jen was back.

Megan knew she should feel elated, victorious. But she was aware of different feelings altogether. Not shame, but something like it. Not fear, but something like it. Not disappointment, but something like it. Among all these elusive emotions, she was also aware of a feeling not unlike immaturity, and that made no sense. She had made dozens of responsible decisions today. But she couldn't shake the feeling. She felt like a child.

She left her parents' room and headed to the family room to wait for her dad and sister to get home, wondering all the while if Cheryl and Adam were back in Phoenix yet. Suddenly her life there seemed a million miles away.

~ ~ ~

It was a few minutes after seven when the phone rang. Dinner was over, and Megan, David, and Megan's family were sitting in the family room with Jen, discussing what Jen should do.

"I really think the wisest thing you can do is call the police," Gordy was saying. "The sooner the better."

"I think so, too," David echoed.

The sound of the phone interrupted them. Trina went to answer it in the kitchen. She came back to the family room with the phone in her hand.

"It's Chaz," she said softly.

Jen's eyes widened.

"It's okay," Megan whispered to her, and she got up to take the phone from her mother. She moved to the entrance of the family room but stayed where everyone could still hear her.

"Hey, Chaz…Yeah, I know…Yeah, me, too. Right…"

Megan looked back to Jen's anxious face. Charlie wanted to chat.

"Um…no, I think that's great…Chaz. I need to…Chaz, something… something important has happened, and I need to tell you about it…Come over?"

Megan looked over at Jen. Jen was nodding her head.

"Well, okay. You're not busy?" Megan continued. "Is Emily your girlfriend? I see…Is she there?… No, that's good. It might be better if I tell you alone. No, it's better if I just wait and tell you in person. Okay. I'll be there in half an hour. Yep, I remember where it is. Bye."

Megan clicked off the button. "You want to come, Jen?" she said.

"I think maybe I should," Jen said.

"Maybe we should come, too," Trina offered.

Megan shook her head. "I don't think so, Mom."

"Well, then at least have David go with you, please?"

Megan nodded. "Okay."

"I think we should pray before you head out," Gordy said.

"Pray?" Jen said.

"Definitely," David said.

Despite having a pretty good recollection of where Nate and Caroline's former house was, Megan still made a few wrong turns. It was a few minutes before eight when she pulled up to the gated entry of the house. She rolled down the window in Adele's car and pressed a button on a raised platform by the entrance.

"Yes?" came a reply from a speaker on the platform. Charlie's voice.

"Hi, Chaz, it's me," Megan said.

"Hey, Meg! Come on down!"

The buzzer switched off, and the mechanized gate in front of them began to open.

Megan eased Adele's car into the narrow driveway, leaving the driver's side window down. The air was laced with the tangy odor of salt. The surf below them could be heard just beneath the sound of the gate's motor.

"Just stay in the car for a few minutes, okay, Jen?" Megan instructed as she drove the car down the circular driveway. "I think maybe I should prepare him first."

"Want me to come?" David asked.

"Yeah, I think I do," Megan replied. She stopped the car in front of a towering wall of bougainvillea. Twilight made the magenta blossoms take on a hushed shade.

"Let's get out before he comes out to greet me," Megan said, hurrying to open her door. "We won't be long, Jen."

Jen just nodded and pulled out a cigarette.

Megan made her way to the front entrance with David rushing to keep up. The arches over the entryway were covered in wisteria vines that sprinkled the tiles below with dots of faded purple. As they neared the front door, it opened. Charlie stood framed in the doorway.

"Megan!" he called out and rushed to embrace her.

He was just as Megan had seen him a year ago: tanned, well-groomed, trim and fit. Charlie smelled faintly of spice, cedar, and mountain air. He wore a baggy T-shirt, long khaki shorts, and flip-flops.

"It's great to see you," he said, holding her tight. He kissed her on the cheek, and then stepped back.

Then Charlie noticed David standing behind Megan.

"Hey! David, right? You didn't tell me you were bringing a friend, Meg," Charlie said, offering David his hand. "How's it goin', man?"

"Great," David said, shaking Charlie's hand.

"Come on in," Charlie said, motioning them to follow him inside. "Sorry you can't meet Emily. She's visiting her sister in San Mateo. You're gonna like this one, Meg. I swear."

"I'm sure I will, Chaz," Megan said.

They stepped into the entryway, which was in semidarkness, the late summer sun nearly gone for the day. Charlie switched on a light.

"Here, have a seat, make yourself at home," he said, throwing a newspaper off a wide leather couch. "You guys thirsty? David, you want a beer or something?"

"No, thanks. I'm fine," David said, taking a seat on a matching chair.

Megan sat on the edge of the couch and waited for Chaz to sit down next to her.

"So, what's this big news you got for me?" Charlie began. Then his face broke into a wide grin. "You two are getting married. That's it, isn't it?!"

"No, Chaz. That's not it," she said, smiling uneasily.

"Really? That's not it?" Charlie looked puzzled.

"Charlie," Megan began, not realizing she had called him that. "I'm going to tell you something that at first you won't be able to believe. And I want you to just hear me out, okay?"

Charlie's smile hadn't quite left his face. "Sure," he said.

Megan looked over to David, and then back to Charlie.

"I got a call yesterday from someone. Someone I haven't seen in a long time. At first I couldn't believe this person was actually calling me, but we arranged to meet today and..."

She broke off and looked to David. He said nothing but his eyes told her what she knew already: No matter how she said it, it would come as an enormous shock. Megan turned back to Charlie.

"Megan, what is it?" Charlie said. He was looking tenderly at her, just like David had the moment before she told him.

"Charlie, Jen isn't dead," Megan said. "She's alive. I've seen her. Talked to her. Jen's the one who called me."

The words came out in a rush. Megan couldn't hold them back. She knew how it sounded. Mad. Ludicrous. But there was no easy way to tell Charlie that Jen had returned. There was no easy way.

Charlie stared at her, saying nothing.

"Chaz, did you hear me?" Megan said.

"I heard you," he said, turning his head slowly to David. Megan could read the look on his face. *Is she crazy?*

"Chaz, I know it sounds outrageous," Megan said, forcing Charlie to turn his face back to her. "I didn't believe it either until I saw her and talked to her. I'm telling you the truth. It's her."

Charlie held her gaze.

"What you are saying is impossible," he said evenly.

"No...no it isn't," Megan said. "We all thought she was dead, but we were wrong! Jen was kidnapped by people who brainwashed her, Chaz. They told her she was really their daughter, that there had been a mistake made at the hospital where she was born. They told her her real name was Sara Curran. They told her so often and for so long that she believed it. They raised her as Sara Curran. It was only a few months ago that she learned the truth. It took a lot of courage for her to come back here."

"Someone is playing a trick on you, Megan," Charlie said, anger tinging his voice.

"I thought so, too, Chaz. I didn't believe her at first, even though she looks just like Jen. She looks just like your dad. Like *you*."

Charlie got up and walked over to the wall of glass that looked out over the sea.

"Chaz," Megan said. "Look."

Megan walked over to him and held out the pair of little girl's socks.

Charlie turned and looked at her and at what she held.

"Chaz, she remembers the day she and I met. Your family had just moved here from Los Angeles. We met in school the first day back from Christmas vacation. We had on matching socks. Socks similar to these. I never told anyone that. Not even you."

Charlie fingered the lace.

"It's her, Chaz. I know it."

"Where is she?" he said.

"Outside. In my car."

"Outside?" he said, his voice breaking.

"She wants to see you, Chaz."

Charlie looked away, toward the ceiling that ended high above his head.

"I'm going to have David go get her, okay?" Megan said gently, keeping her hand on his arm. She nodded to David, and he left without a word.

Megan said nothing during the two minutes David was gone. When the door opened a minute later, David had his arm around Jen and was leading her into the room. She looked as fragile as glass.

"Charlie?" Jen said.

Time seemed suspended as brother and sister stared at each other.

Then Charlie moved toward his sister, and she toward him, and for many minutes after that, there was only the sound of shared regret.

Megan went into Charlie's kitchen in search of a box of tissues as Charlie and Jen held each other and wept. David followed her.

"I feel like we're in the way," she whispered to him, scouring the countertops with her eyes. No tissues.

"I don't think they're thinking about you and me right now, Megan," David said, popping his head into a tiny, adjoining bathroom. "Here's some," he said, emerging with a shiny, black container of tissues.

She took it from him, amazed he knew what she had been looking for.

"Let's just wait a minute," Megan said, watching Jen and Charlie and waiting for them to part, to start laughing, to start healing.

"We've got to call Mom and Dad," Charlie was saying, his voice thick with emotion. He broke away from Jen. "We've got to call them!"

"Come on," Megan said to David, and they started walking back into the main room.

"Megan, grab that phone!" Charlie said to her as she began to walk past a cordless phone sitting on a granite countertop.

Megan picked up the phone and carried it to him. She offered both Jen and Charlie the tissues.

"I must look a mess," Jen said, blotting her wet cheeks with a tissue.

"Not on your life," Charlie replied, looking at her deeply.

Then Charlie sat down heavily on the couch. The leather squeaked in protest.

"Okay," he said and took a breath. He looked at the numbers on the phone. Jen sat down next him.

"Chaz," Megan said, taking a seat on the loveseat opposite them. "Don't tell them everything on the phone. Especially your mom. It's an hour and half drive from Mission Viejo to here. It's too long a drive to have so much on your mind."

"Yeah, yeah, okay," Chaz said, wiping the last of his tears away. "I'll try Dad first."

Chaz pressed a button on speed dial and waited to be connected.

"It's his voice mail," he whispered with a frown, covering the phone. "Hey, Dad, call me as soon as you get this message. I'm at home. It's really important, Dad. I need you to come over tonight. I don't care how late."

Charlie clicked off.

"I think he and Caroline are at the Marine Room tonight with some client he's got to impress. He should be getting back to me fairly soon," Charlie said. "Now I'll try Mom."

He pressed another speed dial number and waited. Then he stood up. He couldn't sit still.

"Hey, Mom!" he said. He sounded nervous. "No, I'm fine…I just…I'm wondering if you and Leo are busy right now… I know it sounds weird, but can you come down tonight?…Yeah, I know it would put you here kind of late, but Mom, something has happened, and I think you will want to be here…Actually Mom, I want to keep it a surprise for you…You and Leo can stay the night…Can you leave right away?…Okay, we'll see you about ten-fifteen or so? Great."

"She's coming," Charlie said as he pressed the "off" button. He tossed the phone onto the coffee table.

Megan noticed that Jen was staring at her brother with an odd look on her face.

"Jen, you okay?"

Jen turned to her. "I'm okay. I was just thinking how wonderful it would be to just call her up like that. To just call her up and say, 'Hey, Mom.'"

Megan moved over to her and put her arm around her. "It won't be long, Jen," she said. "You look so tired. Why don't you rest until your parents get here?"

"Maybe if I could just close my eyes for a little while," she said.

Jen curled up and put her head on the stuffed arm of the sofa. Meg grabbed a loose-knit afghan off the back of the armchair and put it over her.

Within minutes, Jen was asleep.

While Jen slept, Megan put a teakettle on to boil. Then the three of them sat on stools at the expansive bar in the kitchen and drank tea Megan had found in one of the cupboards.

"It's probably old," Charlie said when she asked about it. "I think Caroline left it."

"I don't care," Megan said. "This seems to be the night for rekindling old things."

As they drank, they waited for Nate to return Chaz's call.

"You know, Chaz," Megan said. "When your dad calls back, he'll be within minutes of being here. If he gets here first, you'll have to tell him first. Then you'll have to say it all again when your mom gets here."

"Yeah," Charlie said.

"Telling it is hard," Megan said. "Hearing it is hard."

Charlie looked down at his mug and nodded.

"What do you think we should do?" he said.

"Have Jen wait in another room until they both get here. Tell them together. Then we'll bring Jen out."

Charlie thought for a moment.

"Okay," he said.

Fifteen minutes later, the phone rang. It was Nate.

"Dad, I need you to come by the house. A little after ten. Will you be done by then?…No, it's not bad news, Dad…it's good news, but that's all I'm going to say. Can you come?…Okay. See you then."

Chaz hung up the phone and looked at Megan.

"At ten o'clock, I'll wake her," she said, looking over at Jen.

A few minutes before ten, Megan gently shook Jen awake.

"Jen, we're going to have you wait in your dad's old study while Charlie tells your parents you're here, okay? They're going to be here in a few minutes. It might make it a little easier for them," Megan said to her.

"All right," Jen said groggily. "Can I have a glass of water?"

"Sure," Megan said.

"I'll get it," David offered.

Megan and Charlie led Jen to Nate's old study which now bore the mark of Chaz's life: lithographs of shiny sports cars, large photos of helmeted Trojans on a football field, and two sports trophies. As he flipped on the light, Charlie said, "There's a bathroom in here, so you can freshen up."

The gate's intercom beeped just then, and Charlie swung around toward the sound.

"Someone's here. I gotta go," he said. Then he gave Jen a hurried hug. "It'll all be over soon."

He turned and left, closing the door behind him.

"Here's your water," David said, moving toward Jen.

"Thanks," Jen answered. Her hands were shaking.

She took a drink, and then set the glass down on a narrow table against the wall. Wordlessly, she made her way to the bathroom, went inside, and closed the door.

"Which one do you think it is?" Megan whispered to David.

"Want me to put my ear to the door?" he said. Megan could tell he was not joking.

She nodded.

David walked over to the door and leaned in close to it.

"I think it's Elise," he said after a moment. "I can hear a man's voice, too."

"That's probably Leo," Megan said.

Jen emerged from the bathroom, the sleepy look gone from her eyes. She had brushed her hair. Her cheeks were flushed.

"Is someone here?" she said softly.

"It might be your mom," Megan said. "But I don't think your dad is here yet."

She nodded and walked over to a chair by a window. She sat in it and pulled her legs up underneath her.

No one could think of anything to say.

Ten minutes later another car's engine could be heard outside the window.

"That's probably your dad," Megan said softly to Jen.

Jen just nodded.

Before long the voices in the living room intensified, but Megan couldn't make out any words. But she could imagine them. She could picture Nate walking into his former house and seeing his former wife sitting there. No, standing there.

"What's going on here?" she could picture Nate saying.

Then she imagined Chaz trying to calm everyone down. After that he would do what she'd had to do four times in the last two days: announce that the unthinkable had happened. *Jen was home.*

She couldn't make out the words, but she could tell when Chaz broke the news. A man's voice got suddenly very loud. Nate's, no doubt. A woman began to weep. Elise.

Then Megan heard three words unmistakably clear,

"Where is she?!" Elise was shouting.

More muffled male voices.

Megan turned to Jen. "I think maybe we should go out there now," she said.

Jen rose from the chair and walked slowly to the door. She reached for Megan's hand.

"Ready?" Megan said.

Jen nodded. Megan opened the door and stepped out of the room. The voices were getting louder.

"Why has no one called the police?" Nate was asking.

"We can call them tomorrow, Dad," Chaz replied.

As they neared the entrance to the room, Megan could see a man she didn't recognize standing off to the side with his hands in his pockets. Leo. Caroline was sitting in an armchair, dazed.

Megan squeezed Jen's hand as they entered the room from the hallway. Heads turned. Voices fell silent. Nate hadn't changed in the five years since Megan had seen him. Elise's hair was cut very short and her sun-drenched skin was lined with the tiny wrinkles those who love the sun must wear. But she looked very much the same.

Megan watched Jen look from Nate to Elise, her blue eyes misty. Nate simply stared, incredulous. Elise was frozen in place for only a few seconds. Then she ran to Jen, much like she had run to Megan in the police station the day Jen had been kidnapped. Only this time her arms were outstretched like she was flying to paradise.

"My baby girl, my baby girl," Elise said, wrapping her arms tightly around Jen. She kept moving them like she wanted to increase her hold on her daughter, like there had to be a better way to secure her to her bosom. Nate stumbled over to them and touched Jen's hair. Megan had never seen Nate look so vulnerable. She watched him ease his arms around Jen and his ex-wife, watched him rest his head on Jen's, watched his face crumple into something like agony, something like joy. Charlie moved to join them, putting his arms around the trio of crying people.

Megan was aware of David behind her. She looked back at him.

"Let's go outside," she said, motioning with her head to the deck outside the wall of glass. They walked past Leo who simply stood there in awe. Megan hoped he wouldn't follow them. As they slid a huge sliding door and stepped out onto the deck, Megan could see that Caroline had also fled the room, having crossed over to the bar in her old kitchen where she was now mixing a tall martini.

David slowly slid the door closed behind them. Megan placed her hands on the railing of the deck and stared out at the rolling sea below them. Moonlight was casting a glow on the pounding surf that made it look like electrified lace. Megan couldn't help but think that the ocean below her probably looked exactly like this two days ago, before Jen's call. It looked just like this before

Adele died, before she moved to Phoenix, before Charlie kissed her, before Nate and Elise broke up, before Jen was snatched away before her eyes. It looked this way before all those things and still looked the same now, even when everything else was suddenly different.

"You doing okay?" David said. His voice was soft and kind. He was right next to her. She wanted to lean into him, but...

"I feel...I feel so *young*," Megan suddenly said, finally putting into words how she had been feeling since Jen had called her the day before.

"Young?" David asked.

"I feel so helpless and weak. Like no matter what happens, even when it's good, I can't move past it."

"Can't move past what?" David said.

"It's like no matter what happens in my life, I always feel like that little girl on the sidewalk," Megan said. "I feel like I'm still discovering that the world is big and scary and wonderful. I should be able to handle things like an adult. And instead, I feel like a child."

David moved close to her and leaned his shoulder next to hers. Megan found herself resting her head on it.

"What you're feeling," David said, "is what makes you human, Megan. You don't want to be without powerful feelings in a world as wonderful—and scary—as this one, no matter how old you are."

Yes, Megan thought. She closed her eyes and let David's words wash over her. The peaceful, assuring sound of the surf and David's quiet strength calmed her. It reminded her of another time she had been on the beach with David and he had tried to give her the same kind of advice.

She lost track of time. At some point, the sliding door opened and Charlie poked his head out.

"Megan, my parents would like to talk with you," he said.

She turned and walked back into the house, and David followed.

"Megan!" Elise said as Megan stepped into the main room. Elise came to her and embraced her. Megan could almost smell Elise's drying tears.

"Thank you," Elise said as she broke away.

"I really didn't do anything, Elise," Megan said.

"Yes, you did. She came to you. And you helped her," Elise said, fresh tears springing to her eyes. "I will never forget that."

Nate came over then and hugged Megan as well. But he didn't seem able to say anything. Tall, confident Nate Lovett was at a loss for words.

Megan hastily introduced David to the people in the room. Leo came forward, and Elise introduced him.

After that, it seemed to Megan that she and David should leave.

"Jen," she said softly. "Do you want to stay here tonight?"

Jen nodded and smiled. "My mom is going to stay here, too."

"I think maybe David and I should leave then, okay?"

Jen looked a little anxious.

"You'll be all right," Megan said. "You and your family have a lot to talk about."

"Can you come back tomorrow?" Jen said, reaching for her.

"Of course," Megan said, hugging Jen back.

Megan and David said good night to everyone and then left. They walked up the tiled pathway to the driveway in silence.

"Let me drive," David said, extending his hand for the car keys.

Megan placed them in his hand. She was exhausted.

Once they were in the car, David backed out of the driveway and turned onto several side streets before turning north on Del Mar Heights Road.

"How about some music?" he said, tuning in Adele's radio to the local jazz station.

Somehow he knew she was too tired for words.

"Thanks, David," she said and leaned back on the seat and closed her eyes.

29

Morning sunlight filtered through the nearly closed curtains in Megan's childhood bedroom. She awoke to the sound of a lawn mower outside and the telephone ringing in the kitchen. She turned over and raised herself to a sitting position, glancing over at the clock on the bedside table. It was almost ten o'clock.

After she and David left Charlie's the night before, they had come back to Megan's house and talked with her parents until after two o'clock in the morning. She yawned.

"Megan?"

It was her mother's voice outside her door.

"I'm awake, Mom," she said. She ran a hand through her hair. She felt like she had just run a marathon.

The door opened, and Trina stood there with the handset in her hand.

"It's Jen, honey," Trina said, coming into the room and handing her the phone.

"Thanks," Megan said, taking it from her.

Trina stepped out of the room and closed the door.

"Hello? Jen?" Megan said, trying not to sound like she just woke up.

"Hi, Megan," Jen said, sounding rested but slightly out of breath. "Do you know when you can come over? Things are really crazy here. The police want to talk to you."

Megan stood up.

"They want to talk to *me*? What for?"

"I don't know. They just say they have a few questions. Can you come?"

Megan paced the length of her small room.

"Yeah, I can come. I'll be there in an hour, okay?"

"Okay. Thanks."

Jen clicked off.

Megan tossed the phone on the bed, trying to imagine what possible help she could be to the police. She wished it wasn't a Thursday. David would be at work. She wanted to call him up and ask him to come with her, but she knew asking for two afternoons off in a row probably wasn't a wise thing for him to do. The phone rang again, and Megan picked it up, thinking Jen had forgotten to tell her something.

"Hello?" Megan said, kneeling down and opening her suitcase.

"Hey, is this Megan?"

Megan didn't recognize the man's voice on the other end. "Who is this, please?" she said, standing back up.

"This is AJ. I need to talk to Sara. Is she there?"

Megan froze for a moment. Something wasn't right.

"You must have the wrong number. No one by that name lives here," she said.

There was a momentary pause.

"Aren't you Megan?" the man said.

"Who is this?" Megan said, a flutter of worry in her voice.

"This is AJ, man. And I need to talk to Sara. So you better put her on." The man sounded angry.

Megan fully realized then that the man on the phone was the one who drove Jen out to California on his motorcycle. This was the man who had friends in Chula Vista. And he was looking for Sara Curran, a woman who no longer existed.

"She's not here," Megan said, trying to sound calm.

"Where's she at, man?"

"She's with her family," she said.

"Well, she owes me three hundred bucks."

"Um, can you tell me where you got this number?" Megan said, trying to come up with a plan. A surge of allegiance to Jen swept across her. She didn't want this guy messing things up. ·

"She gave it to me, man. Hey, I want my money!"

It occurred to Megan that she'd had Jen all to herself for just a day—hours, really. Today and every day after, it would be different. Jen would not need her much after today. She might want Megan's friendship, but she really wouldn't *need* anything from her. What Jen had needed most, Megan had already helped provide. Megan decided to do one last thing, done between good friends who suddenly weren't little girls anymore and were now living their own, grown-up lives. One last thing.

"Tell me where to send the money, and I'll make sure it gets to you," she said.

"I don't want you sending it. I want it now," AJ said firmly.

"Well, you're not going to get it *now*," she said, trying to sound just as firm. "Tell me where to send the money."

AJ blurted out an expletive.

"What's this money for?" Megan asked, the edge still in her voice.

"It's what she owes me for bringing her here!" the man yelled. "And I want my money! I'm going back to Texas *today*. She knew that."

Megan rubbed her temple. *There is a way*, she thought...*David will have a fit. So will Mom...maybe I won't have to tell them.*

"Look, AJ, I have to go," she said, deciding on a plan. "But I'm going to leave the money under the door mat at an address I'm going to give you. Are you writing this down?"

"Geez, yeah, I'm writing this down."

Megan gave him Adele's address.

"It'll be there in an hour. Don't come before then."

"It better be there," the man said.

"It will be."

"Fine," the man said.

"Don't call for Sara here again, okay?" Megan said. "You won't find her here. She's with her family...now. And I don't even live at this number anymore. You're lucky you caught me. So don't call for her here."

"You just have the money there, got it?"

"You'll get your money," Megan said.

The man clicked off. Megan was going to have to hurry. A stop at the bank and at Adele's was going to make it tight. But even so, she sat back down on the bed for several minutes to calm her shaking legs.

~ ~ ~

When Megan arrived at Charlie's house in Del Mar about an hour later, the mechanized gate was already open. Five or six other cars lined the circular drive. Two belonged to the San Diego Police Department. Another was an unmarked black sedan with the unmistakable look of law enforcement about it. Two policemen were standing just outside the entrance to the house.

She eased to a stop behind a blue four-door she didn't recognize. One of the cops came up to her and motioned for her to roll down her window.

"If you're a reporter, you're going to have to wait until three o'clock. That's when the family is giving the press conference."

"I'm not a reporter," Megan stammered.

"Can I have your name, then, please?"

"I'm Megan Diamond. Jen Lovett called me and told me to come."

The cop stood up and called out to his colleague.

"This is Megan Diamond. Wright is expecting her." Then he turned back to her. "Okay. You want to follow me? You can leave the car here."

Megan switched off the ignition and climbed out of the car.

The main room that had been the location of such a tender, quiet reunion the night before was now a hectic jumble of activity. Nate and Charlie were there, talking to men in dark suits. Caroline was in the kitchen making a pot of coffee. Another man in a suit was using a small cell phone and writing things down at the bar where Megan had made tea the night before. Two cops were standing by the fireplace, talking quietly.

Jen and Elise were nowhere in sight.

"Detective Wright," said the policeman who had shown her in. "This is Ms. Diamond."

One of the men in suits who was talking to Nate and Charlie turned to her. Charlie turned to her, too, and smiled at her.

"Ms. Diamond, my name is Detective Jim Wright. Can I have a few minutes of your time?" He motioned her to the wide sofa. It looked different in the morning sunlight.

"Sure," Megan said softly and followed him.

"We just have a few questions for you, Ms. Diamond. We need your full name and address, where you work, that sort of thing. Can we start with that?"

Megan nodded and began answering his questions. He wrote down everything she said in a little black portfolio.

"Now can you tell me when Ms. Lovett first contacted you?" he said.

"It was two days ago, late in the afternoon."

"She called you at your parents' house, is that correct?"

"Yes," Megan said. "I was in town for a funeral."

"I see. And did you agree to meet Ms. Lovett?"

"Yes."

"At Horton Plaza?"

"Yes."

"Did you consider contacting the police?"

"I considered it," she said.

"Why didn't you?" the detective asked, with no emotion in his voice.

"Because Jen asked me not to. She told me we could later. But not right then."

The detective nodded. He flipped over to some other notes. It appeared he was going to move on. Megan began to relax.

"Okay, Ms. Diamond," he continued, not looking up at her. "Have you ever been contacted by a Mr. Rudy Curran, a Mrs. Belinda 'Beanie' Curran, or a Ms. Ruth Hobart?"

"What?" Megan exclaimed.

The detective looked up from his notes. He repeated the question.

"Have you ever been contacted by a Mr. Rudy Curran, a Mrs. Belinda 'Beanie' Curran, or a Ms. Ruth Hobart?"

"No!" Megan said. "I had never even heard of those people until yesterday."

"Do you know the whereabouts of Mr. Rudy Curran?" the detective said.

Megan shook her head. "No, I don't," she said.

Detective Wright closed the portfolio.

"Okay. Thank you very much," he said. He stood up. She watched the detective walk over to another plainclothes policeman and begin talking with him.

Charlie came over to her.

"They did that to all of us, Megan," he said softly. "Don't worry about it."

"Why did they ask me about Rudy and Beanie?" Megan whispered back.

"I think they just want to make sure Jen is telling the truth. Come on. Jen's waiting for you."

Megan followed Charlie up the stairs at the edge of the main room. As they climbed, she could see that the policemen and detectives were gathering their things, preparing to leave.

"So that's it? You're done with them?" Megan said quietly to Charlie.

"I don't think so," he whispered back. "Formal charges are going to be filed. Jen will probably have to go downtown and tell her story to the district attorney. But at least for today we're done."

Charlie led her to the back guest room and knocked on the door. Jen opened it.

"Oh, thank God you're here, Megan," Jen said, pulling her in. "Are they gone?"

"I think they're finishing up now, Jen," Charlie said, stepping into the room.

Elise was standing by the window with her arms folded across her chest. "Well, I'm glad that's over with," she said.

"They've been here for *hours*," Jen said, rolling her eyes and flopping down on the bed.

"Since nine," Charlie said to Megan.

"Megan, there's going to be a press conference here at three o'clock," Jen suddenly said. "Can you stay, please? You won't have to say anything if you don't want to. Daddy will do all the talking. Please say you'll stay."

"Sure, I'll stay," Megan said.

"We should think about some lunch. Jen, you need to eat," Elise said, heading for the door. "You think *Princess* Caroline will let me fix something in her former kitchen?" she said to Charlie as she walked past him.

"Mom, I don't think I have much to work with," Charlie began, following her out.

Megan was alone with Jen in the guest room.

"Quite a day already, huh?" Megan said, sitting down next to Jen on the bed.

"It's been exhausting. So many questions. I'm tired of questions."

"I have a few more of Michelle's clothes in the car with me," Megan said, wanting to carefully work her way to AJ's phone call.

"Well, after the press conference, Mom's taking me shopping for some clothes," Jen said. "Hey! You should come! It would be fun!"

Megan didn't think Elise would want to share Jen so quickly.

"Your mom might want to be alone with you, Jen. Maybe next time?"

"Well, okay."

Megan cleared her throat.

"Jen, I got a call from AJ this morning."

Jen turned to her, eyes questioning. "What did he want?"

Megan started to answer but Jen cut her off.

"He wants his money, doesn't he?" Jen said. She stood up. "I want to pay him. I do! I just don't feel right asking my dad for money yet."

"Jen," Megan said. "I took care of it. He should be on his way to Texas now."

"You did?" Jen said.

"It's done."

"Megan, I'll pay you back every penny. As soon as I can, I promise."

"It's okay, Jen. There's no hurry."

"I mean it. As soon as I can."

Megan nodded her head. Then she looked off toward the window, wanting to say something else and not sure how to say it.

"Jen," she began. "AJ seems like a scary person. Like maybe he's not completely safe. If he tries to contact you again, maybe you should tell your dad. Maybe you should let the police know. When he finds out who you are…"

"I know, I know," Jen said. "He does kind of scare me. But he was the only way I knew of to get here."

"Well," Megan said, shaking her head and standing up. "I don't trust him. I wish you had called me from Texas instead of trusting *him* to bring you here. Who knows what could have happened to you!"

"You wish I had called you from Texas?" Jen said, echoing Megan's words.

Megan looked at her.

"Would you have come for me?" Jen asked. But she didn't wait for an answer. She started for the door.

"I hope Mom found us something to eat," Jen continued. "I'm starving."

~ ~ ~

After a lunch of penne and canned spaghetti sauce, Jen and her parents sat down to discuss her schedule for the following day. Leo sat with them as well but said little. Caroline stood off at a distance but stayed within earshot. Elise wrote everything down: doctor's appointment, a stop at the Social Security office, letters to be written to the schools Jen had attended as Sara Curran, more shopping.

"We should have a party!" Elise suddenly said. "A welcome home party! We can have it Saturday, before Leo has to go back."

Elise tore off the top of the tablet and started a new list. No one had really thought much beyond one day at a time. But apparently, Leo was going back to Mission Viejo after Saturday, and it sounded like Elise was staying.

"We could have it at our place in Rancho Santa Fe," Caroline said. "It's private, secure, and quite spacious."

"That's true," Nate said. "Caroline has lovely gardens in bloom right now. It's a lovely place for a party."

Elise was still for a moment, weighing the idea just presented.

"All right," she finally said, looking down at her paper and writing something on it.

"Who will we invite?" Jen asked.

"Everyone," Elise said, looking up. "All our friends."

"I don't think I remember any of your friends, Mom," Jen said, casting a furtive glance at Charlie.

"But they remember you, darling," Elise said. "No one has forgotten you. No one."

Elise and Caroline began compiling the list. Megan was amazed at how well they worked together.

"You'll come, Megan, right?" Elise said, looking up at her. "And your family? And your young man?"

"My young man?" Megan said.

"David," Charlie said and winked.

"Chaz, Emily will be home by then, right?" Elise continued.

"She gets home tomorrow night."

The flurry of party preparations made Megan feel a little out of the loop. Everything seemed to be happening so fast. Before she had time to get used to the idea of a huge party at Nate and Caroline's, the speaker for the outside gate buzzed. The first crew of reporters had arrived.

Within half an hour, the main room was packed with camera crews, boom-microphone operators, TV and newspaper reporters, and floodlights.

Megan stayed in the background while Nate did all the talking. The questions came when he was done, but most were directed to Nate, Elise, Jen, and Charlie. At one point a *Union Tribune* photographer took her picture, but she was unaware that she had been in his viewfinder until after the flash went off.

"Thanks," the photographer said, like she had just posed and said "cheese."

By four o'clock the TV crews had scrambled back to their vans and left for their studios for the five o'clock news. The newspaper reporters were packing up, too. By four-thirty, the house was quiet again.

"Are you sure you won't come shopping with us?" Jen asked her. "My dad's going to tape the news so we don't miss it."

"I think I'll just go home, Jen. Your mom deserves this time alone with you," Megan said.

"But you will come to the party on Saturday, right?" Jen said.

"I wouldn't miss it," Megan said, as she gave Jen a quick hug. Jen held her tight.

"Jen, we better get going," Elise was saying. "The mall is only open until eight on weeknights."

"Bye," Jen whispered.

"See you Saturday," Megan said.

Jen walked over to where her mother was standing. Megan picked up her purse from where she had left it during lunch and slung it over her shoulder. Then she looked over at Jen, now encircled by her mother, father, and brother. They were all talking together and smiling. It looked right. The way it should be. No one heard Megan leave.

On her way home, Megan made a quick stop at Adele's. She pulled into the driveway, left the engine running, and stepped out of the car. Megan walked over to the welcome mat that lay just below Adele's front door and lifted it.

The money was gone.

She hoped it was a sign that AJ was also gone. For good.

30

On Friday morning, Megan emerged from her bedroom at a little past eight to find that her parents had already left for work. Michelle was still asleep.

Her mother had propped up the morning paper against the still-warm coffee pot. On it was a yellow sticky note that read: "Our little hero." Above the fold, in bold letters, was the headline describing Jennifer Lovett's amazing return home after a fifteen-year absence. The main photo was of Jen, flanked by Nate, Elise, and Charlie. A second photo below it showed Jen talking to reporters, explaining the ordeal that wasn't an ordeal. A third photo, smaller still, was of Megan herself, seated on a sofa cushion, with a thoughtful look on her face. Under it the caption read: "Jennifer Lovett's childhood friend, Megan Diamond, who witnessed the kidnapping fifteen years ago, helped Lovett reunite with her family."

"Good grief," Megan said aloud.

She had read most of the article when the phone rang.

It was David.

"Did you see today's paper?" Megan said.

"I'm looking at it right now."

"Can you believe the size of the story? It's huge!"

"This is big news, Megan. This doesn't happen very often. Most kidnapped children gone longer than a day never come home."

"I know."

"I took the day off, Megan," David said.

"Really? How come?"

"I thought maybe you'd like to get out of the house, away from the phone."

"Away from the phone?"

"The wire services have already picked this up, Megan," David said. "It's on all the major Internet news sites. Your phone is about to start ringing, I'm sure."

"What for? This story isn't about me," Megan protested.

"Well, you and I know that, but to the media, it *is* also very much about you. The fact is, those who want more of the story are going to have a hard time pinning down Jen Lovett. Chaz's number is unlisted. So is Nate's. Their homes are gated and protected by security systems. You live in middle class suburbia, and your phone number is in the phone book."

"What should I do?" Megan said.

"Do you want to talk to reporters today?" David asked.

"No."

"Then I'll be over in an hour. We'll think of somewhere to go."

Megan clicked off the phone, put it down and stared at it. Then she unplugged it from the wall. She headed to the bathroom to shower and get ready.

When David arrived at nine, Megan was ready. She wrote a hasty note to her parents and Michelle, telling them she'd be back later in the day and to politely decline any offers of interviews should any come her way. She plugged the phone back in as they left through the garage.

"Just in case Jen should call, I want her to be able to leave a message," she said, following David out.

"Any place in particular you want to go?" David asked as he was backing out the Diamonds' driveway.

Megan thought for a moment. "I know it sounds weird," she said. "But I'd like to get some doughnuts, and then take them back to Adele's."

"I like that idea," he said.

They made their way to the nearest Winchells doughnut shop, and Megan picked out two large apple fritters. Then they swung by Starbucks for two Venti morning-blend coffees. Ten minutes later, they were pulling into Adele's driveway.

"Let's try this one," she said, inserting the most likely looking key on the ring into the keyhole on Adele's back door. The lock turned, and they went in.

The house smelled stale and musty after being closed up for two days. Megan opened a few windows while David set their breakfast on the kitchen table.

"So this house is yours, huh?" David said as they sat down.

"No, not really. I just have the privilege, if I want to exercise it, of living here for the next eight years. If I don't want to, Cheryl and Adam are going to rent it out."

"So, do you want to?" David said, placing a fritter in front of her.

"I don't know," she sighed, looking at nothing in particular and then turning to look at David. "I don't know *what* I want."

"You like Phoenix," David said, taking a bite of his apple fritter.

"Yeah, I do..." Megan began.

"But…" David continued for her.

"But I don't know if I want to stay there after I graduate. At some point I have to move out and live on my own. I can't stay with Adam and Cheryl and the kids forever."

She tore off a corner of her fritter and put it in her mouth.

"I left San Diego because I wanted to find out what I was like away from it," she continued. "I wanted to find out what I'm good at. I wanted to find out what I really believed about God, and I wanted to be free from the past, from what happened here."

David waited and sipped his coffee.

"I found out I love working with autistic kids. I really do, David. They're like brilliant people lost in another world. I think I know what that's like to an extent. And I found out my parents' God *is* my God after all. The same one they taught me to love and fear and to want to know better is the one I *want* to love and fear and know better. And when I left San Diego and moved to Phoenix, I was indeed far away from all that had happened here."

"But you weren't free from it," David said.

"No," she said softly. "I wasn't."

"Why do you suppose that's true?" David asked.

"I guess my mind didn't want to let go of it," she said, shrugging her shoulders.

"And why didn't it?"

"Why do I get the feeling you are about to tell me?" she said, sipping her coffee.

David smiled.

"I have an idea," he said.

"You usually do," Megan replied.

"Come with me," he said.

David stood up, walked over to the front door, and opened it.

"Come," he said, turning back to her.

Megan stood and walked over to him. David stepped out into the midmorning sunshine, headed to the sidewalk at the end of Adele's yard, and began walking up the street. Megan followed.

"Where are you going?" she said, as she came up alongside him.

"We're going to get rid of some stuff," he replied.

David continued past the last house, past where the fenced schoolyard began. Ahead of them were a bench and a bus stop.

"David, what are you doing?" Megan said, concern and doubt making her steps falter.

"Is this where it happened?" he said, stopping at a nondescript square of cement.

Megan looked down at the ground. She pretended like it was no big deal.

"I guess so."

"Okay," David said. "Tell me what happened."

"David, you already know what happened."

"Yeah, I know. Tell me anyway."

"This is dumb."

"Maybe. Tell me what happened," David said, looking at her, challenging her.

Megan sighed.

"I am standing there, Jen is standing here. A blue van comes up to her, a lady starts talking to her, the side door slides open, a man grabs her, the van speeds away with Jen inside. I scream."

Megan met his stare with her own challenging eyes.

"That's not all that happened," he said.

"Okay, fine. Adele comes to help me, the police get called, they ask me a million questions I can't answer, we all wait for a ransom note, there never is one, I grow up without Jen. Satisfied?"

"No. That's not all that happened," David said again.

"What? You want me to tell you my whole life story from that day to this one?" Megan said, clearly peeved. "Is that what you want?"

"No. I just want you to tell me what happened after Jen was taken from you. What happened to her?"

Megan stood on the square of pavement where so much ended and began and said nothing.

"What happened to her, Megan?" David repeated.

"They...took her to Oklahoma," Megan whispered. David didn't look away from her.

"*Then* what happened?" he said.

"They bought her clothes. They told her her name was Sara."

"Did they beat her? Did they abuse her?"

Megan closed her eyes.

Lord, send the ghosts away, send the ghosts away, she prayed.

"No, they didn't," Megan said, eyes still closed.

"Did they *love* her?" David said, almost whispering himself.

Megan opened her eyes. "I think they did, David."

"Were you ever in any danger that day, Megan? Did they take Jen because, as you thought, she was the pretty one?" David asked, his voice softer still.

Megan hesitated...thinking... The people in the blue van never gave her a moment's thought.

"Jen looked like Sara. That's why they took her."

David reached forward and wiped away her tears with his thumb.

"Now that you've gotten rid of the lies, let's find out what you're left with," he said, putting his arm around her and guiding her back in the direction of Adele's house.

"What do you mean?" Megan asked as they walked.

"Well, what are you always left with after you've eliminated all the lies?"

"The truth," she said.

They had arrived back at Adele's. David sat down on the front steps to the house. Megan sat down beside him.

"Out of really terrible things, good things can emerge, Megan," David said. "It happens all the time. That's the truth you're left holding. Can you see the good things that you were left with now that all the lies are gone?"

Megan looked up at David, then past him to the dangling geraniums above his head.

"Adele," she said.

"She loved you like her own daughter, Megan," David said. "She never would have met you had that terrible thing not happened."

More names fell from Megan's lips.

"Cheryl and Adam and the kids. Ian. Cole…"

David was quiet as Megan slowly began to grasp how Jen's disappearance had shaped her, how something twisted and wrong had nevertheless been used by God for better purposes, how the people she had met after the abduction had influenced her, how there had been beauty after and within the misery. She suddenly thought of the canyon, which like so many things was nothing but a memory. She remembered how wild and scary it was and yet how stunning and majestic.

"I had forgotten the beauty of it," she said aloud, though not to David, and he said nothing. Megan didn't feel the need to explain it. She looked up at David as a fresh revelation seized her.

"I never would have met you," she said.

"You think your past is something to be buried and forgotten, but it isn't," David said gently "Your past, all of it—the good and the bad—is what God used to make you, *you.*"

Megan stared off in the distance, to where a tiny bench by a tiny bus stop stood in absolute ordinariness.

"If I might point out one more thing," David said, leaning tward Megan.

"What?" she said.

"What was it exactly that you liked so much about Jen?" David asked. "I mean, *why* was she your best friend? From what you've told me, she was feisty and independent, she challenged her parents' rules, she wasn't afraid to stand up to her brother or any other boy, she had quirky ideas about God. If you don't mind my saying it, she doesn't sound like you at all."

Megan laughed lightly. "She *wasn't* like me. I was so shy and timid, and she was the complete opposite. She scared me sometimes."

"So, what was it, then?" David said. "I'd really like to know."

Megan let her mind take her back to the first day she met Jen. She remembered how Jen stood at the front of the classroom as confident as a movie star. She remembered her beautiful blonde hair. Those crayon blue eyes. And then she remembered how those eyes had locked onto hers when Jen noticed her.

"She *liked* me," Megan finally said. "She liked me just the way I was."

"Megan," David said softly. "She's not the only one."

Megan leaned into David's side and closed her eyes. She didn't want to move from that place of peace and safety. For the first time in as long as she could remember, the world seemed motionless. At peace. *This is the way it is when everything is right,* she thought, *when all is at rest.* The sounds of cars driving past, however, and the far-off barking of a dog, and the squeal of a child playing in a yard nearby reminded her that the wild, wonderful world was yet spinning. Megan knew the tranquility of that moment was temporal, that heartache would revisit her at another time, another place in the future. Turmoil was part of the splendor of living.

In the midst of this new insight, Megan knew decisions awaited her and the outcomes were anything but certain. But as she felt the morning sun on her face, she realized she didn't have to decide anything today. It was enough to know she could choose. She could finish up at ASU and come back if she wanted. Jen might need a good friend in the coming months. *She* might, too. And David's nearness, in so many ways, was a surprising comfort. The future was brimming with options.

Megan opened her eyes and shifted her weight. The cement step was becoming uncomfortable. "Want to go somewhere?" she said to David.

"Sure," he said, leaning his head onto hers.

"Do you care where?" she said.

"Not really."

They stood, and Megan took out Adele's key ring. She reached over to the front door and locked it. Then Megan and David walked down the front steps and started across the grass to David's car.

"How about a walk on the beach?" she asked him as they walked.

"Sounds nice."

They reached the passenger side of the car, and Megan stepped aside.

David smiled at her and reached to open her door.

Susan Meissner is an award winning newspaper columnist, pastor's wife, and high school journalism instructor, and author of one previous novel, *Why the Sky Is Blue*. She lives in rural Minnesota with her husband, Bob, and their four children.

If you enjoyed *A Window to the World*…
you'll also enjoy Susan Meissner's previous
novel, *Why the Sky Is Blue*.

What options does a Christian woman have after she's
brutally assaulted by a stranger…and becomes pregnant?
That's the heartrending situation Claire Holland faces. A
happily married mother when she is attacked, Claire begins
an incredible journey on the painful pathway to trusting
God "in all things." This wonderful first novel isn't a *love*
story…but a *life* story about the rewards that eventually
come with love that takes us beyond our limits.

A Note from Susan Meissner

Thank you for the many ways you have encouraged me as a writer since the release of my first book, *Why the Sky Is Blue*. I love hearing from readers and I welcome your feedback. Please feel free to e-mail me at susan@susanlmeissner.com or write me in care of Harvest House Publishers, 990 Owen Loop North, Eugene, OR 97402.

If you would like discussion questions to use with *A Window to the World* or *Why the Sky Is Blue*, I have some available for you on my website; www.susanmeissner.com.

May God enfold you in His tender embrace,

Susan Meissner

Harvest House Publishers
For the Best in Inspirational Fiction

Susan Meissner
Why the Sky Is Blue

Mindy Starns Clark
THE MILLION DOLLAR
MYSTERIES SERIES
A Penny for Your Thoughts
Don't Take Any Wooden Nickels
A Dime a Dozen
A Quarter for a Kiss
The Buck Stops Here

Craig Parshall
CHAMBERS OF JUSTICE SERIES
The Resurrection File
Custody of the State
The Accused
Missing Witness
The Last Judgment

Sally John
THE OTHER WAY HOME SERIES
A Journey by Chance
After All These Years
Just to See You Smile
The Winding Road Home

IN A HEARTBEAT SERIES
In a Heartbeat
Flashpoint
Moment of Truth

Debra White Smith
THE AUSTEN SERIES
First Impressions
Reason and Romance
Central Park

Lori Wick
THE YELLOW ROSE TRILOGY
Every Little Thing About You
A Texas Sky
City Girl

CONTEMPORARY FICTION
SERIES
Bamboo & Lace
Beyond the Picket Fence
Every Storm
Pretense
The Princess
Sophie's Heart

THE ENGLISH GARDEN SERIES
The Proposal
The Rescue
The Visitor
The Pursuit

Roxanne Henke
COMING HOME TO
BREWSTER SERIES
After Anne
Finding Ruth
Becoming Olivia
Always Jan

Raymond Reid
The Gate Seldom Found

Chris Well
Forgiving Solomon Long